HAPPY HEAD

HAPPY HEAD

JOSH SILVER

DELACORTE PRESS

Copyright © 2023 by Josh Silver
Jacket art copyright © 2024 by Sasha Vinogradova

All rights reserved. Published in the United States by Delacorte Press, an imprint of Random House Children's Books, a division of Penguin Random House LLC, New York. Originally published in paperback in the United Kingdom by Rock the Boat, an imprint of Oneworld Publications, London, in 2023.

Delacorte Press is a registered trademark and the colophon is a trademark of Penguin Random House LLC.

GetUnderlined.com

Educators and librarians, for a variety of teaching tools, visit us at RHTeachersLibrarians.com

Library of Congress Cataloging-in-Publication Data is available upon request.
ISBN 978-0-593-81202-0 (trade) — ISBN 978-0-593-81203-7 (lib. bdg.) —
ISBN 978-0-593-81204-4 (ebook)

The text of this book is set in 11.5-point Adobe Garamond Pro.

Editor: Kelsey Horton
Interior Designer: Michelle Crowe
Production Editor: Colleen Fellingham
Managing Editor: Tamar Schwartz
Production Manager: CJ Han

Printed in the United States of America
10 9 8 7 6 5 4 3 2 1
First American Edition

For all the patients who have
inspired me over the years

HappyHead
Commitment. Growth. Gratitude.
FOR THE ATTENTION OF SEBASTIAN SEATON

Congratulations!

We are writing to inform you that you have been selected to participate in the HappyHead Project as part of its inaugural intake.

Based on the research of Dr. Eileen Stone and guided by world-leading professors, the HappyHead Project is the first of its kind. This cutting-edge program will offer participants the opportunity to find enduring happiness. Completion of the program will unleash your full potential, equipping you with the tools you need for future success.

You will be required to undertake a thirteen-day course of assessments, therapy, and closely monitored nonmedical intervention. For the purposes of complete immersion, there will be no contact with family members or friends for the full thirteen days. Access to devices and the internet will be prohibited until departure.

We ask you to bring the following items:

- Sneakers (no laces)
- Current necessary medication
- One personal item of your choice that does not identify you but is meaningful to you. Place this item in the lockable box provided.

The program will begin on September 1, and you will be granted leave from school or college to attend. Arrive no later than 20:00. Enclosed, please find a questionnaire, options for transportation to the facility, a pamphlet with further information, and a consent form for your parent/guardian.

Please fill out the questionnaire with complete honesty. We look forward to welcoming you to HappyHead. Attendance is mandatory.

Yours in faith,

Professor G. Manning

Professor G. Manning ☺

ONE
Bowie Sky

"I think it's down there," Mum says.

"We've already been down there," Dad says, more rudely than I expected.

"No, it's a different road—look."

"They all look the same."

"No, that one's narrower than the others."

"What does the GPS say?"

"It's not working. It thinks we're in the middle of a field."

"We kind of are in the middle of a field," Lily chips in.

It's unfortunate that I'm spending my seventeenth birthday with my face pressed against the car window for eight hours as my parents and sister talk without coming up for air. But they wanted to see me off. I said they could have done that from the front porch, but they didn't think that would have been meaningful.

I think it would have been meaningful. The *meaning* being that I could have gotten the train and avoided this. I could have seen Shelly last night and said goodbye, and not got up at four-thirty to the sound of Dad waving a box of chocolate Cheerios in my face, claiming they were a *fun treat,* before I left.

Going to HappyHead will do me a world of good, Mum is now saying. I should be thankful that I was selected. Grateful.

"It's a blessing." She loves that word. "Truly," she says as she catches my eye in the rearview mirror. "You've always had a bit of a sensitive nature, haven't you?"

I think she might actually want an answer.

Lily snorts.

"I—"

"And we love that about you, Seb. We do. You've always felt things very deeply." Christ. "Not that it's a bad thing. It's . . . part of who you are. What makes you special." I want to open the door and jump into the bushes flying past us. "I just worry sometimes about how you'll cope. Life isn't easy."

For a while now, there has been a general feeling among my parents and my teachers that something has to come along to really shake things up for me if I am to equip myself for the Next Phase of Life.

When the letter came, they were all very excited.

HappyHead would be the answer.

It had to be.

They all agreed.

The car is packed with my things, so me and Lily are parted by a bulging suitcase, which is definitely for the best. But it keeps digging into my chest when Dad brakes too hard, which he does all the time. I didn't want to bring everything from my wardrobe, but Mum insisted. When I said it wasn't necessary because of the required packing list, she said I could never be too prepared.

"Where even are we?" Lily groans.

"Nearly there," Mum says, unconvinced. "Just a little tricky on these Scottish roads. Let's try and enjoy it."

Enjoy it.

Shelly said she was going to get a bottle of vodka and some weed, and her uncle was going to let us sit at the back of his pub and bring us free drinks.

4:30 alarm, tho, I texted her yesterday. *I'll have to pass if I want to survive the journey. Sry.*

I wanted to go to the party.

I did.

Come on, Shelly replied. *It's your birthday buddy and you're going away for nearly two weeks. You say you're independent, but they have a hold on you, Seb. You're scared of them. Always have been. Goodbye. I really hope you make some friends there so it's not just me putting up with this shit.*

I didn't reply to that. Shelly loves to use full sentences and first-name me when she thinks I'm bailing. And anyway, I don't always do what my parents say. And if I do, it's only to make things easier because I can't cope with the disappointment and the "That's not like you, Seb." Also I've had weed before and it wasn't up to much. I became very dizzy, couldn't feel my body, and threw up in the shower.

Shelly didn't get a letter from HappyHead.

No one else at my school did.

Just me.

Maybe she's jealous.

I can see Mum has opened the parent/guardian pamphlet— now covered in coffee rings and with worn edges—yet again. "Oh, Seb. *Selected.*"

3

"I'm pretty sure it's just random, Mum."

I don't think she has parted with the pamphlet since it arrived. She's read it so many times that she practically knows it by heart and sometimes just quotes bits of it at me, like "nurturing strengths" and "athletics track."

The car is very hot now.

"They must see something in you, Seb. They must. They have to be using some sort of . . . set of standards for the selection process, right? Richard?"

Dad doesn't answer.

"They've never even met me, Mum."

"And," she plows on, "you needed a little boost, didn't you? What with your grades dropping so—"

"Yeah, it's great, Mum."

She turns and looks at me, beaming with hope. "I've signed all the consent forms. And you filled out the questionnaire thoroughly, didn't you?"

I nod.

"Good. *Mandatory.* Gosh. Like the army used to be . . ."

I try to avoid the tone in her voice that can only be interpreted as *please, please, please don't mess this up, son.*

I suddenly feel the familiar twist of dread in my stomach. I pull a Jolly Rancher from the wrapper inside my coat pocket. When I press it to my lips, I realize I can't stop my hand from shaking.

"Can we put *Hunky Dory* on?" I say.

Lily rolls her eyes so much they go completely white. She loves to act as if I don't really like David Bowie, as if I just say I do to try to be interesting. But that's not true.

4

"Fake obsessed," she mutters.

"Just wait, Seb. We need a break from music so we can think." Mum sharply presses the off button on the dashboard so the Lighthouse Family abruptly stops singing.

I've never felt the need to explain my appreciation of Mr. Bowie, especially to my schmucky little sister. She thinks I went seeking something out to make me look a certain way because of how *painfully bland* I am, but I didn't.

Bowie found me.

She wouldn't understand the importance of the first time I saw the lightning bolt shuddering down his face on Shelly's mum's CD case when I was thirteen.

Or that I stole it.

Or that, when I listened to it, I danced around my bedroom in Mum's heeled boots, sometimes crying.

I do not need to tell her that.

And I do not need to tell her that he was the first man I ever liked.

And by "liked" I mean *liked.*

Hot buzzing in my head, can't focus, can't think of anything else, talking to his picture under the sheets, want to tear my chest open and cool the pain of not being together on the cold hearts of everyone who has never felt this way type of liked.

I can smell the cheese-and-onion chips Dad is trying to eat while also holding on to the steering wheel. He lifts the bag and pours them onto his face.

"Oh, darn."

"Eyes on the road, love."

"Sorry."

Lily's headphones start blaring that shitty music she loves. She often says I don't get her music and that it's actually really relevant. It's Christian pop. She loves the churchy pop groups, and for that my parents give her things and drive her to and from freestyle dance class four nights a week and she always has twenty-pound notes rolled up in her purse. She's fifteen and richer than most people I know. I will never understand it, but apparently that's what God will do for you.

"Lily, turn that down. Did we put Seb's regular pills on the form, Richard? I think we missed them. Did we miss them? That's the kind of stuff they'll want to know about. And the course of diazepam last year? Richard?"

"We put it all on the form." I find myself looking for an ejector seat button.

Lily is shrugging her shoulders up and down in some kind of street dance that she must have picked up from all those hours of practice.

"What about the lavender pillow mist?" my sister says. "Do they want to see that on there?"

Mum looks at Dad, worried. "Do they?"

"Funny, Lily," I say. "How's the hip-hop coming along? The classes are worth it, I see."

"Dick," she says.

"Sorry? Didn't hear you." She rolls her eyes. "Louder, Lily."

D-I-C-K, she mouths. "Come on, Seb. You of all people should understand what that is." Her eyes flick from her phone to Mum, and she gives a wicked little smile. She's always threatening to tell them. Blackmailed by a fifteen-year-old. She loves it. Little sadist. She shrugs, casual, in a way that says *Try me.*

She wants to see me squirm.

I don't care. They know. They must.

I turn to press my forehead against the cool window, and it fogs with the hot air from my nose.

I focus on the bright yellow fields.

The sky is electric blue today.

A Bowie sky.

Lily pokes her tongue into her cheek so it bulges. "Happy-*Head.* Sounds like you'll be right at home there, Seb." She leans back, smug, like she's won something.

Not long now. And then some peace.

From this.

Nearly two whole weeks.

I stare out the window and watch as the sky darkens, streaking with purple and pink like a new bruise.

Mum sharply inhales. "Did we put about the childhood bedwetting?"

"Yes, Mum," I say. "Everything was on the form. Just leave it now. Jesus."

The car bumps along the road, and my head bangs against the glass.

"Watch your language," Mum says, sounding hurt.

Lily smiles.

Suddenly Dad slams on the brakes. The inertia pushes me into my seat belt.

"Dad!" Lily snaps. "I really, *really* would prefer not to die before Lola's birthday party next week."

"Sorry, everyone."

I look up at the thick wall of tall reeds that we have nearly just plowed into. The same reeds that have been on either side of us for over an hour now.

My toes are numb, my ass is numb, and I'm desperate for a piss.

"*Blair Witch,* family edition," Lily says, looking out at the swaying reeds.

I reach for my Jolly Ranchers.

"Well, we can't just sit here," Mum hisses at Dad.

The clock on the dashboard reads 7:30. That's 19:30 in military time.

"We have to get there before eight, apparently," I say.

That's what the letter said. *Arrive no later than 20:00.*

"Yes, Seb, we are well aware," Mum says quietly, opening the glove compartment and sifting through the glacier mints as if a map might suddenly appear.

We sit for a minute, with only the sound of the wind in the reeds and my sister's intermittent pissy snorts. I reach down into my backpack to find my phone.

Shelly.

I open the message:

Have fun, Seb. You'll boss it.

Still first-naming, but she's coming around, at least. I text back:

Thnx. If I make it. This effing journey might end me before I even get there. How was last night?

There is banging on the window.

"Shitting hell!" Lily screams.

"Lily!" Mum says, but stops as she turns to see what the rest of us are seeing. The face of a man staring in through the window above my sister's head.

TWO

Sunflowers

"Hello!" the face says, smiling widely.

His teeth are very white.

He stands back and shows us the front of his overalls, running his finger over the pocket on his chest where the word "HappyHead" is printed in bright green lettering underneath a smiley face.

"Oh," Mum says. "Perfect!" She laughs in a way that sounds like she could just as easily cry, then rolls down the car window and sticks out her head. "We seem to be a bit lost," she says in that fake formal voice she sometimes uses.

The man walks around the front of the car, cutting through the beams of the headlights, his yellow overalls bouncing the light back into my eyes.

"Don't worry, it's hard to find." He chuckles and bends down. "Full house in here!" he says, poking his head through the gap in the window so it hovers above Mum's lap.

"Mrs. Seaton," Mum says, holding her hand near the man's face. He takes it, and for a moment I think he's going to kiss it. I think Mum does too, because she gives some sort of stifled squeal, but instead he shakes it enthusiastically and says, "Ah! Sebastian's mother."

"Yes!" she says loudly.

"Hello." He looks directly at me. "You made it."

There is a distinct smell of antiseptic coming from the floating head. Reminds me of that pink ointment mothers put on our mosquito bites.

"Hi," I say to the antiseptic head.

His hair is neatly clipped and gelled into a perfect flip, like one of the T-Birds from that movie *Grease* where they dance on the car. His high cheekbones throw a shadow over the bottom half of his face.

"I'll take him from here, Mrs. Seaton. It's not far to the gate."

"Wonderful," Mum says. "Thank you. Just in time, hey, guys?"

Dad nods.

Lily just stares at the man.

"Right, Sebastian. Let's get your stuff." He's still smiling.

"Right."

A pang of nervous heat radiates in my stomach, making me suddenly feel dizzy. I open the car door and pull my backpack from the footwell. As I stand by the reeds and slam the door shut, the cold wind blows up inside my coat. I shudder.

"Everything in there?" Antiseptic asks, pointing at my bag.

"Yep," I say.

"Current medication?"

"Er, yep."

The sky is ash gray now.

"Personal item?"

"Oh, he's got that!" Mum pipes up from inside the car. "In that funny little box."

"Is it safe?" he asks quietly.

"Huh?" I take a step backward because he is now very close to my face. "Yeah. It's . . . safe."

He holds my gaze. His eyes are very black. I'm not entirely sure what to do.

Then he nods.

"Great!" He slaps my back and winks. "Let's go."

He is smiling again.

"What about the suitcases?" Mum says. "He might need—"

"He won't."

Antiseptic moves in front of the car and stands in his yellow overalls, teeth glinting in the beam of the headlights.

"Sorry, but who are you?" Lily says.

"Lily!" Mum turns. "Don't be rude. Sorry, sir."

"How do you know he even works for that place?"

"Don't worry." He laughs. "You make a good point, Lily. I have some ID that might help." He pulls it out of the front pocket of his overalls and holds it up to the windshield. Mum and Dad lean forward to read it through the glass. "I've been asked to pick up any stragglers on the roads. Most people used the train or our coach shuttle service. We anticipated some teething problems and welcome any feedback you might have. Perhaps a map would be useful next time?" he says, looking at Mum.

"That would be helpful, er"—she squints at the ID card—"Mark. Yes, thank you." I can see she's blushing.

"We wanted to see him off," Dad says weakly, as if it's

12

dawning on him that the eight-hour trip might not have been worth it. "Can we not come to the gate?"

"No need. We're all good from here. Aren't we, champ?"

Champ.

"Yeah, I guess," I say, swinging my bag over my shoulder and joining Antiseptic in front of the car. When I look over at the windshield, I have the sudden urge to get back in.

I clench my teeth, hard.

"Thanks for bringing me all this way." I hold up my hand in a farewell salute.

"It's getting dark." Antiseptic takes hold of my shoulder, and I feel him pull. "Come on."

"Wait!" Mum shouts, and opens her door. She stands in front of me and holds out her arms. I step into them. She squeezes me and kisses the top of my head.

"Just make sure you do your best," she says. "This is going to be great for you."

"Your mum is right," Antiseptic says, smiling.

Dad holds up his hand through the window, reciprocating my salute. "Good luck, son."

The man takes hold of my shoulder again. I look into the back seat and see Lily has her headphones in and is nodding along to something poppy, probably with a wholesome moral undertone.

She catches my eye. "Bye," she says, then mouths, *idiot*.

I turn around because Antiseptic is pulling me by my shoulder again. Harder this time. I hear a door slam and the engine revving behind me.

"Families are difficult, huh, champ?"

I don't really know what to say to this, so I just shrug. The car horn beeps, and the headlights swing over us with the crunch of wheels turning on the dirt.

And they are gone.

Antiseptic sets off, walking quickly ahead of me. "It's not far. Maybe half an hour," he says.

"But I thought we were—"

"Keep up."

"One second!" I shout. "Mark? I need to go."

He stops. *"Go?"*

"Yeah, I need to piss." God. "It's been a long journey."

He waits for a moment, and I watch his back rise and fall as he inhales deeply. He turns, smiling.

"Go in there, quick." He points into the dark reeds.

"In *there?*"

"Where else?"

I look at them rustling. "It's fine. I can wait."

He steps toward me. "You're going to need to be resilient, Sebastian," he says. "It's important."

"Right . . ."

"You can't always take the easy path. At HappyHead."

He is looking at me, and he is definitely not blinking. I look back at the reeds once more.

"I can wait, thanks, Mark. The urge has passed."

"OK," he says. "You can go when we get to the sunflowers. Where it's less dense."

By the time we reach the sunflowers, it's nearly completely dark. I can just make out rows and rows of them, running all the way down to a tall wire fence.

"Go on," Mark says, pointing his flashlight into the field.

The pressure in my bladder hurts now and is making me see white dots dance across the sky. I bite my lip and weave my way between the rows of flowers, their heads reaching up over mine. When I look back, I see Mark silhouetted against the sky, holding what appears to be a walkie-talkie.

He puts it to his mouth. "Not long," he says. "Yes. They were just a little lost. Sebastian is with me now. . . ."

I find a big sunflower to put between us, and as I piss on it, I feel a shudder down my spine. The steam rises around me.

This isn't exactly what I expected.

I don't know *what* I expected, because there were no pictures on the pamphlet, but I didn't think I would be urinating in a field of flowers. It's all a little music-festival vibes for me, and there is a reason I don't go to those.

"Done?" he shouts.

Jesus. I jump, steadying myself. "One sec," I reply.

I glance behind me. In the dark, the sunflowers look a little bit like human heads, floating. Watching. I shudder again and squeeze the rest out, looking down at my new white slip-on Vans. I head back to the path, quickly now.

He must see that I keep checking behind me, because he says, "You don't need to worry." I make a face like he is making false assumptions. "Now come on. We don't want to be late for the introductions."

THREE
Ice Eyes

It's pitch-black, and all I can see is fog. We have been walking for at least forty-five minutes since we came through a huge iron gate in the wire fence.

We haven't spoken much.

I'm pretty sure we crossed a bridge at one point. I can't be certain because I couldn't see beyond the pool of light from Antiseptic's flashlight. But I swear I heard rushing water.

When we finally get to the building, I can't see it all, but I can tell it's huge. The walls are white and shiny. Smooth, like plastic. Small circular windows run the length of it like portholes in a cruise liner. The wall continues until it disappears into the darkness.

"Phone, please, buddy," Antiseptic says suddenly. "Time to send your last text."

I pull my phone out of my backpack, my chunky noise-canceling headphones attached. Shelly says they're old-school. I say they're necessary.

"I'll need to take those too."

I wonder if there are any birthday messages. Something else from Shelly, maybe. Someone from school. I look at the screen.

One message.

Mum.

I open it.

> *Good luck! Mark seemed nice!!! Glad you'll be kept safe. Take your pills!!!!!*

Antiseptic is looking at his watch.

Will do, I reply.

"Sent?" he says.

"Yep."

"We're a little late for the introduction assembly, but no one will notice." He takes my phone and headphones and places them in a plastic wallet he has pulled from a pouch in his overalls. "Anything else?"

I turn out my pockets. My Jolly Ranchers.

"Those too, buddy."

Killjoy. I hand them over to the fun police. Then he shines his flashlight at the wall. I see the faint outline of a door and a small keypad in the white plastic. He types in a code, and there is a *clunk* and a hissing noise.

"Ooh, spacey," I say. "Air lock?"

He looks at me, confused.

I brush it off.

"Just to warn you, people are possibly a little nervous," he says. "You know what teens are like."

I laugh awkwardly, like I've never really thought about it.

When the door opens and we step through it, I realize we

are at the front of a large room. It's a little like the gymnasium at school, except everything is white and there are no windows. There is a white platform in front of us with a white lectern and a white microphone. Facing it are one hundred white chairs, and all but one of them is occupied by a person who looks the same age as me, each with various versions of confused, excited, and nervous emotion plastered on their faces. The door clunks shut behind me, and the noise ricochets around the inside of my skull.

The air lock hisses.

Everyone turns toward me.

Ninety-nine staring seventeen-year-olds.

Antiseptic said no one would notice.

Antiseptic is a liar.

This is my kind of Actual Hell. I want to shrivel up like a dying leech, slither back through the crack underneath the space door, and crawl in the opposite direction as fast as my wretched leech body will carry me.

Antiseptic takes a spot against the wall and points to the single empty chair in the front row.

"Go on," he whispers.

There are others in yellow overalls lining the walls, with similarly shiny teeth, grinning like they are programmed to do nothing else. A little like those perpetually enthusiastic children's entertainers that love an egg-and-spoon race and a ball pit.

One of them, a lady on the opposite wall with a blond ponytail, catches my eye and winks. She waves so much that I worry she might hit herself. I feel Antiseptic's hand give me a small shove. I bow my head, hoping this will make me invisible.

Should I wave?

Casual wave?

Sure.

I lift my hand.

I hear someone laugh.

Someone sighs loudly.

No.

No wave.

Abort.

I drop my hand.

I'm not sure how long they have been sitting here, but it might have been quite a while, because there seems to be a high level of hostility aimed in my direction. The girl who smirked now snorts her annoyance so loudly that a ripple of laughter emanates from her like she is the epicenter of an aggression tsunami. (I am no stranger to aggression tsunamis. They mostly happen in the school environment. They require one total smart-ass and a cluster of suck-ups who are willing to approve smart-ass's snarky comments by way of laughter. Sometimes pointing. Generally directed at one person. Current person: me.)

Don't worry, sweetie! Take a seat! Ponytail mouths.

"Hurry up, fucknugget," someone witty-whispers from the crowd.

I am incredibly hot and realize I haven't inhaled for a while.

Mum says in times like these I must find *inner confidence.* I never really know what she means by this. Maybe it means I should say something charming and fantastic like *Don't worry, you don't need to panic, Seb is here, and these thirteen days just got extra!!!* then jump on the platform and drop into a perfect *shablam,* causing the room to whoop and cheer so I will be forgiven and become the Immediate Favorite.

Instead, I find myself shuffling to the chair, slumping into it, my face burning. I focus my gaze on my backpack, which I have placed over my lap like a parachute I'm about to use to jump out of a plane. Beyond it, on the floor, I can see my new Vans, which are now muddy and have little flecks of yellow on them from pissing in the sunflowers.

This is bullshit.

I feel a layer of cool sweat crawl over my back. I lift my foot as stealthily as I can and wipe my shoe on the back of my trousers, in the hope that the girl on my left with rigidly straight bangs suspects nothing. The yellow flecks of urine do not budge. Her eyes scan me down to my shoes. I see it flash across her face: She knows. She knows that what she's looking at is in fact my very own piss splatter. She looks at my face, seeking an explanation. I give her a smile because it's the only distraction I've got. She raises her eyebrows as if I've just asked her to hook up with me in a dumpster, snarls, then turns her head to the lectern with her hands on her lap, her pleated skirt all neat and perfect like her hair.

I look to Antiseptic for something. I'm not sure what. Help, probably. He smiles.

There's a strange *energy* in the air.

I'm not one to *feel energies* like Shelly says she does, but this one is so intense I can't miss it. It's thick like glue.

Expectation.

People are whispering around me.

"When does this thing start?"

"I'm missing a girls' vacation to Mykonos for this."

"Where can I smoke?"

Somewhere, a girl is telling anyone who will listen that her name is Eleanor and that she is *so* excited to be here, among the *first-ever* cohort for this project.

"I'm thrilled," she is saying. "We need to radiate positivity for this to work."

Someone murmurs in half-assed agreement.

"Some people just radiate *twat*," a gravelly voice says quietly directly behind my head.

When I turn around, the first thing I see is the tattoo right on the side of his neck.

A bird's wing.

Long, dark, oversized sweater with a hole in the seam by his shoulder.

Jet-black hair falling into his eyes.

They flick upward. Ice blue.

Tall. All angular and untidy, like a sketched manga character.

Black nail polish.

He clenches his jaw, and a vein bulges in his neck, making the wing wiggle.

Shelly told me I should try and make some new friends. Maybe I should say hello.

A small scar on his cheekbone catches the light.

"What?" he says.

I snap my head toward the stand. The sweat on my back is seeping through my T-shirt.

"Hey, bro, cool tattoo," I hear the boy next to him say.

"Back the fuck off," Ice Eyes says to him.

The energy thickens to molasses.

"What's your problem, bro?"

"Don't talk to me," Ice Eyes says, louder now.

"Just making conversation."

"Do I look like I want a conversation?"

"Wow. Apparently not," the other voice says. Then, quieter, "You look like you want a good fucking shower, though."

I hear a chair scrape. Before I can turn, Ponytail has scuttled down the row and is standing next to them.

"What did you say?" Ice Eyes is on his feet.

"Hey, fellas, it's a little hot in here. Anyone want a quick cool-off?" Ponytail says in a singsong voice, bright and plucky, like she's giving it her all in a West End production. "Mr. Blake? *Finneas?* Want to take a *breather?*"

Ice Eyes ignores her.

The other one is standing too. I turn my head just enough to see that he's built like a double-door fridge.

"Say it again," Ice Eyes presses.

Fridge Boy snorts defensively. "I said . . . you smell like a urinal."

Ice Eyes raises his fist, and a cold darkness flashes across his face. He's about to swing, when, quicker than I can inhale, Ponytail grabs his wrist, twists it so he turns, and pulls him away. She leads Ice Eyes along the aisle and down to the back of the hall, where they disappear through a door. As if they were never here.

A few people whisper in confusion.

"Pathetic," Eleanor's voice says.

I turn and look at Fridge Boy. He gives a weak little laugh and says, "Coward," then sits back down, folding his arms.

Antiseptic moves forward to stand in front of us. "It's been a long day, but remember, guys, let's approach each other with kindness." His voice is smooth and soft, like something from a meditation app.

"That freak started it," Fridge Boy mutters.

Antiseptic holds his hand out. "Let's leave it now." He stands with his hand in front of Fridge Boy's face for what feels like a little too long. Like he's casting a therapeutic spell.

The room falls silent.

Antiseptic slowly moves back to the wall.

I look at the Overalls. Watching over us. Smiling.

I think about my Jolly Ranchers.

I think about Finneas.

Maybe the pastoral team is giving him a nice cup of herbal tea and a debrief.

The buzz of silence rings in my ears.

"Welcome!" a loud voice booms from the microphone. Suddenly the lights dim. People shush each other.

"Finally," someone groans.

A woman has appeared in a spotlight on the white platform. She is not wearing yellow. She's wearing black. A long, finely tailored coat. Her gray hair is cut neat and short, and her half-rimmed glasses sit on the tip of her nose.

She looks at us. Her eyes twinkle.

"Welcome to HappyHead," she says, her voice strong and deep. Calm. Steady. For a split second, I think we're supposed to clap. Other people do too, because the girl with the straight bangs next to me lifts her hands as if to begin. But before she can, the Overalls standing around the edge of the room all speak at once.

"Hello, Madame Manning," they say. "Commitment, growth, and gratitude give us the happiness we desire."

Silence.

Maybe now is the time to clap.

"Indeed, they do." Madame Manning taps her nails on the edge of the lectern. "We are in an epidemic. An epidemic of unhappiness. The data has shown that without intervention, you, the youth of our country, are in serious danger of many things, but most importantly in danger of yourselves. And it is glaringly obvious that now, more than ever, you need help. A way out."

OK, a little bleak, but sure.

"Friends, here is the good news: HappyHead has the answer." She smiles for the first time. I'm not entirely sure it suits her. "Our radical new project is here to put *you* at the center of your journey into adulthood and give you all the tools you need to fulfill your potential as happy human beings. We seek not only to transform lives but to save them. And you, you lucky people, were selected at random from across the nation and have become the first—the very first—to experience this. You, each and every one of you, are special."

Madame Manning takes a step back from the stand.

A song begins to play.

"Shiny Happy People" by R.E.M. I know it because Dad chooses this one in the car sometimes, when Mum lets him pick.

Madame Manning raises her hand and a large screen descends from the ceiling.

The room goes completely dark. A film starts to play.

Aerial shots of a large shiny white building in the middle of miles of countryside.

Sunflowers.

Grass.

A river.

Teenagers running through trees. Playing soccer on a field. Bright sunshine. Smiling.

"Welcome to HappyHead," a drawling Southern voice says, like something from a Hollywood film trailer. *"The next thirteen days will be among the most important of your life."*

Sad-looking teenagers waving goodbye to their parents.

Unpacking bags in bedrooms.

Eating together in a dining room.

Laughing.

Hugging.

"Here at HappyHead, you will undergo a project created by top experts in their fields."

The HappyHead smiley face appears.

"Because we care about you."

A man in a suit points at us. He laughs.

"You will be grouped together in teams of four."

Teenagers high-fiving. Fist-bumping. Laughing. I assume these people are actors, giving it all the enthusiasm they can muster.

"In these teams, you must work on a number of specially designed assessments. . . ."

Teenagers in a tent.

Teenagers climbing an assault course.

"And we will be watching you."

Overalls furiously tapping their fingers on the screens of their tablets.

"Our team of senior Assessors will always be on the periphery, making sure you are exactly where you need to be, readying you for when you leave. Madame Manning is joined by the internationally

renowned Professor Lindström, our therapy lead, and the formidable Professor Fernsby, our physical tasks expert."

Three people in black, sitting at a long desk, Madame Manning in the middle.

Woman on left looking floaty, long blond hair and a kaftan.

Man on right sharply dressed in suit, thick-rimmed glasses with a wise face. Smiling.

"But try to ignore them. Your job is to complete each task to the best of your ability."

A teenage girl runs over a finish line, pumping the air in joy.

"And always remember: be honest."

A boy is crying. Someone who looks like a therapist hands him a box of tissues.

"We are asking you to trust us."

The boy takes one and smiles.

"So that we can help you."

The therapist nods approvingly.

"You will stay in our Harmony Hall. Fun fact: this hallway is one of the longest in the country, with one hundred bedrooms! All the rooms are numbered."

Scanning down the hallway at speed.

Numbers above doors.

100

99

98

97 . . .

"Each morning a screen opposite your bedroom door will show you a new number. You must move to this bedroom. New day, new room!"

A boy looks up at a screen opposite his bedroom door.

"Why change rooms, you ask? Good question."

Laughing Overalls in the Harmony Hall.

"It's part of our assessment process. We want to see your adaptability.*"*

The boy unpacking his things in a new room, making the bed.

"It's our way of tracking everyone's progress. So early starts for room changes, I'm afraid!"

Alarm clock showing 5:30. A girl yawns and bounces out of bed, smiling.

"We also want to see your initiative *and* resourcefulness.*"*

A girl sharpening a knife in a forest.

"Your intelligence.*"*

A boy rapidly completing a Rubik's Cube.

"Your emotional *and* physical *strength."*

A girl watching her friend cry as she lifts some weights.

"And, of course, teamwork.*"*

A group of laughing teenagers cradling hot drinks by an open fire.

More aerial drone shots. Fields and grass and sunflowers.

The white building.

"A few key rules to keep you all safe."

We zoom in on the forest. A wire fence.

"You may have noticed the perimeter fence. We don't want anyone entering the compound who shouldn't be here. There's no need to go near it."

People sitting around a bonfire, singing.

"Another aspect of safety here at HappyHead is ensuring optimum physical health."

Boy on exercise bike. Girl on treadmill.

"We want to monitor you as closely as possible, so, using

state-of-the-art technology, we will be inserting a small chip just above your collarbone, right here."

A kind-looking lady in a nurse's uniform points to her collarbone.

"The procedure involves one small incision and heals very quickly. This way, we can be on hand if you ever need help."

A boy having an asthma attack on top of a hill. A helicopter lands. Overalls jump out and give him an inhaler.

Boy wipes the back of his hand over his forehead. "Phew!"

"Keep your personal item safe in your bag. You will get your phone back when you leave. Sadly, we allow no contact with family or friends. We want to assess your mental state without distractions."

Teenagers staring at a sunset with their arms around each other.

"You'll love the Cozy Room. During assigned downtime, you can chat and get to know your teammates there, supervised by the wonderful Reviewers. Do not discuss your individual assessments with others unless encouraged to."

Teenagers playing pool in front of laughing Overalls.

"And, finally, remember we are always here for you. This is for you. So when you leave, you will do so with a happy head."

A final shot of teenagers reuniting with their families. Hugs. Smiling.

The sun sets.

The film stops.

The music stops.

Darkness.

I hear the buzz of the screen as it disappears into the ceiling from where it came. I feel a tingling in my feet. No one speaks. I might be mistaken, but did the man say something about putting a chip under my skin?

The spotlight comes back up on Madame Manning. She begins to clap. All the Overalls join her. So much clapping.

"Exciting, hey?" she says.

A whoop from the Overalls.

When I was nine, I went on a weekend away with school. I remember feeling like I might never see my mum and dad again, and I cried and cried. For some reason, I am reminded of that now.

"Let's give our first-ever intake a HappyHead hello," Manning says.

"Hello!" the Overalls say, and wave.

"Now, before we proceed, I must introduce you to the most important person in this building. The reason you are here. The reason you have been given this chance. Please be upstanding for my dear friend, the genius Dr. Eileen Stone."

Chairs scrape.

We stand.

The air lock door opens: *Shumm.*

A lady steps through the doorway. She puts her cane on the floor in front of her to steady herself, and it echoes off the white walls. *Donk.*

She edges forward, her gentle eyes taking each of us in like a turtle slowly blinking in its surroundings after hibernation. She stops, and slowly, very slowly, she takes off her raincoat and passes it to Antiseptic, revealing a multicolored patchwork cardigan, her two long gray wiry braids falling down like rope in front of it.

I mean, what do I know, but this is where *I* would have had the applause.

The reveal. Iconic.

Instead, people just stare in silence.

She must be seventy, at least. She is wearing rain boots.

"And the whack job has landed . . . ," Fridge Boy whispers.

"Shh!"

Cautiously, she makes her way to the bottom of the stage, and we watch in collective, uncertain awe. Waiting for her next move. Some of the Overalls even bow their heads slightly, smiling warmly as she passes them. The admiration for this rural royalty beams around us. Antiseptic overtakes her and mounts the steps, holding out his hand. She takes it.

She is a little . . . shaky. Each rain boot hesitantly finds the edge of the step and pushes her up, one after the other. Everyone is holding their breath. I can feel it. *Hear* it around me.

She makes it, and we exhale as one.

Antiseptic takes a stool from the back of the stage and places it next to the lectern in the circle of light. She looks at it for a second, then turns to face us. She closes her eyes. She doesn't open them for what feels like a little too long to just be taking in the moment. I begin to wonder if she is praying, or casting a spell, or about to ask us all to join her in a meditative chant.

Finally, she speaks.

"Thank you, Madame Manning." Irish accent. Soft. Gentle. I almost want to say *sexy.* OK, maybe not. *Inviting.* "Please sit. All of you. And I will explain."

We do. Like we are under her spell.

She has really kind amber eyes. I notice . . . *tears.*

Yep. She's nearly crying. That's happening.

"You are all in danger." Lovely. "The science is fact. The evidence is concrete. We have seen a drastic rise in emotional dysregulation among young people, the extremes of which are becoming increasingly unsafe. Levels of aggression toward others and toward self are on the rise. Depersonalization and derealization are up. Interpersonal and communication difficulties are areas of significant concern. You are progressively vulnerable to invalidation. *Self*-invalidation. You feel stuck. Lost. Loneliness is an infection so strong in some of you that you no longer know how to function in our society."

Why did she look directly at me when she said that?

"I know this sounds incredibly morbid." Oh, good. "But you are all aware of the shift that has happened in the past few years. Your generation is in crisis. I do not wish to frighten you. We do not blame you. You are victims. And the government has been looking, *searching,* for an answer to this crisis with little success. Until now. They have agreed to trial our project, HappyHead. Born as an idea a long time ago that in theory is strikingly simple, but in reality may be vastly complex. Which is why you are here."

She takes a moment. "Not one of you is the same. The science shows us that your genetic makeup is unique; your predisposition to feel things is set at a different degree—a different *temperature*—from your neighbor. And our lives, our stories, our circumstances move the dial. We are the gun, and our experience pulls the trigger. If this is so, how can a single treatment fit all of us? We are far more complicated than this gives us credit for. Tick boxes and worksheets won't cut it any longer. The treatment must be tailored to suit you. Because here, at HappyHead, we will get to *know* you. And thus we can *push* you. To find acceptance of yourselves. To cultivate a desire to change. To learn skills, progress, and connect. To move forward into adulthood, prepared. This is vital. Without these things, how can we truly experience life?"

Silence.

Do we . . . do we speak?

I am becoming less and less able to decipher when people want actual verbal answers.

"This is the beginning of a remarkable journey. My dear friend Madame Manning will be here on the front line, running the project with her team of Assessors. I won't be staying at the base, my office is a little farther out in the woods, but Madame Manning has agreed to keep me updated. I like to remain in the middle of nature. It's where I find my comfort. And much of my inspiration."

Manning steps forward into the spotlight next to Stone, smiling proudly. "It is always hard to drag the doctor away from her work. And we don't want to detain her any longer." She is taller, more alert, sharper. They are an odd couple, yet somehow they seem aligned. Connected, like sisters might be. Manning clasps the sides of the lectern. "Constantly using her research to perfect the program, *led by the science,* Dr. Stone has created the structure of your assessments, which will begin tomorrow. The Assessors and I, with the help of our wonderful team"—she lifts her hand, gesturing to the Overalls—"will be implementing them. In the morning, after chip insertion, we will begin with a brief individual assessment and then you'll meet your teams. Now, Dr. Stone, we mustn't keep you."

Stone nods. "It is a pleasure to meet you all. You are in the safest hands I know. I would trust Madame Manning with my own life. Welcome, all of you. Welcome to HappyHead."

Manning takes the doctor's hand and squeezes it in a way that makes my stomach give a little involuntary charged pulse. Stone stares at us like she is looking at her long-lost children, then blinks away a few final tears and turns to shuffle across the platform. The clank of her stick on the floor cuts through the air.

Antiseptic helps her down. He gently places her raincoat over her shoulders. And she makes her way back to the air lock.

The door opens. *Shumm.*

Her coat wafts behind her as she leaves. A cloaked, rain boot–wearing Jedi.

Just as the door is about to close, I see Ice Eyes standing outside, Ponytail holding his arm. Stone approaches him and puts her hand on his shoulder. . . .

Shumm. The door shuts.

"Now," Manning continues, "straight to your rooms. Please change into your greens, which you will wear from now on. I will see you all in the assessments. Good luck. Finally, remember: *commitment, growth, and gratitude lead to a happy head.*"

She smiles, steps off the platform, and strides off down the middle aisle to the door.

Everything is blurry.

People slowly begin to stand. Overalls beckon them forward, toward the exits, calling their names. They say things to me, and I am pointed in certain directions, then led down different white hallways, through various white doors. I move past rooms with digital screens opposite them, noting the names of people and colors, all shades of green. Olivia: Bottle Green, Freyor:

Pickle Green, Jimmy: Avocado Green, Ola: Forest Green, Paula: Moss Green, Ahmad: Cyber Green.

I am left outside one of the doors.

Above it, the number 27.

"This is you, Sebastian. The color is your team name. Rest up, you must be exhausted."

Words flash up on the digital screen on the wall opposite my door:

SEBASTIAN: ACID GREEN
YOUR TEAMMATES WILL BE:
ELEANOR BANKS
ASHLEY CHANDA
FINNEAS BLAKE

Ice Eyes.

Tomorrow: 08:00.
Individual assessment: Guided Meditation.
Good luck, Sebastian.

I look down the hallway to see others staring up at their screens. One by one, they enter their rooms. I can hear sobbing, but the hallway is so long I can't see who it might be. I turn to my room and step inside.

Everything is white.

A single bed in the corner. A tray with a piece of salmon, green beans, and an apple sits under the circular window on a desk next to a digital clock, its screen giving off a soft red glare.

Rubber utensils are placed next to it. Green clothes are folded neatly on the chair. Hoodies and joggers. The floor is a soft white carpet. There is a small bathroom with a toilet and a shower, a sink and a mirror.

I empty my backpack onto the bed. My inhaler and my two weeks' supply of pills drop to the floor. I pick them up and pop one through the metallic film.

I place it on my tongue and swallow, the familiar chemical aftertaste bitter at the back of my throat.

There is a song by Bowie that sometimes gets stuck in my head. It's not my favorite, but I can't seem to stop the melody from spinning around and around and around.

From the fifth track on the album *Heathen*. I can't quite remember the words. Something about being afraid. And completely alone.

I sit down on the edge of the bed and wait.

For what, I am not sure.

FOUR

Mellow

That song is playing again. Crying on and on about being shiny and happy and holding hands. I blink open my eyes and see a small white speaker in the corner of the ceiling, projecting the noise so that it bounces relentlessly between the four walls. I am drenched in sweat.

I take in the whiteness of the room. My green clothes folded on the chair. The clock on the desk reading 05:30.

Ah, yes. I am *here*.

I reach for my phone. It isn't there.

My hand feels oddly . . . restless without it. No endless Instagram. No TikTok holes to fall down. No messages from Shelly. Nothing to distract me from my own head.

Just this white room. This could be interesting.

I feel . . . emptier. But not empty. *Lighter.*

Up, Seb.

No one knows me here. No one knows anything about me.

As I stand, I glance through the circular window, down toward a large Astroturf pitch, which is dewy and glistens in the morning light. Beyond, there is a forest. We are pretty high up. Maybe on the top floor—I can't be sure.

I draw a smiling face in the condensation on the glass.

Suddenly I feel dizzy. I hold on to the windowsill.

I can hear people moving somewhere in the hallway, so I turn and make my way to the bedroom door.

This is fine. This is all perfectly fine.

I open it.

The first thing I see is the screen on the wall opposite.

Good morning, Sebastian.
Please have breakfast, then make your way to Bedroom 75.
Your first room change!

At my feet, there is a tray with a glass of milk, a banana, and a large bowl of something gray that might be oatmeal. The girl on my left has her hood up over her head and looks at me, bleary, yesterday's mascara smudged around her eyes making her look like a hungover panda.

"Why?" is all she says.

I don't have an answer.

There is a flashing on her screen.

She turns to see red lettering blinking back at her:

No talking to others in the Harmony Hall, Annabel.

"Ugh," she says. "This is some weird bullshit." She picks up her breakfast, turns, and slams her door.

She seems nice.

Back in my room, I sit at my desk and eat as quickly as I can.

I've never been particularly good with meeting new people. I have been told (mainly by everyone I know) that I sometimes come across as a bit *quiet and intense,* and that it can make other people uncomfortable.

Creepy is how Lily describes it.

I don't mean to be.

Just relax, Shelly always tells me.

I feel a tightening in my chest.

Just Relax.

The worst two words ever to put next to each other and say to me. Like telling a pyromaniac to hand over the flamethrower. Not possible.

I can't eat any more, so I put down my rubber spoon, put on my "greens," strip the bed of its sheets, ball them up into the corner by the door. I open the drawers under the desk to find some Lysol wipes and fresh linen, which gives me a small thrill because I am partial to a Lysol once-over. Using one as a make-shift glove, I clean down the plastic mattress.

When I finish, I throw my backpack over my shoulders, pull the straps as tight as they'll go, and make my way out into the hallway.

Goodbye, Sebastian.

Goodbye, screen.

The hallway is full now, and there is a certain buzz in the air. I take a right, as the numbers of the rooms increase that way, then join the line of people moving like a stream of disorientated and slightly giddy pickles. Some of the eyes traveling in the opposite direction meet mine, searching for any useful information, with a repeating look of *What is happening?*

One after the other after the other.

"Nice and quiet, please! You can meet your new friends later," Ponytail says, barely masking her excitement.

I don't need new friends. I need Jolly Ranchers.

Finally, I reach Bedroom 75.

I don't see Ice Eyes on the journey. Finneas.

I think his accent means he's from Manchester.

When I enter the new room, it's the same as number 27 but different. Smaller. Grayer. Darker. There isn't a window in this one. It's hot. Airless. More like a cell. The previous sleeper didn't take the sheets off the bed, which I think is rude, but also probably fair enough.

Assertiveness.

Adaptability.

I use the Lysol wipes to pull the linen off and make up my new bed.

Better.

Clean is safe.

Before I can sit and catch my breath, the door opens and a female Overall enters. "Only me, Sebastian! How are we this morning?" she says, jolly as Christmas.

Do people not knock here, then?

No?

Sure. That's fine.

She looks at the newly made bed, then nods and types something on her tablet.

"Hi," I say. "Yeah, I'm OK. Hot."

"Oh! Yes, it can get warm in these rooms. You'll get used to it." I miss grumpy people. "Okey dokey!" she says. "Chip-insertion time!"

"Right, yeah, about that . . . ," I say.

"Shh, I work best when it's quiet, if that's OK, Mr. Seaton?"

"Um . . ."

"Sebastian's such a lovely name, but you seem like a *Mr.* to me. I hope you don't mind."

I definitely do. But I nod because I don't know what to say.

"Coolio!" she says. "Now, this won't take a moment. Top off!"

Her name badge says she is called Misty. Anyone named Misty was always predestined to be eternally ecstatic, so I guess I can't really blame her. She begins to hum something that sounds a bit like "Crazy" by Gnarls Barkley, but I could be wrong. Then she opens her bag on the desk and takes out a long needle and a scalpel.

"Don't mind these little guys," she says. "All bark and no bite. Sit."

I do.

My stomach puffs out a bit beneath me like it always does. She notices as I cover it with my arm. "Oh, don't be silly," she says. She pulls on a pair of clinical gloves with a slap and picks up the needle. "Right, slight scratch!"

When Misty says *slight scratch,* what she really means is *new depths of searing agony.* She pushes the needle into my skin a few inches above my nipple and the pain pulsates outward, then tingles into a bizarre numbness.

"Jesus!" I hiss through gritted teeth.

Misty frowns, then bites her lip as she picks up the scalpel.

"Language, Mr. Seaton," she says. She looks at her watch, humming. "Few more seconds . . . And. Now!" She gives me a huge smile and slices a vertical line in my skin, just below my collarbone. I pull myself backward in shock, but she grips hold of my upper arm.

She squeezes it tight.

"Keep still! Thank you, Mr. Seaton. The anesthetic is in place."

She leans over to the bag and fishes around in it, taking her sweet time. I feel a line of thick blood run down to my pale doughy stomach and into my belly button.

The room swims.

Eventually, Misty turns back with a pair of tweezers pinching a small metallic square that looks like a flashing green SIM card.

It beeps.

"That's the sound of it working!" With one very swift movement, she pushes it into the open cut on my chest. The nausea hits me so violently that it causes the roof of my mouth to suddenly fill with saliva and make me dribble. I squeeze my palms together as hard as I can, as this seems to be the only way of stopping myself from throwing up all over her yellow Crocs.

"Very brave," I hear her saying as I fold in on myself. She pushes my shoulder so I sit upright again, and she begins to stitch. "One . . . little . . . suture . . . and . . . it's all done!" She stays focused, her tongue poking out from between her teeth. Then she steps back, marveling at her work. "See! How easy was that?"

I put my elbows on my knees and my head in my hands. "How long . . . ?" I don't really know the end of this sentence.

"Until the anesthetic wears off? Oh, probably this afternoon.

It might start to sting a little right in the middle of an assessment, but you'll be just fine," she says, moving me a bit and wiping the blood off my stomach. She puts a Band-Aid over the stitch and begins packing away her things like she has just visited an old friend for a milky hot drink and a cookie. "It was nice to meet you, Mr. Seaton. I hope I'll be seeing much more of you!"

"Yeah," I say, carefully pulling my T-shirt and hoodie back on. "Thanks."

"Oh, wait, I almost forgot. . . ." She reaches into her bag. I recoil, but she lifts out a small pin badge. A smiley face. She leans forward and pins it next to the zip on my hoodie, right in front of where she sliced me. "There. Now you look the part. Wear this with pride. You need to make your way to Assessment Room three by eight o'clock. Individual Meditation. Don't be late!" She practically skips out the door.

I run to the bathroom and projectile vomit my gray oatmeal straight into the bottom of the toilet bowl.

•••

My encounter with Misty was not what I expected, but I actually feel like I coped with it well, considering. I'm just hoping she saw the way I managed not to pass out (die) on her. Because I've always had a very low threshold for physical pain. Stubbing my toe has been known to result in a short breakdown. So I feel like I—in some way—have already shown improvement.

Personal development.

I follow the screens on the walls telling me which floor to go to. It takes me a while to find it because everything looks the same in this building (white and shiny). By the time I get down three flights of stairs and a long walk along another hallway to Assessment Room 3, the screen on the wall outside reads 07:55.

I stop and wait for a moment.

Meditation.

One of my biggest fears happens to be sitting in awkward silence with other people. It's up at the top of the list, above performing arts and Piers Morgan. Bolting might be tricky. One problem being: I still feel very sick from being cut open. Another: I have absolutely no idea where the hell I am.

Please enter, Sebastian.

The door clicks and swings open a fraction. I push it.

The first thing I notice as I step inside is the smell. The same as when you walk past the entrance of Lush—sweet and welcoming, but also a bit sus. Like they're masking the stench of dead bodies under the floorboards.

"Hello?"

In the center of the white-tiled floor, there is a large cushion surrounded by some potted plants. A vapor machine spurts out little bursts of mist in front of a wooden table with an Assessor and an Overall sitting behind it. Maybe this is what Mum was aiming for when she said she was trying to make the living room more Zen by putting a bowl of pebbles by the fireplace.

Zen makes me nervous. I don't trust it.

I could turn and run. Getting lost in the sunflowers wouldn't be so bad. I could learn to live in the wilderness like that kid who was brought up by a pack of wolves. I've always secretly thought I could really nail something like that.

"Hello, Sebastian. My name is Professor Lindström." I recognize the Assessor from the welcome video. Long, wavy blond hair. Soft features, like someone you would see advertising an all-organic hair conditioner. The Overall next to her is Ponytail. In true fashion, she is smiling so hard she looks a bit deranged.

"Welcome to Guided Meditation," Lindström says, her velvety Scandinavian tone enhancing the vibe of the room. "Please, take off your shoes and enter the space, Sebastian."

"Er . . ."

"The space is safe, Sebastian."

I beg to differ.

"Don't be nervous. The key is to be *open*."

I look to see if the window has heard in the hope that I can jump out of it.

Alas, it hasn't.

They are both staring at me like they are trying to move me with their eyes. I slip off my shoes, step into the circle of shrubbery, and point to the cushion.

"Erm . . . should I?"

"What is your instinct?"

To use it on my way out of the window to break my fall. "To sit."

Ponytail looks absolutely delighted by my response. I see a tablet on the table between them, my name written on it. Ponytail sees me looking and quickly covers it with her arm. "Please do. . . ."

I fold my legs so my body begins to lower toward the cushion. When it makes contact, I look up at them over the top of the table. I feel tiny and stupid all at once. No one is talking. "Very comfy," I say to fill the silence.

"Good," Lindström says. "As this is your first assessment, Sebastian, we shall endeavor to keep it as mellow as possible."

Wonderful.

"This is a short individual assessment so we can get to know you. We don't want to tell you too much, as we are keen to see how you respond."

I haven't prayed (to anyone other than Bowie) in over six years, but, Jesus, please help me out here. My throat is beginning to close up.

"The science behind meditation is well proven. Stress reduction. Increasing compassion. Mindfulness is a gateway to learning skills that can reduce anxiety and increase well-being. Dr. Stone's research suggests that all patients must have a grounding in its principles before they can move forward. It is the first building block, if you will. Have you ever meditated before, Sebastian?"

"Not . . . professionally."

They both laugh gently—and not in a way that makes me feel fantastic.

"No one is a professional at this, Sebastian. It's a process."

"Right, yeah. No. I've not. I've tried to, like, breathe, you know. . . . When I'm anxious . . . or just . . . finding it hard to . . . speak . . . to people . . . Two people is fine. . . . Lots of people is worse, but any amount sometimes . . ." Stop talking. "So I don't make a fool of myself or . . . you know?"

They don't seem to. I laugh like I don't either.

"A focus on breath is a great start, Sebastian. To stay mellow."

God, that word. "Right. Yeah."

"Any questions before we begin?"

"No. Yes. How do I pass this, then?"

"There is no passing. Not today. Just respond the way you feel you should respond instinctively. That's all we're looking for."

"OK."

Instincts.

"Great. Lights." Ponytail pushes something on the tablet.

It goes dark. Except for the ceiling. The ceiling is glowing with stars. At first, I think it's those stick-on ones I used to put on my bed frame, but then I see they are slowly changing size and glowing blue, then warm yellow and white.

I can hear the sound of wind. Wind rustling through branches.

"Just relax." Oh, God, seriously? "Rest your hands beside you on the floor and close your eyes. That's it. Now follow my voice."

I hear Ponytail's rapid finger taps on the tablet and wonder what could be so interesting about me closing my eyes for her to make such hurried notes.

"Focus on your breath."

It feels like it is getting caught in my throat. Like when you chew a paper straw, then try to drink through it.

"In and out. That's right."

My hands are shaking. They always do, though. Can I tell her that? I shift them so they are hidden by my knees.

"How does your breath feel? Describe it."

"Er . . ."

"Are you relaxed?"

No.

"Is it comforting?"

No.

"Yeah. Yeah."

"Use a word." What? "Describe your breath."

OK. Any word, Seb.

"Strong."

"Strong?"

God.

"Ready. I feel ready."

Tap, tap, tap.

"Great. We begin in a forest. A beautiful forest." Right. Forest. Forest. Think. "What does it look like?"

"Big trees." Try harder. "The sun is coming through the branches, and it smells like wood and soil."

"Wonderful. It sounds lovely there."

"It is. . . ."

"Someone joins you."

Suddenly Ice Eyes appears from behind a tree. The blue of his irises sharp against the green of the leaves behind him.

Hi, he mouths.

I feel a twinge in the pit of my stomach.

I smile at him.

He winks.

I feel my cheeks go hot.

Hi, I try to say back.

Come with me, his eyes say.

As I step forward, a twig snaps beneath my foot. I falter. He flicks his hair.

His eyes gleam. *What's wrong?*

I . . .

Lindström's voice pierces through the trees. "This person should be someone you have never met before."

Oh.

Bye, Ice Eyes.

He vanishes.

"This person is wearing a suit. They look reliable. Responsible. They say they know you. That you can trust them. Picture them, Sebastian. In your mind's eye. Can you?"

A faceless man takes Finneas's place in the streaking sunlight.

"Yeah. Sorry."

"Why are you apologizing?"

"Nothing."

More tapping.

Piss it. Focus. *Focus.*

"This person is going to walk with you like a shadow by your side. You begin to move through the forest. Keep breathing." I can taste menthol from the vapor. "Can you feel them next to you?" I nod. "Fantastic. Up ahead, you see a stream. You follow it through the woods, and the trees begin to thin. It leads you down to a shore. It is the sea. You stand at the water's edge. The sun bounces off the waves lapping at your feet. Focus on the waves. Your breath moves with the waves. In and out. Each wave brings in peace."

Does it?

I need to scratch my nose, but I'm scared of what the repercussions will be.

"The waves are your strength, your *attention control.* Notice yourself. All of your senses. Just be *aware.* The wind begins to pick up, and the water starts to become gray. You need to cross, Sebastian. There is an island. You must get to it. But a storm is brewing and it's getting dark. There are two options. You could use the rowing boat on your right. It is small and has only room for one. You would need to leave your person behind. Do you see the boat?"

I look. I see it.

"Yes."

"Or you could ask the person to take you a different way. They say they know one and that you can trust them."

"Right."

"The waves are getting stronger. Lightning flashes. Clap of thunder . . ."

I feel myself jump.

This isn't real.

"How are you feeling?"

"I . . ." My voice cracks. "Yeah. Not . . . fantastic."

"Explain that."

"Just . . ." God. "Unsure."

"What do you want to do?"

"Go back!" I blurt.

"But you can't."

"No?"

"No."

"How does that make you feel?"

Really?

"I . . ." I think I'm panicking. "I hate this."

Oops.

"What do you mean?"

Careful . . .

"I just don't like having my eyes closed in front of you. I feel weird and this is weird. It's making me very uncomfortable. I don't like hearing my own breath, and I don't like this metaphorical sea."

"But it's not a metaphor. The sea is real."

"Right."

The waves surge up around me, rising around my legs.

I am floating. Bobbing.

The boat looks tiny next to me.

I rock forward.

"This feels . . . I . . . I feel stupid. Sorry."

"Do you not feel like you can continue, Sebastian?"

My mum's face. *Please don't mess this one up.*

"No. I can. I can. I just . . ."

"Go on. . . ."

"I don't want the boat."

"Your companion?"

I'm turning now. In the water. A whirlpool.

"I dunno. He's my own imagination. I don't really trust that."

"But he's not. Not here. He might have the answer. So what will you do? You don't have long. There is safety on the island."

"I'll ask him."

I see him next to me. The faceless being. He reaches out his hand.

"Help . . . help!" That was quite loud.

He takes my hand.

"Please open your eyes, Sebastian. The assessment is over."

I open my eyes.

"I'm done?"

I'm panting. I'm *sweating*.

Well. Congrats, Seb.

"That's it?"

Ponytail is still typing. The stars have gone. The lights are bright again. I am in the middle of the potted plants and I feel naked. Exposed. Compromised.

"Yes. Thank you. That's all we need."

Do I just get up and go?

Ponytail keeps typing. OK. Yep. Seems like it.

I stand, slip my feet back into my Vans and turn to the door.

"You lied at the beginning," Lindström suddenly says.

I turn back to her. "Sorry?"

"You said you felt ready. You weren't. Your sympathetic nervous system had already been triggered. Tachycardia developed, meaning your heart rate was incredibly fast. Your body was unsettled. Stressed."

"Right. How do you . . . ?"

"Your chip." Oh. "But then it got better. Once you let it consume you."

"Sorry?"

"That part was promising."

"Sorry . . . I don't . . ."

"Initially, openness is what we are interested in. Your openness with us will be hugely beneficial. And Dr. Stone believes that in order for each person to fully embrace this process, they must start from a place of honesty. *Radical honesty* is what she calls it. Most people have been trained to pretend. To lie. Society has taught us to deny ourselves our truth as a form of defense. But your reactions matched your body readings."

I feel a slight twinge as my stitch catches on my T-shirt. "It doesn't matter that you hated it. What matters is that you told us. You were honest. For the most part. You might be surprised, but most people struggle with that. Well done."

"And you asked for help from your person," Ponytail puts in. "It's good to trust those that offer it."

She smiles. So does Lindström.

It seems real. Like they might mean it.

"Right. Thanks."

"No need to thank us," Lindström says. "Now, in your next assessment, you will meet your teammates. Good luck. And *stay mellow.*"

Oh, look, she has a catchphrase. She puts her thumb up.

"Let me get that for you, Sebastian," Ponytail says as she weaves behind me to the door. "You'll be going to Assessment Room twelve after lunch."

"Mr. Seaton?" Lindström calls as I step through the doorway. "Keep it up. You have promise. This could be very exciting."

...

The lunch hall isn't like the one at school. There is panpipe music playing, and water bottles are being handed out. We are told they are decomposable and free from the threat of microplastics. They look no different to me.

As we enter, we are told to stand in front of a screen in the wall.

"The scanner will read your chip and tell you what you are deficient in. You will then be prescribed a personalized meal, to replenish your needs."

My *needs*? My needs are Jolly Ranchers and Pop-Tarts, so here's hoping.

"Sebastian?"

"That's me!"

"In front of the scanner."

The machine speaks in a British accent.

"Please stand still, Sebastian."

I do.

"A happy gut leads to a happy head."

A red light shines from a little dot above the scanner, right onto my chest where my chip is. The voice speaks again.

"Deficient in: zinc, pantothenic acid, folic acid, B12, tocopherol, vitamin D, and calcium."

Oh. So not much, then.

"Prescribed: chicken and avocado with grains. Kale smoothie. Dessert: citrus fruits, probiotic yogurt with nuts and seeds."

I was hoping for curly fries and turkey dinosaurs. But I'll let it slide just for the fact that I feel like I'm in a space film and I like space films. I always think I'd do *really* well in an apocalyptic space disaster. Shelly doesn't agree.

I'm led by an Overall into a huge room that is completely filled with rows and rows of singular white shiny tables, like an exam hall for one hundred robots. I am taken all the way to the back row and told to sit.

"Your prescribed lunch will be on its way."

"Thanks," I say, like this is all totally normal. I watch the tables fill up in front of me. As more people enter, they seem to stop for a moment, taking in the room like they are suffering from a bout of exam-hall PTSD.

I find myself looking around for Finneas. What did Dr. Stone say to him outside the air lock?

People try to whisper to each other, but Overalls patrol between the rows of tables, shushing them.

"The lunch hall is a quiet zone. We want to remain therapeutically engaged while we eat. Mindful."

And so I have the quietest, weirdest, most clinical lunch of my life. When I finish eating, my chip beeps approvingly. And I am told by someone in yellow that I must now go and meet my new teammates.

FIVE

Bucket

The outside of Assessment Room 12 is much like the outside of Assessment Room 3. Except outside 12 there is a girl standing by the door with two pink clips scraping her hair back so tightly that her forehead doesn't move when she lifts her eyebrows.

"Eleanor Banks," she says, and I realize it's the girl who was *so* excited to be at the introduction assembly yesterday.

"Hi." I put my hand up. My greeting salute.

"Sebastian?"

"Er, yeah. How did you . . . ?"

"You just look like a Sebastian."

"Thanks," I say. Thanks?

"Ashley?" Eleanor shouts excitedly over my shoulder, so shrill that it feels a bit like I've been slapped. A new girl has just arrived.

"It's just Ash," she says. She looks at me.

"Hi, I'm Seb."

Ash points to a spot beneath her collarbone. "How gross was that?"

"It didn't bother me." Eleanor shrugs. "I'd rather know they're closely monitoring my health. And we need to show them we can handle it." She tilts her head to the side in some kind of yogic stretch.

"I suppose," says Ash, unsure.

"I threw up," I say out of solidarity, and Eleanor looks at me like I am something stuck to the bottom of her shoe.

"How was your meditation thing?" I ask Ash.

"We're not supposed to discuss the assessments, Seb," Eleanor cuts in. "Where's Finneas?" She shakes her head and grimaces. "When I saw his name in Acid Green . . ."

"Do you know him?" I ask.

"Well. No. But I saw him lose it yesterday at the introduction. He's feral. How are we supposed to have any fun with him—"

"Feral?" a gravelly voice repeats from behind us. We turn to see Finneas lurking by the wall a few feet away. His eyes scan over us, piercing blue. "That's a new one." We shift awkwardly. "What? Did I ruin all the *fun*?" He practically spits the word, the roundness of it unmistakable. Definitely Mancunian.

Eleanor sighs.

I notice his eyes are bloodshot. The muscles in his face twitch. There is something . . . unsettled about him. Tense. Like a coiled spring.

Ash gives him a small smile. "I'm Ash." He nods at her.

"Hi, I'm Seb," I say. For some reason, my voice croaks, so I cough and say, "Seb," again.

He points a finger at me. "Oh, yeah. I remember."

Acid Green. All together. One little family for two whole weeks.

Experiencing HappyHead.

Making memories.

Maybe we will all be best friends by the end, with our own WhatsApp group, going on camping trips to re-create the experience. I can see it already. Maybe Mum's right. This will be good for me.

I think I'm staring at Finneas. I should stop. But there is the faintest blue and green of a bruise just below his hairline. It wasn't there yesterday.

"You OK?" I hear myself say. He looks at me, and I feel a tingling of heat crawling across my skin.

"I'm fine," he says. He keeps looking at me. "Are you?"

Huh?

Before I can answer, Eleanor butts in again. "Don't be late again, please." She adjusts one of her pink clips. "We've already had a team member be *sick*." She looks at me. "We don't need an *absent* one."

Finneas chews his lip like he is restraining himself. Then Eleanor pushes the handle and opens the door to Assessment Room 12 just as the clock flicks to 14:30.

■ ■ ■

Inside are two Overalls, one of whom is Antiseptic. The other is a small woman with fluffy brown hair and rosy cheeks. Between Antiseptic and Fluffy is the smartly dressed Assessor from the introduction assembly. The physical tasks expert. Fernsby.

They are standing behind a long table against the far wall, and they are all wearing enormous puffer coats.

Weird.

In the center of the room, there's a large plastic bucket the size of a trash can on a metal stand. It's a strange sight—I won't lie. I wonder if it's some kind of abstract-art installation.

Eleanor, Ash, and I stand puzzled in the doorway, Finneas a little behind us, keeping his eyes to the floor.

"Welcome, Acid Green. Please step forward," Fernsby says in his monotone voice, not looking up from his tablet. We do as he says. "You will get to know me as one of your core Assessors. You four have been grouped together because we feel that from your profiles, aspects of your personalities should bring out desirable traits in one another. It will be fascinating to see how you develop together." Eleanor subtly snorts and flashes a look at Finneas. "Now, welcome to your first group assessment. This is called Bucket."

"It's a super-fun one!" Fluffy chimes in. She has something very put-together about her, with her perm and her little cardigan under her coat, but her eyes are wild. Like a substitute teacher set loose.

"This assessment is about knowing the basics of human life," Fernsby continues. "Water, nourishment, is at the core of our well-being. And Dr. Stone strongly believes in the therapeutic impact of problem-solving. It is important for us to accept that problems are a part of life and they can be used to better ourselves. Knowing that we have the capability to make changes at any point is vital for progression. Problems in your life must be viewed as challenges, not obstacles. Now, the rules are simple. All you need to do is to keep as much water in the bucket as possible during the next twenty minutes." He points to it, and I notice there are maybe fifteen different-sized cork plugs wedged into the sides with little strings attached to them. "Nice and simple. Do you all understand?"

No one says anything.

Antiseptic peers up at us from his tablet.

"Sorry," Ash says slowly, raising her hand. "Just to be clear . . ."

"Keep as much water in the bucket as you can!" Fluffy's eyes are practically bursting out of her head. Maybe we should just let her complete the test. She definitely seems the most eager.

"Sure . . . OK," Ash says, sounding even more perplexed than before.

"Right, all clear, then? Good." Fernsby doesn't wait for an answer. He beckons to Antiseptic and Fluffy, who move over to the bucket and yank the strings attached to the plugs, so they squeak against the plastic.

Pop, pop, pop.

Water begins to gush out all over the floor.

Suddenly a loud horn sounds. I jump. Ash lets out a tiny squeal.

Fernsby checks his watch, zips up his coat, and sits himself down, crossing one leg over the other. The Overalls join him back at the table. Fluffy pulls on a pair of gloves and a bobble hat.

A clock on the wall bleeps and begins to count down.

20:00.

19:59.

19:58.

Oh, right, so this is actually happening.

I feel the temperature of the room suddenly drop.

"What the . . . ?" Ash says, pulling her hoodie around her.

We look upward. In the ceiling, a set of vents has opened, pumping freezing-cold air directly onto us.

Oh, shit.

Eleanor is already at the bucket. The three adults begin to tap away on their tablets energetically, watching her. She pushes her hands against two of the holes in an attempt to block them.

Somewhere in the back of my mind I can hear Mum's voice. *Make sure you do your best.*

"This place is fucking strange," Finneas whispers next to me, then backs away toward the wall.

As the water pools out across the floor, I notice small blocks of ice floating on its surface, drifting toward my feet.

"A little help?" Eleanor shouts. She pulls one of her hands away, shaking it out and wincing as the water pours over her. "Guys?" I notice her fingers are turning red and blotchy.

Lindström said *promising.* . . .

You have promise.

"Use your hoodie," I say, stepping forward. "Screw it up and stick it into the bigger holes."

"What?" Eleanor says, trying to use the back of her hands now. Ash joins her and begins to do the same.

"It's some kind of a puzzle," I say, more to myself than the others. "We need to use something to jam into the holes." I unzip my hoodie and start to roll it up. Crap. The material is too thick. I need my T-shirt.

I look behind me to see Finneas skulking in a corner, arms folded, hood up. I turn my body away from him, and as quickly as I can I pull my T-shirt over my head, careful of the stitch. Holding it in one hand, I quickly zip the hoodie back over my pale, goose-bumped torso.

"What are you doing?" Eleanor says as she tries to angle her body to avoid one of the torrents pouring out over her shoulder.

I twist my T-shirt at each end and stuff it into two of the larger holes. I step back.

It worked.

It worked!

Have I won?

I look inside the bucket at the dark, icy water. It is already more than half empty. And the level is still dropping.

"Finneas, can you help us, please?" Eleanor barks.

He starts to pace back and forth, biting his nails. His eyes keep flicking to the adults. He seems nervous.

"I'm not doing this," I hear him mutter.

Out of the corner of my eye, I can see Ash trying to use the flat parts of her arms.

"It's still emptying," I say, pressing my hands onto the bucket, the force of the water pushing back against them. The cold stings like pins digging into my skin.

"You think?" Eleanor snaps, her jaw trembling. "Right, we need *everyone* for this to work." She is loud now, clearly wanting to take charge.

"Please?" Ash says to Ice Eyes, her body shuddering as she tries to twist herself so she can use her hip to block a hole the size of a grape.

He doesn't move.

"Seriously?" Eleanor says to him. "*What* is your problem?"

"Back off," he says quietly.

"I can't cover enough of them," Ash says.

"Use your socks," I say.

"What?"

"We just need to plug the holes. Use your socks."

Ash looks at Eleanor, who nods. She lets go and leans down to take off her shoes, but the icy water cascades over her so quickly that she gasps and splutters. She flails, coughing, then presses her hands back onto the holes. Fernsby taps away on his tablet.

Sodden, she catches her breath. "What are we going to do?"

Right. Focus, Seb.

"Finneas." I turn to the corner of the room. "Can we use your T-shirt? You don't have to come over here."

He looks me dead in the eyes.

I feel a rush of something.

Bowie blue eyes. Electric blue.

"Seb, just leave him," Eleanor hisses. "He's wasting our time. We can do this without him."

But I keep my eyes on Finneas. I try to smile.

"Please," I say gently. "You can just pass it to me. You don't have to come any closer."

He flicks his hair out of his eyes. "This is stupid," he mutters angrily.

"It is, yeah," I say. I hope Fernsby didn't hear that. I meant to just think it.

Ash groans, pushing her back against the leaking holes.

"We can do this." I nod at Finneas. "But we need you."

"Do we, though?" Eleanor again.

He holds my gaze, making a prickling sensation rise in my cheeks. Then he speaks. "Fine." He faces the wall and unzips his hoodie. As he pulls his T-shirt over his head, I see the curve of his back.

Tattoos crawling over it. A dragon blowing fire over his left shoulder blade.

His muscles flex as his skin bristles in the cold.

He zips his hoodie up. The dragon disappears.

I turn to the bucket. It's only a quarter full now.

"This is going to be empty *very* soon," Eleanor says, her back now pushed against the bucket like Ash.

"Just wait," I whisper.

Finneas balls up his T-shirt and throws it at me. It passes right by my head, the scent of something musty mixed with deodorant trailing behind it. I release my hand from one of the holes as I try to catch it, but miss. It drops to the floor.

Eleanor tuts.

"I've got it," I say.

I try to pull it toward me with my shoe, but end up tilting forward into a questionable lunge, the freezing water pouring down my back and into the elastic of my joggers.

Christ alive. This is hell.

Then I feel him next to me. He leans down and whispers so only I can hear, "Why the hell do you want to please these people?" He picks up the T-shirt, screws up the ends, and pushes them into the holes.

I straighten up.

"Right," Eleanor says, not acknowledging him. "Everyone pull your sleeves over your hands; it doesn't hurt as much. Leave the holes at the top—just block the bottom ones."

Finneas steps forward into the space next to me.

He looks . . . upset.

"You don't have to," I whisper.

He turns to me for a moment, and I see a flash of something across his face, something I can't quite translate. Confusion, defeat, pain—a mixture of all three? But then he pushes his hair out of his eyes and steps right into the gap. "It's fine." He presses himself against the remaining leaking holes.

He closes his eyes. He doesn't flinch.

"Thanks, Finneas," Ash says after a while.

He nods. "It's Finn," he says quietly.

We lean, limbs tangled around each other, pushing our body parts against the bucket, arms outstretched like we are praying to some weird water god.

The flow leaving the bucket slows. There are only a few trickles now.

I exhale.

A wave of relief crosses Ash's face. *What the hell?* she mouths, water dribbling down her nose.

"Well done, guys!" I say loudly so Fernsby can hear my encouragement.

Tap, tap, tap.

Eleanor is concentrating. Counting. "This should work," she says.

She's right.

I look at the clock.

05:23.

05:22.

05:21.

I watch Finn's face, his closed eyelids quivering.

How did he get that bruise?

Eleanor mumbles something to herself about people needing

to get over themselves. The atmosphere around the bucket is definitely frosty in more ways than one. Acid Green has not got off to a roaring start with communication, but that's fine. Good, even, because it gives us somewhere to go. Yes. Our personality clashes give us something to work with.

Four minutes left.

The tapping of the tablets has stopped. Is that good or bad? Probably bad.

What do they want from us? Connection?

Yes. Of course. I should try to forge a connection between us.

"Should we get to know each other?" I say.

Eleanor darts me a look so disapproving that I want to jump into the bucket and be rolled into the woods never to return.

Ash smiles at me, probably out of sympathy. "It's a little hard to talk right now," she says through chattering teeth.

"Yeah. Sure. No worries."

My arms have gone completely numb.

I think about Shelly. I wonder if she will be going to the pub tonight.

Three minutes.

In my head, I recite as many lyrics as I can from *Hunky Dory*. In a moment of confidence, I hum to distract myself from the burning-ice agony, but stop when Eleanor says it is adding to the pain.

My body no longer feels like it belongs to me.

00:03.

00:02.

00:01.

Horn.

Oh, sweet Jesus, thank you.

"Right." Fernsby stands. "Stay where you are while we measure the water."

Antiseptic and Fluffy walk over and lower a tape measure into the bucket. There is not very much left. A few inches at best.

Tap, tap, tap.

"Step away from the bucket," Fernsby orders.

We do, and the rest of the water glugs away pathetically.

My whole body throbs. "Well done, everyone!" I try, but no one is listening. I shake out my arms in an attempt to regain some feeling in them.

Ash falls to the floor, panting. Finn pushes himself back toward his favorite place, the wall. Eleanor stands. Like it was nothing.

There is a clicking noise from above, and the cold air from the vents stops.

"How much?" Fernsby asks.

"Two hundred and fifty-three milliliters," Antiseptic replies.

"OK." Fernsby's eyes scan us. He clicks his tongue a few times, thinking.

I can't tell if he's impressed by Acid Green's noble attempt.

Then he speaks. "Interesting that you didn't just put the plugs back into the holes of the bucket. But the T-shirt stuffing was highly imaginative."

Oh, shit.

I can't look at Eleanor because I can actually hear her fuming.

"Now for the next part of the assessment." Huh? Next part? "Through there. Now, please, all of you." Fernsby points to an outline of a door in the wall that I didn't notice before.

Without me really understanding what is happening because

my brain now seems to have the consistency of a Slush Puppie, the door suddenly slides open and we are ushered through.

A wire cage stands in the center of the room. There is a single bulb above it, gently swinging on its cord.

Finn backs into the corner.

The cage looks just about big enough to fit the four of us.

"In you go," Fernsby says from behind us.

Nobody moves.

"How long?" Eleanor asks.

"Until the end of the day," he says.

"What?" Ash says.

"So . . ." Fernsby looks at his watch. "Just under five hours. This is a test of endurance."

Five hours?

Antiseptic and Fluffy enter. Fluffy holds an eco-friendly HappyHead bottle in her hand, half full of what appears to be bucket water. "Two hundred and fifty-three milliliters exactly— to see you through." Makes sense, I guess. "See, I told you it was a fun one!" she adds.

Finn is now pacing around the walls of the room. He keeps scratching the side of his head.

"We can do this," Eleanor says.

"Lots of word games!" Fluffy winks.

Ash is shivering. "But . . . I'm claustrophobic. . . . Like, actually." Her face is stuck in an expression of terror.

"We want to see you lean into your ability to endure tough situations," Fernsby says.

I can hear the ticking of Antiseptic's watch. He is staring at the side of my face.

You can't always take the easy path, he said by the reeds.

Eleanor is looking at the cage, drumming her fingers on her arm. "I'll do it."

"Will I fail if I don't?" Ash asks.

"No one fails here," Fernsby says.

She drops her head, embarrassed. "I think I'll leave it, then. . . . Sorry, guys."

"I see." Fernsby makes a sharp tap on his tablet. "Right. Boys?"

I look at Finn. His hands are shaking as he brushes the wet hair out of his face.

Oh, God.

Five hours.

The image of my parents' faces enters my head. Hopeful. *Desperate.*

"I'll give it a go," I say.

Finn looks at the cage, shaking. "No way," he says quietly.

"Very well." Fernsby makes another sharp tap.

Before I can think, Fluffy is leading Ash and Finn out of the room and I am crawling into the cage with Eleanor just behind me.

Antiseptic padlocks it shut.

The light flickers off above us, and the area below my collarbone gives a sharp twinge.

SIX

Eternity

Running my fingers along the skin on my hand, I feel the deep grooves of a grid pattern. I think back to this morning, the meditation. I take a breath and exhale as slowly as I can, attempting to expel the fluttering in my chest. *Stay mellow.* See, I'm learning.

I hear Eleanor's stomach rumble. She sits up, takes a sip from the bottle, then lies back down again. I hear the air moving in and out of her nostrils. She is very close to the side of my head. Somehow, she actually still smells good. Floral.

How long have we been here?

Two hours. A day. Eternity.

In the darkness, my thoughts play out like a film. I focus on them to take my mind off my numbing body.

I kissed a girl once.

To say we dated might be an overstatement, but we definitely saw each other in a room with no other people in it on at least four occasions.

I was fifteen.

I really liked Chloe.

I don't know how the kiss came about—the exact sequence of events. She just kept looking at me like I was going to do it. Like she was *waiting* for me to do it. Every time I said something, she had this expression on her face. She wasn't listening to me. She was thinking, *It's about damn time, Seb.*

I remember the feeling of the kiss. It's hard to describe.

Here goes.

It was a bit like an episode I saw of a reality dating show Mum always watches but pretends she doesn't. One of the men had to kiss a woman he didn't want to for a bet, and when he did, everything about his body tensed up like it didn't want to be there. His body was pulling him in the opposite direction, so he was leaning, *slanted* almost. His hands were behind his back and he was hanging on to her by his pursed lips, nothing else. I always remember how tightly screwed up his eyes were, like it was pure hell. When he opened them, he just stood for a moment, staring.

And there was a sort of gleeful look on his face.

A look of relief. He had done it. He had won.

That was how it felt to me.

Chloe still texts me occasionally. She once messaged me to ask whether I ever really liked her. She has a real boyfriend now who has a job working for his dad as a mechanic.

I kissed a boy once too.

There were several differences between that and the Chloe kiss. First main difference: it wasn't relief I felt when it was over. I wanted it to continue. Second main difference: my little sister saw and told nearly everyone I know. Third main difference: he never texted me again.

My fingers still have that damp texture you get after swimming for too long, like withered prunes. I press them together. Numb.

Everything is numb.

My clothes are still damp.

Eleanor keeps shifting her position.

"You OK?" I whisper.

"Yeah . . . of course."

"Can you imagine if there were four of us in here?"

"Can't believe they gave up."

"Right . . . I guess it would have been a bit warmer."

"It just *bothers* me," she snaps. I don't say anything. She continues anyway. "I don't understand people who don't try."

My tailbone is pressing into a wire rung, sending a shooting pain down my legs.

"People are good at different things," I say. "Not everyone wants to succeed at lying down in a cage."

"Hmm. Well, I'm sure they'll get marked down."

Marked down?

"What do you mean?" I whisper. "Who knows what they're writing?" I nod in the direction of the three glowing tablets. "Probably marking down the two idiots who said yes."

She moves her arm, and it clangs against the cage. "Ouch," she says, and I feel her press her hand to her mouth, stifling the pain. She shakes her arm out. "That's what's wrong with our generation. No tenacity. Everyone wants to take the easy option. I'm sick of it. Ash is claustrophobic, so I get it. But that guy Finn, he's a total waste. . . ." She stops herself. Breathes. "Anyway, we'll be the ones reaping the benefits." I don't know who talks like this, other than my parents. "What room are you in?" she whispers.

"Er . . . seventy-five."

"Right."

"Why?"

"I think the closer to one, the better," she says, and turns over.

"Huh?"

Silence.

The period of time that follows could be any length. I have no idea. At some point, we run out of bucket water.

Things start to blur a bit: my head swims. I ball myself up as tightly as I can. My whole body aches, and I am shaking uncontrollably. I try not to think about how my life has led me to this point. I must be drifting in and out of sleep, because I am dancing with David Bowie at a masquerade ball, when a horn sounds and the light above us flickers on, its brightness stabbing into my retinas so I have to shield my face.

Eleanor is already crouched upright.

Fernsby is standing by the door.

"You should be pleased. The assessment is over." He smiles at me and nods. The kind of proud-teacher nod that I've seen people at school receive when they ace an exam. Or smash a time on the athletics track.

"To your rooms, both of you. Quickly now. Get some rest: you've earned it."

We exit, trembling, into the bright lights of the hallway.

• • •

Back in my room, my fingers shake as I pick up the rubber spoon, making it hard for me to put the steaming soup to my lips.

I stare at the digits on the clock.

20:04.

The screen suddenly goes blank.

I lower the spoon onto the tray, and I'm about to pick up the clock and shake it when writing begins to scroll across the screen.

Hello, Sebastian. . . . Careful. Your chip tells us your body is below average temperature: time for a nice hot shower.

I quickly finish my food, then take off my sodden greens and hang them on the radiator. I step into the shower and feel my body ease as the warmth covers me.

Sweet Jesus. *Warmth.*

The last five hours melt away. The water swirls into the drain beneath me, the dirt from my body muddying it, mingling with the foamy suds. I see the single stitch on the top of my chest, dried black blood crusting in the knot. Under the skin, every now and then, a small green flash.

This is all a bit . . . I don't know. Totally bonkers.

But I'm showing *promise.*

I've not done that before. Not to my knowledge.

I can hear Mum's voice somewhere in my head. *It's fine, Seb. Stop overthinking.*

I let the rain of the shower drum into the top of my shoulders until they are bright red. When I get out, I wipe the condensation from the mirror and look at my reflection. The dark rings around my eyes seem to make my face sag, pulling it downward.

Ugh.

I look away and wait for the steam to mist the mirror up again, then brush my teeth.

I find pajamas in the desk drawer, put them on. I then take my pill, wrap myself in a blanket, and sit down on the bed.

I suddenly remember my dad's reaction when I told him I didn't want to join the local football team. His genuine concern for my *development*. His disappointment as he said, "Don't worry. We'll find something you're good at."

Maybe HappyHead will be the thing I'm good at.

● ● ●

I'm woken by a banging.

A slamming noise. Out in the hallway. A boy shouting.

I sit up. The darkness makes my vision swim.

Silence.

Maybe a bad dream. Maybe . . .

Footsteps in the halls.

Someone running.

I stand up and tiptoe to the door. I open it a crack and peer down the length of the hallway.

I can see shadows in the distance. A flash of yellow. People entering a room. I can't tell how many.

"Get me out!" a voice screams. I push the door open a fraction more.

"Finneas, you're having a nightmare. Please try and relax."

It's him.

Ice Eyes.

My stomach turns.

"No. No!"

"Into bed, Finneas. That's it."

A yellow figure turns and scuttles up the hallway toward me. I pull the door closed quietly, holding my breath. Fear pulsates through me.

Fear of what?

I tiptoe back to my bed and pull the covers over my head.

Muffled noises continue. The occasional cry. A shout.

I'm not sure how long it takes for the noises to stop.

But eventually they do.

SEVEN
This Is My Head

That stupid song is playing again.

05:30. The sour taste of tiredness coats my tongue.

I pull myself up and open the door. The screen outside beeps at me.

Good morning, Sebastian.
Please have breakfast, then make your way to Bedroom 32.

Thirty-two. That's closer to one. What was it Eleanor said? *The closer to one, the better.*

At my feet, granola, melon slices, and a yogurt. Mum would appreciate the meal choices here. Not that there's much choice involved.

I suddenly notice how hungry I am. I take the tray to my desk and shovel the breakfast into my mouth. I then strip the bed, wipe it down, and take my now-dry greens from the radiator.

I dress and go out into the hallway.

It's a bit buzzier this morning. I turn left and pass people heading to their new rooms, all in green. Green, green, green.

I overhear one Green talking about how amazing he did yesterday. How his Assessor stopped their group and asked him to demonstrate his technique to the rest of the team, and how he was *mortified, but happy to help.* Another Green asks him what the assessment was, but then they both get shushed by a lurking Overall.

And a third Green is *super happy* with the way she meditated. She says she wasn't surprised, as she has had lots of practice because her mum is a part-time life coach.

"I can't do that stuff," mumbles a mousey boy.

Life-Coach Spawn shrugs and moves on.

A few others hang their heads, eyes to the floor, looking a bit . . . disappointed in themselves.

I don't hear anything about a bucket or a cage, though.

"Good job on your first task, guys!" the Overalls say as we waddle to our new rooms.

I pass a boy ranting at one of them. "This is a joke. I didn't agree to this mind games bullshit."

The Overall nods. "Frustration is a natural and valid emotion. Do not be overwhelmed by it. Embrace it. Only you have that power."

The boy just stares at him, confused, then sighs and joins the stream of people.

When I get to Bedroom 32, it's much bigger than 75, with a large window and even an armchair. Everything white and slick. The shower is a massive walk-in one. I feel like I'm on a vacation in Ibiza.

I hate to say it, but maybe Eleanor was right. This is kind of cushy.

The clock does that thing again.

Hello, Sebastian. Please join team Acid Green in Assessment Room 18 at 10:00. Lateness is not tolerated at HappyHead.

. . .

Eleanor is already outside when I get there, limbering up. She looks no different. She's fresh and bright. Still smells like a bunch of wild daisies.

"You look exhausted," she says.

Sometimes just *hello* is OK.

"Yeah," I say. "Yesterday was intense."

"I thought it was good." Course you did. "You ready for today?"

"I think so. You?"

"Always."

Jesus, she's terrifying.

"Where are the others?"

Before she can answer, the clock on the wall turns to 10:00. The door swings open and standing on the other side is Madame Manning herself, arms wide open, welcoming us.

"Ah. Good morning, Sebastian and Eleanor. Come in." She's wearing a black suit, stiff and crisp. I notice a momentary warmth behind her formality, underneath the neat lines crinkling around her gray eyes. "Quickly, please. Join your teammates."

When we enter, Ash and Finn are already there.

There are four white plastic seats with connected flip-up desks placed in a circle in the center of the room. Each desk has a single sheet of paper and a pencil on it. Ash is in the corner. She looks at us apologetically, probably feeling guilty about not joining us in the cage yesterday. I smile as if to say, *Don't worry about it,* but Eleanor gives me a nudge with her elbow as if to say, *Stop encouraging her.*

Finn stands by the window, staring out at the Astroturf and beyond, over the thick mass of trees that rolls away toward the horizon. I make my way across the room as casually as I can and look out to see a group of Overalls patrolling the running track that loops the bright green of the playing field.

He doesn't say anything.

The bruise by his hairline is darker now.

The skin under his eyes is streaked with tiredness.

He has his hands pushed deep into the pocket of his hoodie. There is something about him that almost . . . radiates. An energy. Half *pensive* . . . half . . . *angry*?

If Shelly were here, she would know.

I get nightmares too, I nearly say to him. But I don't. I realize I'm probably staring, so I turn away.

Antiseptic has arrived. And Fluffy. Unsurprisingly, they are both smiling. *Hi, guys,* they mouth. Fluffy raises her eyebrows excitedly.

Manning steps into the center of the circle. "Could we all join?"

Everyone takes a chair except Finn, who stays rooted to his spot by the window.

Manning waits for a moment. "Finneas?"

"I'm good here, thanks."

"Please, Finneas," tries Fluffy. "This is a place of acceptance."

He slowly turns his head and eyeballs her. "Is that so?"

She tries to hold his gaze, then drops her eyeline, momentarily flustered. Manning puts her hand gently on Fluffy's shoulder. "Don't worry, Barbara." Of course that's her name. "He can stay there if that's where he feels safe." I don't dare look at Eleanor, but I can tell she's seething.

"So today we'll be engaging in the simple but wonderfully useful exercise of Drawing Therapy," Manning continues.

OK, no. No thanks.

Finn snorts.

Ash rolls her eyes.

Eleanor is positively beaming.

"Art can tap into our subconscious and help us communicate our feelings when we find it hard to do so verbally. So, to get us going, draw what happiness looks like to you. You have five minutes."

I stare down at my blank sheet.

"Off you go."

I hear the scratch of pencil lead on paper.

I'm so busy sneaking looks at Finn's outline framed in the window that when Manning speaks again I realize I have been making my version of happiness completely absentmindedly. I look down at my picture and immediately try to hide it with my arm. Maybe we'll burn them as an act of liberation or something.

"Right, time's up. Let's show our pictures."

Damn.

"Eleanor, you go first."

Eleanor stands. "My picture is in two parts." She looks so

pleased with herself. "This is me winning a trophy. I'm on the top of the podium, as you can see here." She points to a beautifully sketched girl. The two stick figures she has drawn in second and third place are crying. "But as you can see *here*"—she points again—"I am giving my winnings to someone else." Eleanor has quite literally drawn herself handing someone a ten-pound note. "To be in a place where I am able to give, to support those who are less fortunate, will make me truly happy. That's what I want."

If she could drop a mic, she would.

I notice in her picture her eyes look unhinged. A true likeness.

Manning nods. "Generosity is vital to happiness. Very good." She turns. "Ashley?"

"Erm, yeah." Ash sheepishly holds up her page. "It's quite abstract. This is me with my family. We're in a sort of field— a sort of happy land, I guess. Surrounded by flowers—tulips are my mum's favorite. And it's peaceful. The sun is shining. . . ." She trails off. "Sorry, it's a little basic."

"I like it, Ashley. I like the energy it gives. Good job."

Ash gives a little smile.

"Sebastian." I slowly stand and hold up my sheet of paper. "I can see you've drawn a . . . Is that you? And your . . . Is that your *brain*? Would you like to explain?"

I look at my drawing and want to ball it up, swallow it, and run.

"Erm, yes. This is my head. My brain. And it's sort of full of mess. A dark storm cloud, a crow. I think those are . . . yes, those are cockroaches, a dead tree, and, um, that's barbed wire. . . ." What have I done? "But all the mess is falling out onto the floor, see?" I copy Eleanor and point like I am delivering a presentation. *"Here!"*

"So . . . this is your brain falling out of your head?" Manning looks at me with a mixture of pity and fascination.

"Erm . . . I guess." I try to lighten the mood. "All my worries gone!"

"Interesting." She pauses. They all stare. "Eleanor and Ashley have drawn themselves with other people when experiencing happiness. You haven't. Would it be too much to wonder if loneliness has been a part of your life?"

I suddenly sense Finn's gaze fix on me. Would it be too much for me to stick this pencil in my eye?

She spots Finn looking and turns to him. "Finneas, it's a shame you don't want to participate. Look at all the good work we are achieving." He snorts again, making me feel like we are all five years old. "We have learned something about your teammates through this exercise."

He is still looking at me.

"Yes," Fluffy chips in. "Very insightful."

Manning addresses us all again. "It's been an intense first few days, I know. Professor Fernsby fed back that there may have been some anxieties that surfaced during yesterday's session. As we will all be working closely together, I think this is a good time to debrief and clear the air in a therapeutic manner. There is no judgment. No reason to feel guilt or shame. I would like to invite us all to enter a conversation in which we are equal, if you would be willing?"

I'm good. Let's not do that. Please nobody say anything.

Eleanor raises her hand.

You've got to be kidding.

"Eleanor, yes."

"I'd just like to say thank you. I feel like I'm already learning and growing so much. Especially yesterday. I learned that I can work in a new environment and think quickly. And that I'm willing to attempt all the challenges we face. I think it's good that we're getting to know every angle of our team. It will only make us stronger."

God.

Manning smiles. "Thank you, Eleanor."

Then she looks at me.

Oh, God. No. No. No. Please don't. . . .

"Sebastian? Anything you'd like to add?"

It's OK.

I'm OK.

"Erm. Yeah. Sure. Thanks. I'm . . ." Unprepared for this. Dying for it to be over. Unable to access the words I need. "Er . . . I'm . . . I'm grateful."

Is that enough? Please be enough.

"We love gratitude here, Sebastian. Dr. Stone has placed a great emphasis on gratitude in her design for the program. It helps us look outward, away from ourselves, which can benefit us all."

Phew.

"Ashley?"

Ash looks like she doesn't really want to contribute either. "I'm sorry if I was terrible yesterday."

"That's OK, Ashley," Eleanor says before she can stop herself.

"You weren't terrible, Ashley," Antiseptic chips in. "You're all finding your feet." He smiles warmly at her.

"Thank you, Mark." Manning nods. "This isn't easy, but

we are incredibly proud of how your cohort is taking to Happy-Head. Let's go deeper. Be *critical*. What could you have done better? Eleanor?"

I see a twinge of surprise in Eleanor's eyes. Just a flash. Then she smiles, making a thoughtful face as if she is considering this seriously.

"I could have been more assertive," she says. "I think I should follow my instincts and take the lead when other people are floundering." Floundering? "Some of the team needs direction. . . ."

Manning holds her hand up to stop Eleanor's flow. "Who?"

"Well, Finneas definitely needs to be shown that he"—Eleanor makes a face like she is contorting her thoughts to form something more palatable—"is in a *safe* place to participate."

Oh, nice. She's good.

"Why?"

"Because he's resistant. Scared, maybe."

"In what way?"

"He just seems to want to isolate himself. He shouldn't have to do that. It's good to make friends and trust people."

"Don't speak for me," he suddenly says flatly.

Manning turns her head to him. We all do. "Finneas, if you've got something to say, please join us. Or perhaps you could draw how you're feeling, if that makes it easier."

Silence.

I hate this. I hate it. I'd rather be buried alive.

"Perhaps . . . ," Ash says, saving us all, "perhaps we just need to get to know each other a bit better. It's OK that people have different styles, isn't it?"

"We need to be *critical* in order to grow. What did you do wrong yesterday, Ashley? In the spirit of being critical?"

"Well . . . I guess I don't take the lead that often. I can be a bit quiet."

Manning drums her manicured nails on her tablet.

"Is that bad?"

"I don't like that word," Manning says. "Bad. Let's ask if it's *helpful*."

"Well . . . Erm . . ."

"It's not. Your ideas count, Ashley. You should have that confidence."

Ash tries to sink her face into her hoodie, looking like she now wants to dissolve.

"This may be hard," Manning goes on, "but it's the process. To grow, to change, we have to understand which aspects of ourselves we can improve."

Suddenly Finn turns. He steps into the circle in such an abrupt way that everyone leans back. Then, like he's been put on slo-mo, he sits. His eyes fix on Manning.

"Thank you for joining us." She remains calm.

He picks up his pencil and begins to draw.

We all watch.

A flame. A dragon. It's all angular and twisted.

The dragon looks a bit like him. Breathing fire. In the flames searing out of the dragon's mouth, he etches the word "LIAR."

He presses so hard that the pencil lead snaps. I flinch.

He holds it up to Manning. "Done."

"Interesting," she says without any emotion. "Now that

you're here, Finneas, would you like to explain why you didn't participate in the rest of the assessment yesterday? Ashley said she's claustrophobic, but you never gave a reason, I hear." There is the slightest edge to her voice.

A pause.

"You know why. Because of what happened before it."

A bigger pause.

"We're not discussing the individual meditation assessments, Finn—"

"That wasn't exactly *therapeutic,* was it?" He cuts her off. "How did you get your hands on things that I've never shown *anyone* before? Where the hell did they come from?"

"What's he talking about?" Ash whispers.

I shrug.

"In the *spirit of being critical,* Madame, it's pretty *fucked up.*"

Manning is looking at him in a way I cannot read. She then exhales and says evenly, "Like I said, Finneas, we are not here to debrief the personal assessments. Just the group session. You and I can discuss your meditation together later."

"No, thanks. You're good."

"Well then, it appears you may need a breather."

"A breather?" He laughs, then suddenly stands.

"Mr. Blake . . . please calm down," Fluffy tries. "We want to help you. No one wants to see you like this."

"Like what? Like *what?* Don't tell me you don't get off on this. You love it! Seeing people going *mental?*" he shouts, banging the side of his head with his finger. "Isn't that what you want?" He turns, picks up his chair, and throws it at the window. It crashes into the glass, and the white plastic splinters across the floor.

I hear Ash yelp.

"Isn't this what you want to see? Aren't I giving you something *to work with?*"

"As you can see, Finneas is really struggling today." Manning slowly puts her hand out toward him. "Your peers are here for you, Finneas." She looks at us. "Aren't you?" We nod. Yes. Yes. "We each have our difficulties, but, Finneas, you must surrender to this process. We are here for you."

He has his back to the wall now like a caged animal, ready to pounce.

"I want to see her. I want to see Dr. Stone."

"That's not how this works."

"Does *she* know how this works?"

"Of course. This is her vision."

"I want to see her."

"You can't."

"Why?"

"This is a real shame." Manning gives a small nod. On her command, Fluffy and Antiseptic approach him. Just as they reach him, Finn lets out an almighty scream.

"No. NO!" Before I can really compute what is happening, he pushes Fluffy so she falls backward and hits the floor, hard. Then he bolts out the door, tears flooding his eyes.

Manning goes after him.

"Everybody remain calm," Antiseptic says.

I suddenly realize I am at the doorway, watching him pelt down the hallway, Manning walking swiftly behind him.

"Back inside the room, Sebastian. Now." Antiseptic pulls me back into the room and shuts the door.

What the actual—

"Hell." Ash has her hand over her mouth, her eyes wide with panic.

Eleanor is helping Fluffy sit upright. She then shakes her head, looking at us with a mixture of shock and complete certainty. "He's an *animal*."

Fluffy stands and brushes herself off. "Gosh." She turns her head and smiles. "Well," she says, her voice shaking, "I think we need to debrief the debrief!"

She chuckles. No one else does.

Then we hear a noise from outside. We edge over to look out the window, and I can see Finn sprinting into the woods, followed by a pair of Overalls.

Antiseptic puts his hand on my shoulder. "Let's get some lunch, and then you can go to the Cozy Room to cool off. That's enough for today."

I look down at Finn's dragon, now crumpled on the floor.

EIGHT

Worker Bee

The designer of this building really showed their versatility when deciding how cozy the Cozy Room should be. It's white, shiny, and smooth, like the rest of the place. Even the seats look hard and slippery, so we've chosen to sit on the beanbags instead.

It's getting dark outside. There's still no sign of him.

In the corner of the Not-at-All-Cozy-Room, Antiseptic perches on a swivel stool. There is a pool table (white) and a bookshelf full of books (all white). The *pièce de résistance* is a little ice-cream cart with wheels and a red-and-white-striped canopy. Fluffy stands underneath a sign that reads: *Ice cone? Lots of flavors to choose from! A great way to chill out!*

Eleanor is talking at full speed about how we should lodge a complaint, or that we should at least *forcibly encourage* Finn to leave our team. She's going on about other boys she has seen around the building that she thinks look like a better fit for Acid Green.

"I don't know if we can just steal other team members," Ash says.

"Worth a shot, if it means getting rid of that *brute*. Seriously, he should be put down," Eleanor says, then makes a beeline for some kind of games shelf. She starts to pull out the boxes.

"This is all a bit weird, isn't it?" Ash says quietly to me once Eleanor's out of earshot.

Just a bit.

"Yeah, I think she's going too far."

"No. This whole thing. This place."

"It's always hard at the beginning of things like this," I say, like I'm an expert at the beginning of things like this.

"Hmm, I dunno." She twists her hair in her fingers.

Eleanor beckons us over, not even trying to hide her elation at having found a chess set and the incoming thrill of beating us both. "We can make a scoreboard and do a tournament throughout our time here—keep our competitive edge going even when off duty," she declares like a drill sergeant.

Ash shrugs. "Not much else to do around here." She joins Eleanor with an unenthusiastic sigh. I miss my Jolly Ranchers, so I make my way to the ice cream cart.

It's been a while now. I wonder where he is.

Maybe he got out. Maybe they took him somewhere quiet. To help him calm down. Perhaps Lindström is giving him some extra therapy. Yes. They must be prepared for stuff like this. Have a dedicated adjustment team or something.

What did she show him in his meditation session?

"Any toppings?"

I look up. Fluffy is dishing out a huge scoop of blue sorbet. "It's all low calorie!"

Not sure that's what I wanted to hear.

Maybe Ash is right. This is a bit . . . weird.

"No thanks."

It was odd seeing him scream. Crying like that. He looked really . . . young. Like a little boy. His eyelids all swollen and his cheeks red.

"Bubble-gum-yum-yum, I call it," Fluffy is saying, her perm practically bouncing as she balls the sticky gloop. I wonder if she's been secretly chugging the stuff herself to get over the incident.

The incident.

I take my cone. As I pass Ash, she looks at me like she's in desperate need of support with the chess tournament. Eleanor is sketching out the scoreboard on a piece of paper.

I decide to go to the balcony instead.

"You guys enjoy," I say, and Ash throws me a look.

As I push open the sliding glass door, the cold air hits me. I look out over the trees, which are turning black in the dimming light.

Where is he?

I notice a plume of smoke spiraling upward between the trees and a faint smell of firewood. I follow the gray stream to a chimney poking out between the branches. Is that where she lives? Stone.

I lean my elbows on the railing. I breathe. Inhale the woody tones.

For my fifteenth birthday, Shelly thought it would be a good idea to do an all-nighter in a field. We took our sleeping bags and some XXL bottles of cider and headed for the forest just off the roundabout. She told me to invite people. Said it could be fun, like a big woodland party-type thing where I could show people the *real me*. But I just wanted the two of us to get tipsy and listen to music on my new speakers.

We borrowed Mum's big tiger-print rug and bought about seven tubes of Pringles and some marshmallows. We found a spot that was kind of in the middle of the woods, but still close enough to the road that I could hear the traffic in case we needed to run for help. We lit one of Shelly's dad's disposable BBQs that we'd taken from the garage.

We drank the cider and danced around to *Blackstar*. Then she played me some of the stuff she likes. It was all waily and deep, and I said it felt very emo and she said that should be perfect for me, then. It was the first time she ever asked me about boys I liked. I said I liked absolutely no one.

I then went on to prove her emo comment to be correct by talking at length and with frantic drunken passion (as she put it) about how I thought love should feel. That you would know immediately because it would feel *physical*, like a cold, or the flu, like a big, achy flu, and how I'd not felt that yet.

Except with Bowie.

She said Bowie didn't count.

I said it did.

At some point, I was sick inside my sleeping bag. Waking up the next morning was probably the grimmest experience of my life.

Clunk.

The door slides open behind me, and there is the *cccchhh futtt* of a match striking against the side of its box.

I turn.

And he's here.

He's back.

Ice Eyes.

"Oh, sorry," I say.

Hi. I meant hi.

His hood is over his head and his hair, poking out from under it, is wet. He is wearing fingerless gloves. He looks like something from a fashion magazine.

Just act like everything is fine. Because it is. It is.

"I love that smell," I say. He looks at me. "The matches. It's . . . I dunno. Nostalgic."

Nice, Seb. Awesome.

I don't know if he heard me, but he doesn't respond. He just moves around me and leans on the railing to my left, putting the cigarette to his lips. He inhales.

I look out over the trees and down the hill. There's a tension in my stomach. I can feel it creeping up into my throat. A fluttering. Like a tiny bird trying to find its way out. And I'm suddenly very aware of him next to me.

His breath.

His body.

I don't think I'll mention what happened during Drawing Therapy. It's probably been swept under the carpet by now. He won't bring it up.

"Apparently I have to resolve things," he says.

"Sorry?"

"Earlier."

"Oh, no. I mean, you don't. You seemed to have everything sorted . . . fine. Under control."

Ugh.

"I've been told to apologize," he says. "In case I made you scared. Uncomfortable."

"Oh, you don't need to. You didn't," I say. I turn back to look through the glass to see if anybody is watching. I see Manning talking quietly to Antiseptic by the pool table. "It was nothing."

"Yeah."

"Well, not nothing. Just . . . nothing to me. I was fine. Hardly noticed. Maybe not nothing for you."

Jesus Christ, Seb.

He sucks in deeply on his cigarette, and I watch the hot glow of the embers sizzle and crack. The dark rings around his eyes make the blue even more vivid, and I can see the beginnings of stubble, an emerging shadow on his cheeks.

"Hi, boys. How you doing?" Antiseptic is suddenly standing in the open doorway behind us.

"All good," I say, then look at Finn. His eyes seem to be following the plume of smoke from the trees, up into the air.

Antiseptic steps toward us. "Listen, champ. You shouldn't really be smoking that. You were supposed to hand those in." Finn inhales deeply, turns, and blows smoke at him defiantly. "I have a vape you can use."

Finn looks at him, completely dead. No expression. Antiseptic smiles and passes him what looks like a fat purple pen. "It's tobacco flavor. Better than nothing."

Finn slowly lifts his hand and takes it, then slides it into his hoodie pocket.

"Great to see you getting to know each other," Antiseptic says. He catches my eye and nods in a way that says, *Good, yes, making friends is a great plan; good idea.*

He slides the door shut and puts his thumb up to me through the glass.

Finn scratches his nose with his fingernail, the black polish now chipped.

Make friends. Sure.

"I like your gloves. I wish I could pull off that kind of thing. I tried a trilby once, but it didn't work, so I stepped it down to just a baseball cap. But I got told I looked like a prepubescent child, so . . ." God Almighty. Change. Tack. Seb. "Where are you from?" I ask.

He casually begins to pull up his sleeve and shows me his wrist, where there is a tattoo just above his gloved right hand.

A bee.

"The worker bee," I say. His eyes meet mine and momentarily brighten, and the bird in my stomach makes a sudden frantic attempt to escape.

The corner of his mouth turns upward slightly. Is this him smiling?

"Manchester," I say.

"Yeah. How did you know?"

Because of *Coronation Street.* Don't say that, though. "I've not been, but I know a bit about it. Nineteen seventy-two. Bowie played the Hardrock Concert Theatre."

"Yeah?"

"In Manchester."

He nods.

"There's a recording of it. On YouTube. It's not very good quality, but try it. When you get home. Or get your phone back. Whichever happens first."

"I'll do that."

"It's mint." It's the only Manc word I know. I saw it on Noel Gallagher's Twitter and always liked it. I suddenly worry I haven't used it right, but he turns to me and his eyes twinkle.

"It's *mint*?"

"Yeah."

"I see. Well, I must check it out, then."

"You must."

"Where are you from?"

"Me?" Yes, you, *idiot.* "Er, I'm not sure you've heard of it," I say. "I'm from a small town called Woking specifically." God, who talks like this? "Sorry . . . I'm just a bit . . ."

"Polite," he cuts in.

"What?"

"Polite."

Oh, great. It's official. I'm a total catch.

"Oh, not really," I say, trying to laugh. "I just meant . . ." I trail off. Nervous. Incapable.

I'm suddenly very hot.

"It's all right. It's good."

Is it? Is it really?

"It's warm," I say. It isn't, but I am.

"Good job you've got that, then," he says.

"What?"

He points at my ice cream, which I now see has completely melted all over my hand.

"Ah! Yeah. Yes. Doing its job."

He taps his cigarette and gray ash falls to the ground far beneath the railing. As he exhales the smoke, his body relaxes. I try to discreetly wipe my hand on the front of my hoodie, but the green fibers attach themselves to the sugary syrup. My instinct is to put it to my lips to lick it off, but when it touches my mouth, I can feel its furry texture. I pretend I'm just scratching my chin.

"So you're into Bowie?" he asks me after a moment.

"Oh, yeah. Always."

"Interesting." He pulls up his left sleeve, the arm without the bee this time, and on his inner forearm he reveals another tattoo—a lightning bolt, the outline of one, the exact shape of the one from the cover of *Aladdin Sane*. It's as if it jumps from his skin and strikes me right in the face. My stomach contorts.

No way, Ice Eyes. No effing way.

OK. Be chill, Seb. Be chill.

"Oh, nice. Nice. You like him?"

"Oh, yeah. *Always.*" He winks. Just a small one. Like it almost didn't happen.

How can a wink make my stomach feel like that?

"Ha!" is the noise I make to this. "You have a lot of them," I say, trying to steady my voice. "It's good. Means you don't have to answer questions, just show people tattoos instead. You can avoid conversation. I might try it."

He smiles now. It's undeniable. I can even see his teeth between his parted lips.

Did I do that? Did I make that happen?

"How many do you have?" I continue.

"Lost count now."

"Well, I like them."

"Thanks."

"I bet your parents had something to say. Isn't it illegal at our age?" God, I sound like my mother.

He doesn't respond. Move on.

"Your school must *love* them."

He scratches his cheek. "Oh, yeah. What was the word they used . . . ? *Disgusting*."

What did Eleanor say? *He should be put down.*

"Well, that's not very nice," I say, like the absolute stud I am currently presenting myself as.

"Nah. I'm used to it. I kind of like it."

Silence.

I can feel Antiseptic's gaze from behind the closed glass door.

"I wonder what's around here," I say, looking out across the woods. "Maybe we'll do some day trips into the local area or something."

Then he points. "Look," he says.

I follow the line of his finger. Out on the path running up alongside the Astroturf is a team, four of them in their greens, carrying what looks like a selection of tools into the forest. Two Overalls. An Assessor. Fernsby, in a long black coat, leads the way. They are walking quickly.

"Probably some kind of nature therapy. Dr. Stone said she uses nature—"

"You really think that? Really?" he whispers sharply. "Come on." He looks at me. Like, right at me.

Into my brain.

Into my mangled thoughts.

"Seb," he says. "You know there isn't . . ." He stops. He looks back at Antiseptic, who holds his hand up to us through the glass. *Hi!*

What? What do I know? There isn't what?

All OK, boys? Antiseptic mouths.

Finn nods and puts his thumb up.

98

Antiseptic smiles at us.

Finn puts his hand on the railing and then winces, retracting it quickly.

"You all right?" I ask, but he doesn't answer. He just shakes his hand out for a second and looks back toward the team, who have now disappeared into the woods.

"I wonder what's going to happen tomorrow," I say, trying to sound excited.

Finn waits for a moment, still staring, his eyes not completely focused. Then he snaps his head away and squashes the cigarette butt into the rail of the balcony, marking its perfect whiteness with a dark black circle. He flicks the butt over the edge, sparking a cluster of red embers that flutter and die in the cold air. "Yeah," he says quietly. "Me too."

Antiseptic slides the door open. "Can I get you anything? All OK?"

There's no escape from these bloody Overalls.

"Feeling better," Finn says, a bit brighter. "Thanks."

"If you need anything . . ." Antiseptic puts both thumbs up this time, grinning. "Just ask. We're here to help!"

"Can I have one more ciggy?" Finn says. "Then I'll use your vape."

Mark sighs but seems pleased Finn is relaxing. "Sure, Finneas. Just give me the matches when you're done." He leaves, sliding the door shut behind him.

Finn takes out his pack of cigarettes and matches. "See you around, then, Seb," he says, balancing a cigarette between his teeth. He doesn't look at me.

Pretty sure this is my cue to leave. "Right. Yep. See you around."

I enter the Cozy Room and reluctantly join the girls. Eleanor proceeds to beat me at chess, twice. Ash tells me she's hoping there is a proper physical assessment soon because she's a fast runner and good at triple jump. She's on the school track team.

Finally, the balcony door slides open and Finn heads toward us.

"I wanted to apologize to you all," he says. "I didn't want to scare anyone. It wasn't my intention. I'm going to try my best to do better. We're a good team, and I'm aware of what's on offer here. I want to use it to help . . . help me." He looks at Fluffy. "And thank you for being understanding. I overreacted. I'm sorry."

"Don't you worry. We're all here to learn."

"Well done, Finneas," Antiseptic says.

"Don't worry, Finn," Ash says kindly.

"Let's hope you mean it," Eleanor puts in, not looking up.

"I'm off—early night," he says, and holds out his gloved hand to me. "Good night."

I take it. He shakes it. I can practically hear Eleanor's eye roll. When he lets go, I can feel a piece of something flat and sharp in my palm.

He nods subtly.

I close my hand tight and put it in my pocket.

"Night, then," he says.

"Yeah, *night,*" Eleanor says, lining up the chess pieces on the board again.

He leaves.

"Right, one more, anyone?" she asks.

"Sure," I say.

This time I win.

"I must be tired," she says.

When we are told that our duration in the Cozy Room is over, I say goodbye to the girls and am led back to Bedroom 32 by Fluffy.

I keep checking it's in my pocket. That it hasn't fallen out.

The dinner tray is waiting for me on my desk. Pasta tonight.

I sit with my hand in my pocket and wait. When I hear the slam of doors down the hall quiet, I pull out the piece of card. A torn-off strip of the cigarette pack.

I unfold it.

Something has been scratched onto the white side with the dark soot from the burnt end of a match.

There's no way out, Seb.
I need 2 show you something.
2morro.
Tell no one.

NINE
Positive Influence

05:30.

His handwriting looks like him.

All jagged and scrawly.

Last night I woke up terrified that my room might get searched. That Misty might return with her clinical gloves and go rooting through my pockets, or other places. So I stuffed the note in one of my socks and slept with it on.

I need to get rid of it.

Swallowing it had crossed my mind, but I think that only happens in films. Instead, I tear it into as many pieces as I can, head to the bathroom, drop them into the toilet, and press the handle until there are no bits left floating on the surface.

I don't really know what it means. I mean, I know what it *means*. . . . But I don't know what he wants to show me.

Tell no one.

I should probably focus on all the *promise* Lindström says I have.

There's no way out, Seb.

In the hallway, the screen tells me to go to Bedroom 29. Only three doors down. It's a bit bigger again, with a nice soft rug and low lighting. The windows have fancy shutters. I eat breakfast, take my pill, and sit on the edge of the bed.

I look at the clock screen and wait for the digits to turn into words and tell me what to do next.

My stitch tingles.

I think about his bee tattoo. His wet hair. His chipped black nail polish.

Shelly once told me that I always try and see the best in people and that this is a terrible mistake. Absolutely the worst trait a human can possess, she said. One that will only get me into deep, deep shit one day.

I told her I struggled to understand why. She said it wasn't surprising I struggle to understand because I grew up asking *What Would Jesus Do?* (I had *What Would Jesus Do?* written on the front of my school planner and on a bracelet that I wore for a significant period of my childhood.) She said the reality is most people are just out for themselves and that I should be careful. I told her I chose *her* as a friend, so I can't be that bad a judge of character. She reminded me that, no, I didn't: my mum forced me to ask her to be my friend.

And she did. Mum said I need people around me who have *real confidence.*

The clock goes blank.

Hello, Sebastian.
Please join team Acid Green outside on the Astroturf at 11:00
for your next group assessment: Survival.

I wonder if Finn is just a bit muddled. I know what Mum would say. *Stay out of it. You're doing well. He's just trying to derail you.*

His message was a little dramatic, I must admit. Maybe he's playing a game. Maybe it's an undercover assessment! Like those murder-mystery role-play things my parents' friends play at each other's houses. Passing notes, clues . . .

Yes. That must be it. Something like that. Right?

There's no way out, Seb.

I feel a sudden surge of panic and my throat tightens.

There's a knock at the door.

I immediately stand. "Hello?"

It opens a fraction. Perfume instantly wafts in—*sweet*, apples, oranges . . . Smells expensive, like Harrods.

Then I see the short, styled gray hair.

Manning.

"Good morning, Sebastian. Is this a bad time?"

"No. Not at all . . ."

I find myself fighting the instinct to kneel or bow.

"Oh, good. I'm just checking in with people. Please, sit. How is everything?"

"In here? Yeah. Good."

She closes the door behind her. I sit on the bed, pulling the sleeves of my hoodie down and brushing the creases out of my joggers. I place my hands neatly on my lap in an attempt to appear more proper.

She looks over the top of her glasses at me, then scans the room. She has a certain formality about her. A precision to every movement. It makes me scared to move. To speak. In case I do it wrong.

She folds her arms and focuses her gaze on me. It suddenly feels tiny in here.

"Are you settling in, Sebastian?"

"Yes," I say. I cough and shuffle, trying to relax myself.

"How is your . . . ?" She points to her clavicle, and I understand she means the chip.

"Oh, yes, great. No problem at all."

"Good."

"Yeah. It's amazing, isn't it?" I say. "Hardly notice it."

Silence. Maybe I should stand up, show her around. There isn't much to see, but I guess the view is nice.

"I wanted to talk to you about Finneas."

A wave of nausea hits me.

"Mark said you'd had a little chat with him yesterday, in the Cozy Room?" I slowly nod. "This is wonderful to hear. I think it would be really useful to nurture that relationship. I would like you to use it." Use it? "To guide him a little bit. Encourage him to engage. You are not blind to the fact that he has been struggling. And we don't want him to leave, not until he's really given this a go." *There's no way out, Seb.* "We feel the program could really help him. And people like Finneas need positive influences to follow. It's part of the reason we grouped you together."

A positive influence.

Me.

I cross one leg over the other, like I'm in an important interview, and try to sound considered. "Yes, we had a little chat. . . ."

"On the balcony."

"That's right." I am aware that I'm making my voice more formal than usual, in the same way that Mum does.

"What did he say?"

"Sorry?"

"How was he?"

"He was OK. Just . . . you know." I make a face, like *You know crazy Finneas!* Then feel like an idiot.

"Hmm," she says, which I can't quite interpret. She makes her way to the window and looks out over the Astroturf and beyond. She stands pensively, as if she is weighing something up in her mind. "It's beautiful here, isn't it?"

"Yes. Really stunning," I say with confidence, because I'm sure that is what people say in this kind of meeting. Is this a meeting? She feels so . . . *corporate.* Like she would run some huge bank in the city and go back to her mansion in the country on a Friday night to check that the pool has been cleaned for her weekend guests.

I take in her neatly manicured hands, the white tips of her nails—perfect little half-moons. And a bracelet with a clasp in the shape of a small anchor with something small etched into the side. I am aware I can stare too much, so I look down at my bare feet.

My socks on the floor next to them. Where the note slept.

The note. I definitely flushed it all away. *Didn't I?*

Could the toilet have regurgitated it?

Oh, God. Toilets can do that.

She turns back toward me and leans against the windowsill. I shift again, crossing my legs the other way, and lean onto my arm like I am very casual. She pushes her glasses up her nose for a moment as if she is waiting for me to say something.

"Is there anything you wanted to ask me?" she says after a long pause.

"Erm . . . No. Not really."

"Or . . . tell me?"

God. The note.

"Not that I can immediately think of?" I make it sound like I'm really trying to think.

There is another pause. She scratches her perfect nails on her perfect sleeve. "I think this will be a really positive friendship to nurture, Seb. For everyone."

"Yes indeed."

"But be careful. I don't want him affecting your progress. Your journey is just as important."

"Of course. But I'd be happy to help, if that's what you'd like? If he's struggling."

"Thank you. You're showing an openness; that is what we are looking for. Dr. Stone is very pleased with you."

"Is she?"

"I'm constantly giving her feedback. She's eager to know if people are taking well to the program. If you need our support, we're here. You can tell us anything, Sebastian."

"I appreciate that," I say.

"There's something about you, Sebastian. We're very excited. Keep it up."

I feel a strange tingle down my spine that might possibly be pleasure. *Something about you.*

She pauses for another brief moment as if giving me a final chance to speak, which I don't. Then she heads to the door.

"Good luck this afternoon, and be brave. Fearlessness is something we love at HappyHead." She turns the handle and disappears out into the hallway, leaving behind the sweet smell of expensive fruit.

...

By the time I get to the Astroturf, the others are already there. My newly formed dysfunctional family, Acid Green, all shivering in the mist. I stride toward them with an unusual degree of confidence. Antiseptic, Fluffy, and Fernsby are there too, tablets in hand, wearing big yellow fleeces. The other teams are disappearing off into the forest around us.

Fernsby looks at his watch. "Let's get going—we've got a big day ahead."

Finn has his hood over his head and keeps his eyes down.

Be a positive influence.

He doesn't look at me or even seem to register I've arrived, which feels a little rude. Especially after last night. Maybe he didn't mean what he said in the note. Maybe it was just a joke.

I look back at the huge building. It's like a spaceship has landed in the middle of the Scottish countryside. I catch sight of the glass roof—it is shaped like a dome. I hadn't noticed when we arrived in the dark.

"Sebastian, focus, please," I hear Fernsby say. "We are about to enter the forest. I don't want anyone getting lost."

"I thought we might be doing some athletics today," says Ash, disappointed.

"Well, maybe this one will suit you in other ways," Fluffy says brightly. "It's another fun one. Promise."

We walk for maybe half an hour through the woods to where the trees become thicker. When I look up, I can no longer see the sky. There is a deep earthy smell. The silence makes me shudder.

"Let's press on."

There is no path to follow now.

Eleanor and Ash stay at the front with Fernsby. He leads us over tree roots and across a stream, guiding us around boggy ground covered with wet moss. We push through bushes and ferns, and everything becomes denser—heavier.

Finn lingers at the rear of the pack, Antiseptic often stopping to wait for him.

"Stop lurking back there, young man!" Fluffy calls out cheerfully. But he keeps his distance, sometimes vanishing for a moment so we have to stop to wait for him. Still, he always reappears.

When we arrive at a little clearing in the trees, Fernsby puts his hand in the air. The ground is flat and covered in dead leaves.

"This is it," he says, and I spot three chairs and a folding table underneath a low tree. We all stop. "Welcome to Survival. One of you must be in charge of *food,* one of you *clean water,* one of you *shelter,* and one of you *fire.* Four essential needs for human survival. Trust your instincts. Be confident. All of these things need to be presented to us before the fall of darkness." He looks up. "Not as long as you might think. You will be assessed as a team and for your individual contribution. Within the vicinity are hidden items that might help you, if you can find them. If you see a Do Not Pass sign, you are heading into prohibited territory and must turn back immediately. Off you go."

They head over to the folding table and sit down.

"Right," Eleanor says, taking charge. Learning from the debrief. "Well, someone will need to get wood before it gets wet.

I think it's about to rain. Nothing's going to light if it's damp. I did some survival stuff in Scouts."

"No shit," Finn mutters from behind us.

"What was that?" She turns to him. "Go on?"

He smiles. "I said sounds good." He puts his thumb up.

"I'll do shelter," Ash says. "I used to go camping with my dad. I can figure something out."

"Great," Eleanor says. "You do fire, Finn."

"No," he says.

"No?" Eleanor repeats. "Why not?"

"I'm not doing fire." He begins to pace around us on the edge of the clearing.

"Didn't you say you were going to *try harder*? This would be one great way of doing it." She walks toward him.

"Hey, guys . . . ," I start to say.

"I'm not doing fire," Finn repeats calmly.

"I think you should tell us all why you can't do that," she says in a matter-of-fact tone. "After all, we are a team."

She turns back to me and Ash for support.

"Look, I'll do fire. Finn can do food," I say. "It's not a big deal."

"Finn seems to think it is. *I* think it's pretty selfish." Eleanor moves quickly to stand directly in front of him, arms folded. "We can't always just do *what we want*," she says loudly so the Assessors can hear. "We have to compromise."

They all look at their tablets in unison.

Tap, tap, tap.

Finn takes a step toward her. "You're saying all the right things, aren't you?"

"Guys—" Ash tries to interject, but Finn continues.

"What do you know about this place?" He is looking down into her face. "Miss HappyHead . . ."

"Excuse me?" Eleanor takes a small step back.

"Finn, leave it, please," I say.

"I'm just curious as to why you're so mad at me," he says. "Is there something in it for you?"

"Ugh, please." Eleanor laughs. "Freak."

He is very close to her now. A flicker of darkness flashes in his eyes.

"Thank you," he whispers. "I try my best."

"What is the *matter* with you?" she says. "Get away from me."

"You two, come on!" Ash shouts. "The sooner we do this, the sooner we can leave. None of us want to be here. Let's work together."

Fernsby, Fluffy, and Antiseptic keep tapping away.

"There's no point fighting." Ash puts her hand on Eleanor's shoulder. "Just let Finn do food. . . ."

Eleanor inhales. "Fine," she says after a moment. "Finn can do food."

He is breathing heavily.

"Finn?" Ash says.

"Yeah, I'll do that," he says, his eyes still on Eleanor.

"Great. I'll do fire," I chip in.

"That leaves you with clean water," Ash says to Eleanor. But she is already marching off into the surrounding trees as it begins to pour with rain.

■ ■ ■

I scurry around, trying to get as much wood as I can from the ground of the clearing, piling it up under my hoodie to keep it dry. I then find some pine cones to use as kindling. There is something I like about it, the smell of the wet outside. *Fresh.* It enters my brain and expands, giving it space.

I should ignore Finn until this assessment is through. That's the wise thing to do. I don't want to be derailed. I want to find wood and make a fire. There are bits of bark under my fingernails now, and my hoodie is soaked.

Ash has begun to build a structure around a tree in the middle of the clearing—a bit like a tepee with long branches and logs balanced against the trunk. She is covering it with moss and leaves to make a protective canopy.

"Looks good, Ash," I say.

"Thanks. My dad's obsessed with the TV show *Survivor.* Put your firewood under it," she suggests.

As I do, I realize I like standing under it. It makes me feel enclosed. Protected.

I like Ash.

She helps me arrange stones beside the shelter to make a firepit. She then brings me some of the drier moss she has collected that she says will hopefully catch fire easily. We watch as Eleanor starts to angle branches to allow the rain to drip painstakingly from the leaves into a little tin pot she found buried in the undergrowth.

"She told me I need to do better." Ash lowers her voice. "That I need to *go for it* with the challenges. And she's always asking what my room number is. Telling me I need to try and get a lower one."

"Oh, yeah. She does that to me."

"How does she know these things?"

"It was probably in the small print. I didn't get that far."

I need 2 show you something.

I haven't seen Finn for a while.

"I'm going to see if I can find something to start the fire. Maybe there's some matches somewhere." I know he has some.

I weave around the edges of the clearing, turning over rocks and looking under leaves. I find a spoon, a pan, and some nails.

I cross past the Assessors' table so they can see my loot.

Tap, tap, tap.

Then I see him. Crouching down behind a fallen tree a little out of the clearing, with a handful of what looks like some sort of fungi. I'm no foraging expert, but I don't know how edible black mushrooms with yellow spots are. Unless they're a particular *type* of mushroom. Which would be interesting. Maybe we could all get high together. Shelly would love that. She would probably actively encourage it.

Right.

Positive influence.

Here goes.

I make my way cautiously toward him. He looks shattered, to be quite honest, the black rings around his eyes streaking harshly into his cheeks.

"Hey!" I say loud enough so the adults can hear. "Maybe I can help you forage? We could do it together?"

Wow. My sexiness just went through the roof. Not.

Tap, tap, tap.

He looks at me like he couldn't give a toss about foraging and has no idea what I'm talking about. His ice eyes look panicked.

I swallow.

He shifts himself farther behind the tree, out of view of the Assessors. I follow.

"Did you read it?" He is barely audible, speaking out of the corner of his mouth.

Erm . . .

Ignore him, Seb.

Step

back

into

the

clearing.

I nod. "Yes."

Damn.

"Good. Come with me."

Oh, God.

My feet feel bolted to the ground. He turns and begins to move off into the woods. I sense the adults watching through the branches.

"Yes, great idea! Glad you're on board!" I shout. I turn and smile at Antiseptic, then lift my hand. *Cool! I've got this covered. No sweat. I will "positive influence" all over everything. Just you wait.*

God Almighty.

I follow Finn as he strides off into the woods.

It's fine. This isn't a big deal.

I keep my eyes on his back, but he doesn't turn.

We walk quickly for maybe twenty minutes. I'm not sure how far out of the clearing we're allowed to go. This could be what Manning meant when she said they loved people being fearless. Or it might look like we are deserting our teammates and not being clever with our time, considering the limited daylight.

This probably isn't when I should be thinking about this, but the greens really suit Finn. The tracksuit all baggy and hanging off his pointy frame, the hood throwing moody shadows over his face, even the dirt on his shoes looking like it is meant to be there. I glance down at myself. I look like a wannabe rapper, like a big baby rapper, and yet we are wearing the exact same thing. How has that happened? I look up.

Where are we?

Turn back, Seb.

We weave on and on and I am no longer sure where we are, but he seems like he knows.

I see a yellow sign nailed to a tree.

DO NOT PASS

Shit. "Finn. *Look,*" I hiss.

"Not far now," he says.

I swallow hard.

Turn back turn back turn back.

He walks straight past the sign as if it's invisible.

"Finn?"

"Quickly." He moves forward into the trees.

Before I can stop myself, I follow him, panting, trying not to twist my ankle every time I trip. "Finn, did you see the—"

And then he stops. He stops because there is nowhere left for him to go. Because we are suddenly at the fence. The perimeter fence.

It looms up above us into the air, maybe ten feet tall, the wire rungs crisscrossing over themselves all the way up to the top. Finn stands, his eyes alight, looking at it. I wonder if it's best to just tell him that we could always boil down nettles and make some soup, if we're really stuck for ideas. That it might be best to get back to the *task in hand*.

"OK," he says. "We don't have long."

Long for what? I really don't think this is a good idea. Whatever this is.

"What are we doing?"

He looks over his shoulders both ways and waits for a moment, listening. He then pulls off one of his fingerless gloves and holds up his hand to my face. There is a white bandage wrapped around it.

He peels it back to reveal a long burn, blistered and red, wet, running across the center of his palm.

"What is that?" I say. "Are you OK? That looks really—"

"The fence."

"What . . . do you mean?"

"The fence is electrified. There's no way out."

I am still staring at his hand. "How—"

"I tried to leave. Yesterday."

"Wait . . ."

"After our session with Manning. When I ran out . . . I tried to find her, Stone, but I couldn't. So I tried to get out. . . ."

"I don't know what you're—"

"You do, Seb. This place is messed up. Look." He pulls off

his other glove and holds out his other hand, the bandage a pinky yellow from the leaking blister underneath.

"The fence is for our safety . . . ," I say, but I suddenly feel unsteady. "There's a gate. It's how I got in."

"The gate is locked."

"But . . ."

"I tried to climb over it."

"No—it's probably locked to keep things *out*. I don't know, bears and stuff. You know?"

Oh, Christ, what is happening?

"Seb, stop kidding yourself."

"No."

"No?"

"I think we should find some edible berries and get back to the clearing before the fall of darkness."

At this, Finn turns away from me and takes a few steps toward the fence.

"Why are you showing me this? I don't—"

"Seb, come here." His voice is oddly calm. "Come on. Come and stand here."

Argh, shit.

Shit.

No.

I step forward and a twig cracks beneath my foot, sending a burst of hot panic up my spine.

"Trust me, you need to come here. Just for one moment."

Trust me.

I take another step forward and another, until I am right next to him.

This is not good.

Not good.

"Careful," he says. He leans his head forward toward the fence and then presses his finger to his lips.

I stop.

And then I hear it.

mmmmm-K-mmmmm-K-mmmmm-K-mmmmm-K

The hum of an electrical current with the click of a charge cutting through it.

"There's no way out, Seb."

My body moves before my brain can. It turns me away from him, and I begin to walk quickly, my heart pounding in my ears.

"Where are you going?" I hear him hiss behind me.

Back to the clearing. Back to the clearing. Back to the clearing.

I pick up my pace and start to run.

"Seb, *wait*!"

Why did I follow him?

I feel sick. This is not what I want. I want to make a fire and go back to my strange white room and wait for the screen to tell me what to do.

Where am I?

Everything looks the same.

Trees. Lots of trees.

Just keep moving.

I can see a building up ahead. Like a little hut.

That's odd. I don't remember that.

I need to make a fire.

I need to get up into the top bedrooms. *Closer to one.*

Past the little hut.

Run.

I put my foot on something. *Crunch.* Oh, God.

I trip. And I'm falling.

I hit the ground and get a mouthful of dirt.

"What are you doing all the way out here?"

I lift my head to see a figure in a raincoat and boots leaning over me.

Dr. Stone.

TEN

Chicken

"If you want to plow through my vegetable patch, you might find it useful to keep your eyes on the ground," Stone's voice says from somewhere above me. "There's a lot going on down there. Do you need a hand?"

I try to spit out the mud I inhaled, but it just dribbles down my chin.

"Oh, God. Dr. Stone!" I splutter. "I'm so sorry. . . ." I try to scramble to my feet only to slip back down hard onto my bum.

"Please, don't be." She points to a nearby wheelbarrow, and I use it to pull myself up.

I look around for Finn. Did he follow me?

I am in the yard of a small stone hut with a chimney sending a streak of smoke up into the air. The one I could see from the balcony. I assume this is her office. There are rusty gardening tools and rows of plants peeking through lines of soil—the vegetable patch where I landed.

She follows me with her eyes, intrigued. I brush my hands

together, the dirt caked onto them, and try to look as calm as possible.

She's very *still*.

I nod at her and smile, giving a little laugh. *What I am I like, eh?*

She just looks at me.

"How did you get here?" she asks cautiously, like she's figuring me out.

"I . . . got lost. We're in the middle of a challenge. Survival."

"Ah! Survival. Yes. I designed it."

I wish I had never followed him. Then I wouldn't be here, embarrassing myself in front of her.

"Well, it's great. I'm really enjoying it," I lie. She continues to stare. "I was just helping my . . . friend, my teammate Finneas."

"Ah, yes, Mr. Blake."

"You know him? I was helping him look for food. One of the requirements." She nods. "Sorry, I didn't mean to disturb you. I should find my way back. Don't want to keep my team waiting."

She probably thinks I've abandoned them. Fantastic.

"There's no need to apologize, young man."

"I . . . You're very busy."

"Not this second."

"Right. No. OK."

"What's your name?"

"Sebastian Seaton."

Not to be arrogant, but I kind of thought she might know my name after Manning said she had been reporting back, but she doesn't seem to recognize it.

Never mind. Now she just thinks I'm the twat who squashed her lettuce.

I stand up slowly and wobble a little as the image of Finn's hands resurfaces in my numbed brain.

The blisters.

The blood.

The fence.

mmmm-K-mmmm-K-mmmm-K-mmm-K

"You're shaking," she says.

I can't hide it this time. Even my head is trembling.

"Ah, yeah," I say. "Sorry."

She takes a step toward me, pushing her plaits behind her shoulders as she does. Then she groans and makes a face. "My eighty-two-year-old body has been trying its best to betray me of late, Sebastian. I won't have it, though. I won't."

"You don't look eighty-two." She actually doesn't. Her honeyed eyes peer out from her translucent skin, alive and bright.

"That's kind. You're very polite."

God. Again? "I should probably go. Thank you for . . . helping me."

"You're still shaking." Damn it. "Shall we go inside and have a chamomile? I just put a pot on."

"I . . . Shouldn't I get back?"

"Hmm?"

"To the trial. The assessment?"

"That's up to you. Taking a moment is always helpful. You seem rattled. You can spare five minutes, I'm sure."

Rattled.

Is this a test? It's probably best that I agree.

Her raincoat reminds me of my grandma's. I can see a tissue poking out from the sleeve in the same way hers always did.

"OK," I say. "Thanks."

She raises an eyebrow—*right decision*—and gently puts her hand on my shoulder. It weirdly makes me feel like I might cry, and I suddenly remember her putting her hand on Finn's shoulder outside the air lock on the first day. She begins to make her way over to the stone steps that lead up to the door of the hut. She looks small, like a badger waddling its way back to its sett after a big day of pottering about.

I take one last look around for Finn, then follow.

She strains as she lifts her foot onto the bottom step.

"Here." I reach a hand out to help her.

She takes hold of it without a second thought, gripping it tight, *really* tight. Something makes me stop for a second. It's almost as if I feel something pass through her hand into mine— a message. *I get it,* it says. *I understand.* The words sort of travel up my arm and into my chest, and they settle me, just for a second. For a moment, I feel a stillness, as if she is trying to say *It's all right.*

She could also just be trying not to fall over.

I follow her into what appears to be a living room.

It's strewn with papers and files and books. Some of them are open, covering the desk, others piled high around the room. There are fluorescent Post-its stuck all over the walls. It is like a cluttered antiques shop, with an old grandfather clock, teapots and little china cups, compasses, and lamps with dusty pink shades and tassels. A fire flickers in the small fireplace. I hardly know where to stand, so I edge in with my back to the wall as she makes her way over to a kitchenette in the corner.

She starts shuffling around, turning mugs upside down to let teaspoons and old tea bags fall out. As she begins to run them under the tap, I look at the papers dotted around the floor and on the tatty leather armchair. They're called things like "Therapeutic Engagement," "Nature and Nurture," "Regulation of the Emotions," and "Skills for the Anxious."

"Survival was designed to bring people back to basics," she says as she lifts a teapot and begins to pour its contents into a couple of mugs that may or may not be clean. "We are so *distracted* in the modern world. It's important for us to reconnect with our gut instincts. Human initiative is spurred by the need to survive. We are more resourceful, more resilient than we think we are, Mr. Seaton. In this day and age, we are led to believe we need to rely on the external for us to make healthy, beneficial choices when in fact we have the ability within us."

She mumbles softly, like she is talking as much to herself as she is to me. "Really, this whole thing is about figuring out that it is all available to you without needing to look very far at all." What is? What's available? "You follow?"

I nod because she's smiling and handing me a steaming cup of yellowy-green liquid.

"Thanks," I say.

"Please, sit."

"Sure." Where?

I find a seat on the arm of the leather chair.

"How are you finding it all?"

"Me?" Yes, Seb. Continue. "Yeah, I'm enjoying it. Some of it is a little . . . I don't know. I never thought I'd be good at any of this." I stop. She just watches me. "I think my parents really want me to do well, you know. They want me to go to a decent college and to find"—oh, God—"more confidence or something. I know I need . . . *something,* anyway." OK, wrap it up. "I'm really glad to be here, to be able to contribute. I just hope I can learn lots and make you all proud. That's all I want from this venture."

Venture? Wow.

I flush pink and hold my mug up to cover as much of my face as possible. I smell the floral scent of the chamomile, and the steam is hot against my cheek.

I look around, trying to think of something else to say. And I see there are some framed photographs on the desk. One of them, slightly hidden behind some papers, is her, standing with a man with thick black hair, a chiseled jawline, and bushy eyebrows smiling openly into the camera lens.

Antiseptic. Mark.

But younger.

He isn't smiling like he usually does. This is different. Like a *proper* smile. One that doesn't look . . . fake.

Next to it, in an old silver frame, is a black-and-white picture of a girl standing between two people who appear to be her parents, both dressed very smartly.

None of them are smiling.

"Who are they?" I ask. I realize I'm clammy, like I've just been sick.

Stone shuffles along the rug, weaving her way through the piles of books, and picks up the photograph. She looks at it for a moment, then speaks softly. "I used to be like you. Clever, but unsure. Very unsure of myself. My parents wanted so much for me, from such a young age. It was powerful—the pressure I placed on myself to make them proud. I felt it strongly. Lots of my friends seemed to be able to brush it off, but it sat inside me like a little apple seed and it grew. I knew I needed to be a *success,* to make something of myself, for *them.* I made it my unconscious life goal. It didn't even matter what *I* wanted, just that they could look at me and say, *Yes. You did it.* But they never did. They never looked at me and said that. And it quietly destroyed me. Do you relate to that?"

Ha.

"Well . . . maybe."

"When I created HappyHead, my main objective was to give people the chance to see that they themselves are sufficient to achieve happiness. Everyone is, as they are. The pursuit of perfection is a myth. It will spin its web of lies, and within that we will lose ourselves. HappyHead is a safe place in which you can flourish, Sebastian. I know that word is thrown around nowadays. But to feel safe, *really safe* within ourselves, isn't easy. And I want you to take that with you, armed for the difficult world out there."

Yes. See. *See?*

Finn was wrong. The fence. Wrong. Wrong about it all. Wrong, wrong, wrong. I feel relief cover me like a balm, and I exhale.

"I understand," I say.

She blows on her tea. The silence is nice, and I am surprised that I don't feel the desperate urge to fill it.

I feel calm in here. Contained. I'm not shaking anymore. I take a sip.

"Chamomile always does the trick. I needed it too. I've not been feeling quite myself recently." She shakes her head, seemingly frustrated, then says quietly, "Finneas will find a good friend in you. I've been told you have been supporting him. He just needs a little time."

So she *has* heard of me.

I should ask her about the fence. Why it is electrified. Because that is still a little strange.

"I was wondering—"

Suddenly there is a noise outside the door.

A voice. "Mr. Seaton?" I snap my head around.

The door is thrown open, and a man with thick-rimmed glasses and a big yellow fleece stands in the doorway. I jump, nearly falling off the arm of the chair, my hot tea spilling over my fingers.

Fernsby. Red, blotchy, and very out of breath, like he's been running for some time.

Stone doesn't seem alarmed. "Albert! How lovely of you to join us."

"Doctor . . . ," he says. "I'm so sorry. I was—"

"Everyone is apologizing today," she says, a little wearily.

"I thought we had lost Mr. Seaton. Is he disturbing you?"

"Oh, the opposite. We were just taking a breather together. Isn't that right, Sebastian?"

"I got lost," I say, because he sounds a little angry.

"Would you like some tea, Albert?"

"Oh, no thank you, Doctor. I think it's best I get Mr. Seaton back to his assessment."

"Of course," she says. "I think he's ready now."

I don't really want to leave.

"Sebastian?" He looks at me sternly, like I should move.

"Thank you," I say to Stone, and put my mug on a coaster. "It was nice to meet you."

"You too, Sebastian." She watches as I weave my way to the door.

"Time is ticking," Fernsby says, taking my arm.

"I hope you find your safety here," she says as he pulls me through the doorway. "And your friend Finneas too." She smiles, almost knowingly.

Fernsby pulls my elbow. "We will leave you to your gardening, Eileen."

Then we are out onto the steps and down into the garden, and he is pulling me through the woods, his hand tight. But not the same tight grip that Stone had. This one is angry-tight. "You shouldn't be disturbing the doctor. . . ."

"But—"

"It's going to be dark soon and you still need to make your fire. Look." He points above the canopy of trees, and I see a few streaks of smoke rising above them. "The other teams seem to be making headway. Acid Green needs your help."

I feel like he is waiting for an explanation.

"I think I just lost my way," I say.

We walk quickly in silence, so I try and ease the awkwardness. "She seems nice," I say.

He doesn't respond. Just keeps dragging me. It kind of hurts now.

Finally, I can hear the others farther ahead.

"Did Finn manage to find any food? I told Madame Manning I would—"

Fernsby stops. Stops dead. Turns to me.

"Listen. We like you. You just need to be a bit more assertive. OK?"

"Uh-huh, yeah. Yeah. I agree."

"You're a bit . . . distracted. Stay focused. And don't go disturbing Dr. Stone again."

All right. I nod.

"Look under there," he says, pointing to a bush. "Quickly."

I duck down, and under it I find a small duffel bag poking out of the soil. I pull the strap, and the bag comes loose.

"Open it," he whispers.

When I do, I see a butcher's knife. A big one.

"You'll need that," he says.

"Right . . ." I take it in my hand, feeling sick all of a sudden.

"Go on, now." He gives me a little push in the small of my back. I walk quickly with Fernsby right behind me until we reach the clearing.

He crosses it and sits back in his seat next to Antiseptic and Fluffy.

I see Finn. He is back. With the rest of them. Standing in a circle around something.

He momentarily flicks his eyes to mine. *Don't say anything.* He blinks, then flicks them back down to whatever it is they are staring at.

I look into the center of the circle. A small wooden crate with something white and fluffy inside. It is moving. I look closer. It's a chicken. It stares out with its bulging eyes.

Puk, puk, pukaak.

"Where did you find it?" Finn asks Eleanor.

"Over there in the trees," she says, like he is terminally stupid. "Better than your suspicious mushrooms." I see he is still holding them. "So we have food. Anyone have any ideas how it's done?" she asks bluntly.

I watch them look blankly at each other.

Puk, puk, puk.

I feel the cold wood of the handle of the knife trembling in my palm.

"Guys!" I shout. They turn.

"Where the hell have you been?" Eleanor snaps.

I lift the butcher's knife into the air. "This might help."

"You're kidding." Ash recoils. "We're really doing this?"

"Well, *Finn* is," Eleanor says.

· · ·

Eleanor is holding the chicken by its legs now, so it's swinging upside down. "Let's not waste time."

Its wings start flapping.

"Maybe the mushrooms are enough?" Ash says hopefully.

"Maybe they're poisonous," Eleanor cuts in.

"We can keep looking," Ash says. "There might be something else."

"It's getting dark," Eleanor says.

She's not wrong.

She moves to a tree stump not far from the unlit fire. "This will do." She turns the chicken on its side.

It struggles.

"Come *on.*" She looks up at us. "I need your help."

Ash hesitates, then leans down and grabs its feet.

"Finn, take the knife," Eleanor orders. "We don't have time for any nonsense. Let's just get it done and complete the assessment."

Finn takes the knife from my hand.

His fingerless gloves.

His hair in his eyes.

He doesn't look at me.

I follow Ash and take hold of the chicken's body, the feathers silvery and spiky in my hands. I can feel its heartbeat.

Dumdumdumdumdumdumdumdumdumdumdumdum.

"Let's just take a second," I say.

"Present all of them before the fall of darkness," Eleanor says. "We have no time, no thanks to you disappearing. And we currently only have shelter. Well done, Ash, by the way."

Ash isn't listening. She looks like she is about to keel over.

Eleanor makes sure we have a hold, then lets go of the chicken and stands back.

"One quick movement," she says to Finn.

"Is this really necessa—"

"Shh." Eleanor cuts me off. "He needs to concentrate."

His eyes focused, Finn lines up the knife above the bird's neck.

Ash looks away. I can hear her quietly crying now. "This is insane," she mutters.

"Don't be a baby," Eleanor whispers. "Finn. Now."

He bites his lip. I can see the muscles in his neck tensing. Then he drops the knife.

"Pathetic," Eleanor hisses. She steps forward and picks it up. With one hand, she holds the chicken's head. With the other, she raises the knife.

Thwack.

My body jolts.

Thick dark blood pours over the wooden stump.

ELEVEN
Hell Is Other People

I don't think Eleanor is a psychopath. I just think she wants to win. At everything.

But I might be wrong. This might just be me *seeing the best in her.*

According to every true-crime TV show, you can't label anyone under eighteen a psychopath. You would say they are *callous with unemotional traits.*

So . . . Yeah.

We managed to present all four components just before the fall of darkness. Ash found a flint and blade fire lighter, so Eleanor was able to boil her rainwater without Finn having to reveal that he still has his matches.

Shelter, fire, clean water, and food.

The food bit happened in a frenzied blur of pots, pans, and cutlery found in the bushes. Feathers, slimy pale flesh, and flames.

"Well done, Acid Green," Fernsby now says, inspecting our

offerings. He sticks a thermometer into the chicken, then stands back and looks at the temperature gauge. "It's cooked." No shit, it's black. "Time for dinner." He smiles. As does Fluffy. As does Antiseptic.

"Huh?"

"You made your dinner. Time to eat."

Antiseptic holds out a stack of what are probably eco-friendly decomposable plant-based plates.

It appears they are not joking.

"What the—" Ash takes a few steps backward.

"There is no food prepared for you up at the facility tonight, so you will go hungry otherwise. We had faith in you to suc-ceed, which you did. And it looks very . . . edible."

We stare at the charred chicken corpse. Eleanor takes his cue and begins to hack it apart with the knife. I watch as she picks up a chunk with a rusty fork, a string of sinew still attaching it to the rest of its body.

"Wing, anyone?"

I watch Ash weighing up her options, no doubt considering what Manning said yesterday about growing and changing.

"OK," she says, and I can practically hear her whole being protest.

"Seb? You like breast?" She looks me dead in the eye without any irony.

"Um . . . If that's what's going . . . sure."

She hacks at it some more and plops a lump onto one of the plates. "Here you go." She looks at Finn.

"I'm not hungry," he says, and takes himself off to the edge of the clearing.

"You should use your shelter to eat in," Fernsby says brightly.

The three of us sit in the shelter and pick at the charcoal flesh, drinking lukewarm cups of rainwater.

"Well, we did it, guys." Eleanor is delighted. She picks a rogue twig out of her drink.

Ash looks at me as she nibbles on something that resembles scorched gristle. "We definitely did *something*. . . ."

I smile at her.

Eleanor notices. She suddenly grabs my hand.

"Hey, nice work on finding the knife," she says in a weirdly soft voice that doesn't suit her. "Keep it up." She smiles at me in a way that makes me uncomfortable and not just because she has what looks like a bit of chicken feather lodged between her teeth. Her eyes linger on me a little too long; then she pouts her greasy lips. I think she might be . . . *flirting*. But I have been wrong before about what flirting looks like.

I shrug, pretending this isn't making me want to swap places with the chicken remains.

She squeezes my upper arm, making me flinch. "Oh, you have *muscles* under there, do you?"

I'm so confused because I definitely don't, but also because *what is she doing?*

"Not the last time I checked," I say, and I mean it.

She shuffles her bum so she is now very close to me. "Don't be so *hard* on yourself; you're very strong." Why did she stress that word?

Just say something. Anything.

"The first time I went to the gym I fell off a treadmill. Haven't been back since. So definitely no muscles under here."

She suddenly laughs very loudly. "Seb! You're funny too."

How is that funny?

I try to swallow a suspiciously chewy bit.

She is still holding my arm.

Ash raises her eyebrows in a way that says *Good luck.* An abrupt noise suddenly makes us turn. Fluffy is fervidly banging a metal pot with a spoon. "Time to get back," she calls out. "Early start again tomorrow!"

Eleanor stands. "Well, it was nice to hang out, Seb."

We must have different definitions of the word "nice."

"Yeah, same."

She then brushes her hands on her joggers and heads off to join the adults.

"Wow," Ash whispers. "Subtle."

I decide I should forget about it. As we walk through the woods back toward the building, I watch Finn in the growing darkness, moving in and out of Fluffy's flashlight. Biting his nails. His face hollow in the shadows. Eyes a little wild.

Don't think, Seb.

The fence. His hands. The blisters.

Stone said we are safe here.

Finn has to be wrong.

■ ■ ■

The image of the chicken blood has stuck to my brain, seeping into my thoughts, thick and deep red. I stand in the shower and try to rub it away with soap, then dig my palms into my eye sockets. When I open them, red dots explode all over the tiles like fireworks.

Why. *Why?*

Good morning, Sebastian.
Please have breakfast, then make your way to Bedroom 36.
At 06:30 head down to the assembly hall
for a special announcement.
Bring your bag with all of your belongings.

I've slipped down seven whole rooms. Maybe it was the Stone thing.

Stay focused. That's OK. I can do that.

A special announcement?

Maybe Eleanor has been arrested for being a danger to chickens. And to me.

I eat my breakfast and join the throng of people moving up and down the hallway.

Today is a new day. *Stay mellow.*

As I make my way down the corridor to the assembly hall, I catch snippets of conversation between various team members.

"I nailed it yesterday. Quite literally."

"You hammered two pieces of wood together, and they barely stood upright. I wouldn't get ahead of yourself."

"Can't help being good at this stuff. Just comes naturally."

"I did well with the water."

"Oh, wow, you absolute warlord."

"I heard something about a *reward*. Like something special for people who do well."

"I just want to get into a good college."

"I just want my phone back."

"We're here to compete, not to live stream to your three followers. I want to win this thing."

"What do you mean 'win'? I don't think that's the point."

My head is spinning. I try to keep my eyes down so I'm not drawn into any conversations.

Focus.

We like you, Fernsby said.

The buzz of anticipation follows us into the hall. We all have our bags over our backs like a troop of zealous Scouts. Some people stop whispering, and I realize it's because at the front, on the stage, are Lindström and Manning. They both gaze out at us expectantly, glowing, sort of luminous.

They look so . . . wealthy. Like the two of them enjoy decompressing in their second homes by the coast.

"Settle down, please!" Antiseptic shouts from somewhere behind me, and I suddenly remember the photo on Stone's desk.

I decide to sit in the front row with all the eager ones. To show I'm not off in an alternate reality. *I'm focused.* But I wish I hadn't when they begin to turn around and shush the others.

Eleanor is here, naturally.

I look behind me. I don't see him.

Focus.

"Welcome, welcome," Manning says into the microphone. "How wonderful it is to see you all together again. It is a joy, simply a joy, to get to know you. We are very impressed. Most of you are really throwing yourself into this. Your commitment is exciting."

The Overalls lining the walls start clapping. We all join in like obedient seals.

Where is he?

"I think it proper that I let Professor Lindström introduce your next assessment." She takes a step back, and Lindström, with her perfect bouncy hair and wafty clothes, breezes up to the microphone. She makes a noise into it that is a bit like a purr.

More applause.

I turn and see Finn has joined a few rows behind. He looks worse than yesterday. His gloves are still on.

His eyes meet mine. His ice eyes.

A heat courses through me. Total unexplainable *heat,* and I don't know where to look.

"Sorry," I say quietly, unexpectedly.

The girl next to me side-eyes me, then shrugs like I'm probably just mental.

Don't trust them, he mouths. *Do not trust them, Seb.*

I snap my head back around to the front, my spine tingling.

"Hello, all," Lindström begins.

Breathe.

"One of the main tenets of Dr. Stone's research is that we must learn to build therapeutic connections with others, in order to progress. Therapeutic connection is one of the most consistent predictors of happiness. Humans are sociable creatures, biologically inclined to pair up." She clasps her hands together, intertwining her fingers. "When relationships are positive, we feel contentment and an overriding sense of peace. When they are negative, the worst in us emerges. We become anxious, depressed, and lonely. The components of a therapeutic connection may be emotional or intellectual. This may even progress to physical attraction."

"Oh, yes, miss! We gonna be knobbing in the woods, then?" some Total Bro shouts from the back.

Most people laugh. Not many in my row do. I definitely don't because this all sounds horrific.

Lindström hardly reacts. Just stares at Total Bro until his face drops. There is a fizzing around me at the prospect of what this means.

"Your maturity will play a part in finding that connection," she adds with a hint of passive aggression.

Hell is other people. Who said that? I agree. But it seems that the rest of this room doesn't.

"We want you to find your match."

Silence. Just . . . dead silence.

A girl giggles. "My mum said she was kind of hoping I'd come back with a boyfriend. This could be perfect!" she then whispers giddily.

God, please no.

"Shh. Now," Lindström continues, "this might be an exciting prospect for some of you, but we are also aware that it will be a frightening one for others." At least she's aware. "Connection is not easy, but we are here to push you. We want to send you out into the world with the tools you need. After an initial interview, you will be regrouped to give you a larger pool of potential candidates to connect with." Candidates? "Ultimately the goal of this assessment is to show your capability for a therapeutic connection with someone. It is exciting to think you might find that here. Don't force things, but do throw yourself into this. Open yourselves up to the experience."

Can't we go back to murdering animals?

She lifts her hand and runs it through her hair, all billowy and serene, her silky caftan wafting around her. "If you would all like to follow me up to the roof, it's time to take you to a very special place. Serenity."

TWELVE
Serenity

The roof. The actual roof of the building.

This building has at least seven stories, according to my breathless count. So that is very high.

Which means I am cautious. Scrap that. I am seriously terrified.

Everyone else seems thrilled.

Breathe.

We are told to remain quiet. We ascend, left hands on the side rail, backpacks knocking into each other as we spiral our way upward.

I saw Finn just before we left the assembly hall but then lost him in the swarm of green flocking toward the promise of potential romance.

Don't trust them.

"Don't dawdle, please. Keep moving."

A group of girls ahead of me talk in hushed voices, speculating about what we will find at the top. One with shiny red hair thinks we will be given drugs and have a massive rave and maybe an orgy to see if we can connect on a more *spiritual level*. She hopes it's the drug ayahuasca because apparently ayahuasca is *mental* and *amazing* and makes your connections *otherworldly*. All I know about ayahuasca is that Shelly's cousin took it in South America and pooed himself while thinking he was talking to God.

There is an Overall behind me. He is tall and muscly with blond hair. Ayahuasca Girl keeps looking back at him. "Maybe they want to see how well we therapeutically connect with figures of authority," she says, gazing in his direction. The others fall about laughing, and he tells them to be quiet.

We finally get to a door, and Muscle Man stops us.

There are no more steps.

He overtakes the girls so he is at the front of the line. Ayahuasca Girl pretends to sniff him as he pushes past. The others think it's the funniest thing they've ever seen. He then puts his hand on the metal bar that runs along the door. The panic bar. I remember being told once at school that you can only open them one way, so you can't get back in. Just saying.

"Please . . . Can you try and calm yourselves before we enter Serenity?" Muscle Man says, trying his best not to show that he is losing his patience. "For this assessment to work, we need you all to be on your best behavior."

"Oh, yes, *sir* . . . ," Ayahuasca Girl says.

Giggles erupt.

He ignores her and turns to the door.

Anxiety nips at me.

"Wait," I say.

Muscle Man stops.

"What is it?" he asks sharply. The girls look at me like I had

142

better not crush their dream of a rooftop romance with Muscle Man.

"I just wonder if it has been checked—the roof." I swallow hard, trying to steady my voice. "Risk assessed, for dangers or whatever? I'm just wondering if the drop is visible. It could potentially be off-putting and not conducive to a therapeutic environment. Know what I mean?"

He blinks at me like I'm some kind of health-and-safety twat.

"You talk too much" is his answer.

He pushes the panic bar, and the door opens.

■ ■ ■

I step out of the dark of the stairwell, and my feet touch what appears to be grass. I rub my eyes to make sure what I am seeing is not some anxiety-induced vision.

It is bright. *Sunshine.*

In front of me on the roof—the actual *roof of the building*—stands a large white marquee, and beyond it is what I can only describe as a garden. Not a shitty garden like you get at the end of the street by the corner shop, but some fancy one. Opulent, *lush.* All flower beds and rows of colorful bushes. Fairy lights weave their way into the distance, and I catch the twinkling blueness of a small body of water. A pond with lily pads and a fountain.

Dotted around the pond are structures that resemble igloos, white and shiny. Maybe fifteen of them. And around each igloo is a white circular wooden fence.

It smells fresh, like oranges and cut grass.

It's *warm.*

I look up.

We are under some kind of vast Perspex dome. *This* is what I saw when we were going into the forest. Huge lights shine down from tall metal structures. It reminds me of when we were in elementary school and we had to make mini ecosystems in glass boxes and kept them heated with special hot lamps.

I feel like I am trapped in one of those. Like I'm an ant. A Bowie song plays somewhere in my brain. Something about a *glass asylum* . . . Which one is that? God, I can't remember. I'm rusty.

I look back to the door behind me—a concrete box jutting up from the grass. A stream of teenagers continues to emerge, blinking eagerly into the lights. People stand around me, staring.

"Holy shit, it's like Willy Thingy's Chocolate Thingy," someone says.

"How did they do this? Crazy!"

"I wonder if those lights will give me a tan."

That's it. That's the song. "Big Brother," the tenth track on *Diamond Dogs*.

"Join the others and no talking," Muscle Man says, pointing to a large huddle of Greens forming under a group of little trees.

Trees. On the roof.

We make our way over to them.

"Bye, sir," Ayahuasca Girl whispers.

He looks back at her, deer-in-headlights.

She pouts and swans off.

I see Ash and Eleanor together under a low-hanging branch with white blossoms. No sign of Ice Eyes.

"Seb! Have you seen this place?" Ash grabs my arm. "It's insane!"

"Where's Finn?" I ask.

Eleanor shoots me a look: *Why do you care?*

"No idea." Ash shrugs.

"Hopefully they've sent him home," Eleanor says. "It's pretty clear he doesn't want to be here. We'd do so much better as a team without him."

There is a pause that feels sticky. Like she really wants me to say something, to agree. But I exhale instead, making a whistling noise. "It's pretty amazing up here, isn't it?"

"It's incredible," Ash says.

Eleanor folds her arms, annoyed I didn't join her hate train. "Very impressive."

Ash nods. "Beats creepy forests and beheading chickens."

I look around for his dark hair.

Don't trust them.

What does he know? Eleanor is probably right.

He might be dangerous. He pushed Fluffy. Unprovoked.

Yes. Dangerous.

Suddenly there is a hushing that sweeps through us. Lindström stands at the top of a grassy mound at the front of the crowd. Beneath her feet are daffodils planted in the shape of a smiling face. Which is odd . . . If Mum has taught me anything, it's the annual blooming patterns of flowers. Daffodils should be well and truly dead by now.

To the left of us, under another group of trees, Manning and Fernsby stand next to each other, watching. Wearing sunglasses.

And on the edge of this sea of eager, hustling bodies, just in front of them . . .

The wing on his neck. The black hair. Head down. Finn.

I feel a strange relief. He's OK. He's here. He seems out of place in this sunshine, like he's a shadow cutting through the brightness. His skin catches the light, and he squints, holding his arm above his eyes.

He looks a bit . . . *fallen angel–y* in this light. And I feel this weird pull.

Fernsby keeps glancing at him.

Lindström taps her mic.

Dunk, dunk, dunk.

"I'm going to try and get a better view," I say to the girls. I don't give them time to answer and begin to push my way through the crowd toward him. I just want to ask him what he meant. . . .

Eleanor follows me with her eyes, so I duck behind a huddle of Greens.

She's so . . . observant.

I can see the top of his head. Messy black hair. He's leaning against one of the tree trunks now, apart from everyone else.

There are Overalls everywhere, circling like yellow flies.

"Welcome to Serenity! Isn't it beautiful here?" Ripples of "Yeah, bruh, this is sick," "So nice!" ensue. I look up to see Lindström on her mound, completely in her element. Therapy God, everyone hanging on her words. I slip sideways between clammy bodies as she continues.

"Serenity has been built using state-of-the-art technology. We are within a climate-maintaining bubble to keep the atmosphere exactly as we need it. Dr. Stone's research shows that more meaningful relationships are developed in brighter weather and warmer climates. People feel more open and relaxed, which is what we want from you." She smiles.

I glance over at Manning. Smiling. Fernsby. Smiling. Everyone smiling.

"I can feel how excited you all are. It is very encouraging. You will each have a brief consultation with the Assessors, and then you will be assigned to a pod"—she motions to the igloos—"in a new group this time."

"Watch it," someone says as I stand on their foot.

"Sorry."

I can see the tree ahead. His lanky, leaning frame.

"This is all to be *enjoyed*. You've done brilliantly so far," I can hear Lindström saying. "Have fun. Be yourselves. Only then can we truly assess your capability for connection."

People are clapping.

"Hey," I whisper.

He doesn't hear me.

I move closer until he is right in front of me. "Finn."

I reach out to tap him on the shoulder, and he begins to turn.

Suddenly I hear a voice directly behind me. "Sebastian. This way." Muscle Man.

"No! Wait . . . I just . . ."

As he ushers me toward the line that is forming in front of the marquee, I turn back to the tree.

But Finn is gone.

■ ■ ■

"Wait your turn." Muscle Man drops me between two boys. The shorter of the two actually spits in his hand and slides it through his disheveled hair like it will suddenly make him irresistible. He sees me watching and grimaces.

"What are you looking at?" His voice is plummy and clipped.

All right, Spit Boy. Don't flatter yourself.

"Nothing," I mumble.

"Good," he says, then looks me up and down and snorts.

The Overalls begin spacing us out to form a line that trails from the tent all the way back to the door.

A couple of girls are also trying to do things to their hair.

Boys take their hoodies off and roll up their sleeves. One starts doing push-ups on the grass. I see other boys snarling at him.

Some girls act like they aren't watching him. He does have a lot of muscles.

"I don't know how push-ups will make you good at connecting," one comments.

"I do," another says, biting her lip.

One by one, we are sent into the tent for the initial consultation.

There are rabbits on the lawn. Actual rabbits. I look back to see Eleanor and Ash farther down the line. Eleanor is rolling up her sleeves and putting her hair into a tight bun. Ready for battle. Right down at the end, near the door, Finn stands on his own.

Don't trust them.

I shake my head like it will remove the memory of his voice.

"Stay in line, please."

"Sorry."

I notice that the flowers next to the marquee spell out "serenity."

Yes. Serene, Seb. Maybe it will be fun?

I look closely at the grass. It's . . . fake. The flowers too. Plastic and polyester. It's all fake.

I am suddenly at the front of the line.

"Right, your turn." Muscle Man gives me a little shove. I look at him, *bit rude,* but he just plasters on a smile. He pulls back the entrance flap and leans down. "Be honest," he says quietly into my ear.

OK.

Inside the tent, there are large white cushions scattered over a fluffy carpet. My feet sink into it. Ahead is a table with candles flickering gently, a box of tissues placed dead center. An empty chair.

On the other side of the table sits Lindström. She has a halo of daisies in her hair, giving Therapy God realness. Behind her, a little farther back, sit Manning and Fernsby with tablets in hand. Here they all are. Together. The Three Musketeers. Staring at me.

I wonder if they are friends. If they hang out. Go out together on a Friday night.

"Come in, Sebastian," Lindström says so invitingly that I immediately start moving toward her. There is something oddly *seductive* about her.

I get to the chair. I know what to do this time. Manning taps away on her tablet.

That's right. Watch me work, Madame. I put my backpack on the floor in front of me and sit decisively.

Lindström looks at me with her big doe eyes, all calm and soft. I try to ignore the trickle of sweat that weaves its way from my forehead to my left cheek.

"This won't take long," she begins. "I will ask some simple questions. Try and ignore those two." She waves a hand at Manning and Fernsby. "The questions will be about you and who you are so we can place you correctly into a pod." She lifts her glass of water to her lips so I see the cucumber slices floating in it. "How do you feel about that, Sebastian?"

How do I *feel* about that?

Let's see. . . . It sounds completely horrific.

"Ask away." I smile.

An intense anxiety builds behind my solar plexus. There is a pressure emanating from the Assessors. An expectation.

"Let's begin," Lindström says. I lean forward eagerly. Confident. Ready. "Do you like yourself, Sebastian?"

OK, right.

Not ready for that.

Not ready at all.

"I . . ." I cough.

They wait. Their fingers poised above their tablets.

"It's a fairly simple question," Lindström says.

Really not. I make a weird gurgle.

Openness and honesty. That's what she said the last time.

I breathe. "Not particularly."

Lindström suddenly seems a bit upset. Disappointed.

Quick. U-turn. Laughter is always good. I throw my head back. "Ha! Joke!"

"That was a joke?" She sounds unsure.

"Yes! Just . . . trying to be funny."

"You think it's funny that people might not like themselves?"

Oh, God. "No, definitely not. Just . . ." My face begins to tingle.

"So you do like yourself?"

"Of course. Yes, I do."

"Good. That is a good starting point."

They all soften now.

"It's OK to admit that you like yourself, Sebastian," Lind-ström says, like she's speaking to a child. "It's OK to know your strengths."

"Uh-huh, yep."

"In fact, you need to. So *what* do you like about yourself?"

Ugh.

"Well, I like that I have a good sense of humor, as you just witnessed."

Nice transition, Seb.

"Humor is great. Yes. Laughter *is* important."

Phew.

"Name three of your strengths."

Just say positive words. "Honest. Articulate. Thoughtful."

"Wonderful. We like honesty, Seb."

"Definitely honesty. It's really important to me."

"Of course. What qualities do you admire in other people?"

More good words. "Bravery. Confidence. Loyalty."

"Fantastic. We really appreciate loyalty here at HappyHead."

"Oh, loyalty is *everything*."

"So you're loyal?"

I suddenly remember Shelly asking me if I would take a bullet for her and then being upset by how long it took me to answer the question. I won't mention it.

"I'd like to think so." Come on, Seb. "Actually, I know I am. *Fiercely* so."

Too much?

"Good. What about respect? Obedience? Are they qualities you admire?"

Obedience . . .

"Oh, one hundred percent, yes."

"Elaborate."

"Well . . ."

Lindström looks at me dead-on. I can see Manning and Fernsby behind her, watching with anticipation.

Big on obedience. Easy. All those years at Sunday school boil down to this moment.

I inhale. Then go for it.

"I think it's a misconception that obedience is just doing what you're told. I see it as an opportunity. If I'm completely honest, I don't know what I'm doing most of the time. I feel like I'm guessing, fumbling my way through. Actually, it's arrogant to think I can do this on my own. Obedience means having trust in those around you and knowing that their example is worth following. One of the most important things we can do is choose who to be obedient to. Who we will follow. That choice is fundamental to who we will become. We learn our values from them and then we don't have to guess because we are shown the path by those who have"—go on, do it—"already walked it."

Mic drop. I sit back.

Lindström's eyes widen. She smiles.

I smile.

Behind her, Fernsby and Manning are smiling.

We all smile.

Nailed it.

"That's a very thoughtful take, Sebastian. Well done." *Thoughtful.* "Nearly there. What kind of romantic relationship interests you?"

Er . . . Shit. "Romantic?"

"Yes."

"With . . ."

"Perhaps you could describe your ideal female counterpart."

Female.

OK.

Not

sure

what

to

say

now.

"Seb? What qualities do you like in a potential partner?"

"What do I like? Right . . . Well."

His wing tattoo.

The smell of the damp smoke hanging on his clothes.

Fallen-angel types.

"I think . . . Maybe . . ."

His wet hair in his eyes.

His *energy.*

"Someone sensitive," I say. "But they also know who they are."

"So she needs to know what she wants?" She. *She.*

"Is something the matter?"

"Oh, no."

"Are you sure?"

"Uh . . . yes. Yes. I suppose . . . they . . . need to know that."

"You like a strong-minded girl?"

What can I say to that?

"Yes. That is correct."

I have the sudden urge to punch myself in the face.

"Have you been in love before?"

"Love?"

"Yes. Do you know what it *feels* like?"

Er . . . "I think I do, yes."

Tap, tap, tap.

"What does it feel like?"

"Like the flu. Like a big, achy flu."

"The flu?"

Tap, tap, tap.

Change direction.

"Or . . . ," I say. Come on, Bowie, help me out here.

"Yes?"

"It is like . . . an opening door, I guess. A key we must turn, or a flame . . . It is freedom." "Love Song," from *The "Mercury" Demos.*

"Interesting." OK, that was a bit intense, but better than the flu. "Thank you, Sebastian."

I pick up my backpack and stand.

"One last question. Would you die for someone you love?"

Huh? "What . . . like, hypothetically speaking?"

No answer. Would I?

"I guess if I felt like that for someone . . . I would do everything I could to keep them safe."

"Thank you, Sebastian. Well done. Again, your openness is impressive. Here, take this T-shirt."

She takes a fat black marker and scribbles "36" onto a white sticker that is already stuck to its front, then presses down its edges where they have peeled away slightly from the green cotton.

"It now has your room number and pod name on it."

"My pod name?"

"Yes. The signs will show you where you need to go."

154

I take the T-shirt. Underneath the scribbled "36" is a smiling face and the word "Integrity" printed in curly yellow lettering.

"Any questions?"

Why did you just ask me if I would die for someone?

"No. Actually, yes. Will Dr. Stone be here with us in Serenity?"

"Why do you ask?"

Because she doesn't scare me like you do. "No reason. I just wondered if she would be seeing any of her project in action."

"She is busy working on her research, I'm afraid. But I'm sure she'll be glad to hear of your respect for her. Now, off you go to Pod Integrity. And, Sebastian?"

"Yes?"

"Give this your all and you won't regret it."

■ ■ ■

I walk down the wood-chip path following little signposts that point me to Pod Integrity. Some point in other directions. Pod Perseverance. Pod Tenacity. Pod Fortitude.

I keep replaying the conversation but can't really remember much of it.

I remember saying I liked honesty and then not really being honest.

I didn't lie. Did I?

She. She. She. Female counterpart.

But it's OK. They were smiling.

God. My stomach twists.

I stop.

Pod Integrity.

Inside the wooden fence, a little stream trickles calmly through the middle of a cluster of plastic rose bushes. The lawn is elegant. Fake . . . but elegant.

The pod looks like the top half of a peeled boiled egg. There are no windows.

There is a screen above the shiny white door.

Welcome, Sebastian.
Have a glass of homemade lemonade.

A hatch next to the door slides open, revealing a cold glass of lemonade. As I sip it, I actually make a little moany gasp. God, that's good.

What a lovely day.
Welcome to Pod Integrity!
When you have a moment, take a look around the lawn.
There is a picnic rug, some games (best played in pairs!),
outdoor dining, and a cozy swing chair with some
blankets for when it gets chilly in the evening.
In you go, Sebastian.

Suddenly the front door moves to the side—*ssshhhuuum*—revealing a large, circular room. It is bright. Airy. Smells like that thing all my mum's friends love. Sandalwood.

I stick my head inside and look around. "Hello?"

I see four bunk beds pushed against the circular wall, surrounding a long wooden dining table in the center. A screen hangs above it. It is very Lindström. Everything is light wood and clean lines, very minimal Scandi. Clutter-free. The opposite of my current brain state.

"Hey!" A boy's face appears in mine. "I'm Raheem." He points to the sticker on his T-shirt. "Number forty-three."

"Hi," I say brightly. My room number is better than yours. Ha. "Er . . . I'm Seb. Number thirty-six."

"Come in, man," he says. "There's some food on the table. I think we help ourselves."

"Thanks." I look at the little finger sandwiches with the crusts cut off and take a tuna one. My mouth is so dry it quickly turns to a paste and becomes hard to swallow, sticking to my teeth. I gulp my lemonade.

Raheem looks a bit like a jock in one of those teen horror films who survives till the end. All tall and strong and conventionally handsome. I suddenly notice a girl sitting on one of the lower bunks, spreading her stuff out onto the mattress.

"I'm Anoushka. Number sixty-one."

She seems sweet.

"Seb. Thirty-six. Should I just choose a bed?"

She shrugs. "Yeah, I think so."

I pick the bottom bed of the bunk next to her.

"This is nice," I lie. "What now?"

"We wait for the screen to tell us something, I guess," Raheem says.

• • •

Over the course of the next few hours, more people join us in Pod Integrity. Someone tries to start a group conversation, but it fizzles out quickly.

Spit Boy has joined, with the number 48 on his T-shirt. He says his name is Matthew Parry-Brokingstock. He struts around with his chest out like he owns the place.

A striking girl called Lucy arrives. She hops onto the bed above Raheem and stretches out, leaning her head on her hand like she's in a photo shoot for some trendy magazine. She seems effortlessly cool. One of *those*.

A small boy called Malachai enters, immediately hiding in the shadows of his top bunk like a scared mole in his glasses. Then a very quiet girl takes the bunk above me. The sleeves of her hoodie are wet and frayed where she seems to have chewed them. She says her name is Betty.

Bunk Buddy Betty.

Number 81. Wow, that's not good.

"Is there a toilet?" Anoushka whispers.

"In there," Raheem says, pointing to a door in the wall.

It's getting dark outside. The fake sun is setting.

The pod door slides open one final time.

Shhhuuum.

My body tingles a little, hoping that it will be him.

A silhouette lingers in the doorway against the red sky.

I know this person. But it's not who I want.

"I'm Eleanor. Number five." She enters like she is floating through the air and takes the final bed, the upper one on the bunk opposite me. When she sees I'm here, she waves her fingers at me. She then does that weird pout smile again. The flirty one from the forest.

The lights in the pod dim and the screen above the table turns on.

"Shh," Lucy says. "It's happening!"

A smooth female voice narrates the words on the screen, from speakers above us.

> Hello, Pod Integrity. Welcome to Serenity.
> Please take a seat at the table and bring your
> personal-item box with you.
> Girls on the left. Boys on the right.
>

I had forgotten all about that. I root through my backpack and drag it out from the bottom.

I pull out the chair next to Malachai and sit. I try to smile at him, but he just pushes his glasses up his nose.

It feels like a weird cult assembling.

> Look around you. Look each of your
> pod mates in the eye.

My brain crumples like a piece of screwed-up paper. Eye contact with strangers. Worse than the devil.

> Boys, look at the girls.
> Girls, look at the boys.
> These are your potential partners.
> Your potential matches.

God.

Really knowing someone else. This is delicate work.
Could you couple up with someone on the other side of the table?
Do you have the potential for this connection?
The openness?
The maturity?
The integrity?
Dr. Stone's work shows that making ourselves vulnerable is scary
but can lead to true happiness.

Betty has gone bright red.
Malachai looks like he just developed a hernia.

Place your personal item in the locker under the table.
These will be used in due course.
Do not discuss them with anyone.

One by one, we lean down under the table and deposit our
items in what looks like a large safe by our feet.
Matthew Parry-Brokingstock goes last.

Please push the locker door shut.

He does. The door clicks.

Well done, all.

The smooth voice gives a gentle laugh.

You have just one day to see if you can match with someone here.
We believe this kind of connection is achievable in this short

amount of time in these conditions.
There are four boys and four girls, so all of you have
the potential to couple up.

What is happening?

Now, to bed, and no talking to each other tonight.

"Is it finished?" someone whispers.
The screen lights up one final time:

Tomorrow.
Time to get personal.
☺

THIRTEEN
The Bathroom Pact

Eleanor's hand is over my mouth. I taste the sweet tang of hand cream.

"*Shh*. Come with me," she whispers.

I can hear the others sleeping in their bunks as I slide off the mattress. The air is still and close like a hot summer's night, making my T-shirt stick to my skin. There is a faint warm glow from night-lights in the ceiling.

She takes my hand and pulls me toward the bathroom door.

"Wait, what are you—"

She abruptly puts her hand over my mouth again. "Don't. Speak," she hisses.

Like a spy on a mission, she opens the bathroom door, pushes me in, then closes it. A fluorescent light flickers on above our heads. I look around for somewhere to stand that'll give me a bit of distance. But it is very small in here, so I just perch on the toilet seat.

"OK, so what's going on, Eleanor?"

"I want to talk to you."

"In here?"

"I don't want you to wake anyone. You can be a bit awkward sometimes. A bit clunky."

Clunky. Wonderful.

She folds her arms and starts to pace in small circles, her bare feet slapping on the tiles as she goes. *Pat, pat, pat.*

"I have an idea. We want the same thing, right?"

"We do?"

"Yes. To do well here. At HappyHead."

"Oh, right. Yes, I suppose."

"We do. I can see that, Seb."

"Sure."

"So about the room numbers. If number one is the best, that means I'm the top-numbered female in Pod Integrity, by a long way. And you're the top-numbered male. Quite a bit lower in the rankings than *me,* but that shouldn't matter too much. I hope."

All right, Regina George. "You think the numbers really mean something?"

"Oh, come on, don't be thick. It's pretty obvious they're rating us, isn't it? I mean, I'm number five, and *Finn* is eighty-something. . . . All the mental ones are down toward one hundred. And I have a feeling it will benefit both of us if we each try to connect with a high-ranking number here in Serenity. You might even get yourself into single digits. . . ."

"What are you saying?"

"We should try and match, Seb. Me and you. This is clearly one big assessment. And it's the best way to impress them, don't you think?"

I think this room is getting smaller.

"Er . . . Maybe. Probably."

I try to control my eyes. Don't look terrified. Don't.

"Don't your parents want you to go to a top university?"

"Huh?"

"HappyHead could make that happen for you, Seb."

"How did you know that?"

"What?"

"About Cambridge."

"Oh. I just . . . All parents want their children to go to Cambridge."

"Yeah, I guess."

She continues pacing in a small circle, biting her nails like she is thinking hard. She drops her voice. "Look, I think there are benefits other than the university recommendations, if we end up impressing them. We need to do really well here."

Pat, pat, pat.

"Do you understand what I'm saying, Seb? This is a huge opportunity. . . ." She trails off. "And, let's face it, I've noticed a bit of *something* between us already. Some *chemistry.* I don't think we should deny that." I feel like my brain just left my skull and splatted on the wall behind me. "Intellectually I might be stronger, but emotionally I think we can get there with a little work. I know our desires and values match, and that's ultimately what they want. It will benefit you to couple up with me, Seb."

God, she really loves herself, doesn't she?

"I—"

"Just . . . trust me, OK?" The fluorescent light above her makes her eyes look like she is some mythical hypnotizing devil creature. One of those siren things that lure sailors to their deaths. "We need to match low. There's something more to all of this. Something bigger." I suddenly remember Finn in the forest asking her: *What do you know about this place?*

"So what do you think, Seb?" She takes a step toward me. "This could help us win."

"*Win?* Win what?"

"You know what I mean. I can tell they think you're great, Seb. Doesn't that feel good?"

Dad's face flashes into my brain. *We'll find something you're good at.*

Am I going to make a pact with Eleanor Banks, spawn of Lucifer?

"OK." What could go wrong?

"There's potential for something *deeper* between us. My gut tells me I'm right. Right?"

Wrong.

So wrong.

Mnhrn is the noise that comes out of me. I stand up from the toilet seat to see if this makes her back off. It seems to have the opposite effect.

She leans forward, opening her arms. I think she wants a hug, which makes my bum tense up. "This is going to be great. And it could also be *fun.*" She winks one of her fluorescent devil eyes. I let her clasp my body, leaving my arms by my side like a rag doll. "Don't tell anyone." She brushes her cheek next to mine. "This has to be a secret."

"Yeah." I try to stop my voice from trembling. "No problem."

"We're going to need to think like each other so they see

we're compatible. I mean, we *are,* but let's really show them. And since I'm the lowest number here, I think the best way to do that is for you to think like me, since my instincts are obviously aligning more with what they want. Yes?"

Where did they find this girl? "Sure."

"You think you can do that?"

Do I think anyone can do that? "I can try. Definitely."

"You're a good person, Seb. Let them see that. OK?"

"Er. Thanks. OK."

"And . . ." She leans right in. "I think you're sexy."

She squeezes my butt.

I see white spots.

"Thanks," I think I say. Can't be certain. My mouth is so dry it's like I've chewed the toilet paper.

She looks at me like she's waiting for something.

"You . . . too," I lie.

"Now, back to bed, and quietly."

• • •

There was a time when I really wanted to be a Good Person.

It was all I wanted. I thought it was our ultimate aim in life as human beings. Our Biggest Goal. And, once we reached it, we would be happy. Because we deserved it.

And I thought it would make people *like* me. Shelly told me it was never going to happen. Not that people would never like me. That I would ever be a good person.

"It just doesn't exist," she said. "*Good* isn't a thing."

My parents and my school and my church didn't seem to agree.

We discover how to be good by watching and learning from the examples of others. Our leaders.

I think some of that might have been on one of Mum's inspirational fridge magnets.

When I told Shelly this, she raised her eyebrows. "What makes *them* good people?" she said.

"They do the right thing," I said.

"And what is that?"

"Respecting others. Getting their approval. Succeeding."

"Right," Shelly said. "You give that a go. If you believe that."

Sometimes I think I still do.

■ ■ ■

When I wake a few hours later, I wonder if the bathroom pact with Eleanor was just a disturbing dream. I glance over at her bed to find that she's staring directly at me. Her eyes still have the residue of the fluorescent glow pulsating outward like she is telepathically trying to transmit a message into my brain.

Think like me.

We're connected.

I think you're sexy.

Right. So . . . It did happen.

I slide my pills out of my bag, pop one through the foil, and take it. Everyone is getting up now. In their pajamas and a little bleary, not really knowing what to do or where to stand.

The screen lights up:

Good morning, Pod Integrity.
Gather around the table. Breakfast is served.

You have some Reviewers to keep you company.
Try to ignore them.

The door of the pod opens, and in come three Overalls with their tablets. Fluffy. Ponytail. And Muscle Man. Ready to *tap fucking tap*.

Pod Integrity, time to get to know your potential partners.
Let the conversation begin.

We sit around the table, awkwardly eyeing each other up over the bowls of fruit and baskets of croissants. People talk about themselves mostly. The Overalls hover around us, making notes.

Raheem is telling Lucy all about his plans to own a chain of barbers. Betty and Malachai seem to be keeping themselves occupied by mixing different cereals together and discovering the best combination. Matthew is just talking. Loudly. About his incredible house and his dad's cars and his thousands of TikTok followers who call him inspirational when he posts his workouts. "It's crazy. Hard to get used to," he says with zero modesty.

Where is Finn? Which pod is he in?

For the most part, Eleanor successfully manages to keep me focused on her. She steers our conversation to the future, talking about things like family plans and wanting to be leaders of the fields we choose. I just agree because I'm scared of her. She keeps touching my arm. I try to bring up my childhood desire to become a baker, but she practically barks at me, making me stop in my tracks.

168

We talk about our favorite films. "*Mean Girls* is good," I say, trying to think like her.

Her eyes light up. "I *love* that one!"

At one point, Lucy tries to strike up a conversation with me. Eleanor literally stands between us. "Seb was just telling me about his huge stamp collection," she declares.

"Oh," Lucy says, and turns back to Raheem.

Eleanor shrugs. "We can't take *any* chances."

We spend the rest of the morning in the garden playing giant Jenga and Twister. I keep scanning my eyes over the little fence to the pod beyond, looking for any sign of him. Greens are enjoying themselves together on the lawn in the midday sun. I can see Ash sitting on a picnic blanket, talking to a tall boy with a big smile.

I find myself loitering at the edges like he might do.

"Seb!" I hear Eleanor shout.

Jesus. "Coming."

Why does the bathroom pact feel so binding?

"Come to the swing seat with me, Sebby."

Sebby.

We sit and talk, Eleanor loudly enough so Fluffy can hear, about things like traveling and our hopes and aspirations. I keep turning my head to see if I can see Finn in one of the other gardens.

"You can get quite distracted, can't you?" Eleanor says.

"Huh?"

"Never mind."

"Everyone, back inside," Muscle Man suddenly calls out. "It's time for a different kind of game. Someone is here to see you."

Fernsby is sitting at the head of the table in his crisp suit. "Good afternoon, pod mates. I trust you have been enjoying getting to know each other in this beautiful setting. I look forward to hearing the feedback from the Reviewers. Please stand by your bunks."

We do as he says.

I notice that our personal-item boxes, all various sizes, are now open and placed on the table.

"This activity is called Blind. We are using it to assess your initial instincts about each other. As you know, each of you was asked to bring a box with a personal item that means something to you. Those personal items are all here, in front of me. You will look at each of them and take the item you feel you most connect to. Obviously, you can't pick your own."

"Aw, sorry, Matthew," Lucy jibes.

"You must all put these blindfolds on, and one at a time you will be selected to come up and choose. There must be complete silence. The game will begin on the buzzer."

Eleanor looks at me, panicked.

As subtly as I can, I move my finger in the shape of a lightning bolt in the air in front of me.

What? She squints.

Which is yours? Quick.

She just stands there, her eyes wide.

A buzzer sounds.

Looks like I might be matching with Betty after all.

"Everyone, put your blindfolds on."

We do.

Maybe, if I'm left till the end, I won't have a choice. . . .

"Sebastian, you have been randomly selected to go first."

Great.

I feel Betty next to me. "Good luck," she whispers.

"You have three minutes, Sebastian. We believe this gives you enough time to follow your intuition. Don't overthink this. Your time starts now. Blindfold off."

Don't overthink? Perfect.

Eleanor. Eleanor. What does she like? Not much, going by everything I know about her so far. . . .

Fernsby nods in that way he does. That *I believe in you* way. I slowly make my way around the table and peer into the first of the unlocked boxes.

Right. Think like Eleanor.

A skateboard.

Nope.

A handwritten booklet. I flick through its pages. Hundreds of quotes from "Shakespeare" and "Jesus" and "Grandma."

Possibly.

A designer handbag. Chanel.

Maybe.

An old copy of *War of the Worlds.*

I mean, maybe.

"Two minutes, Sebastian."

God, I don't know her at all.

A pair of studded Doc Martens.

Doubt it.

A pair of Beats headphones.

No.

On the next chair, my favorite Bowie vinyl, *Aladdin Sane.*

His shock of red hair, eyes down. The lightning bolt slicing across his face. Hello, friend.

"One minute left."

Shit. Come on, Seb.

I approach the final box. Inside it, a brooch. Silver. A sunflower.

I pick it up and turn it over. Etched in the back of it, "GM." Tiny. Hardly readable.

Finn's voice comes into my head. *What do you know about this place, Miss HappyHead?*

"Ten seconds, Seb."

I pick it up. "This one. I connect with this one."

"Please return to your seat."

I do.

"Put the blindfold back on."

Fernsby hands it to me, and I pull it over my eyes. Everything goes black, and I hear my heart drumming through my body.

"Eleanor, it's your turn. Please step forward."

I hear her approach the table.

"Three minutes, Eleanor," Fernsby says.

The clock starts. I sit in darkness. Everything feels longer in darkness. I can hear her shuffling around, picking things up.

"Two minutes left, Eleanor."

She shuffles along. I hear the headphone wires.

More rustling.

"This one!" Eleanor shouts. "I connect with this one."

She'd better have Bowie in her hands.

We sit through the next half hour of people taking their turns. One by one, they choose their fate. I clutch the brooch, my palm moist with sweat.

"Well done, pod mates," Fernsby says at last. "You have completed the personal-item task. Now take off your blindfolds and see whose you have chosen."

I lift my hands to my blindfold and pull it off my head. As I do, my eyes go straight to Eleanor.

There she is. Smiling at me. Cradling David Bowie's face in her hands.

I hold up the brooch nervously.

Yes, she mouths. *Yes!*

Tap, tap, tap.

Miss HappyHead.

What does Finn know?

Ignore. Ignore. Ignore.

Bad. Bad. Bad.

You're a good person.

Everyone around me is finding out whose item they have chosen. There is the meeting of eyes. Smiling.

"No way!"

"Well, I didn't expect that."

"Interesting," Fernsby says. "Very interesting." He stands and clasps his hands in front of him like he has had a fantastic day at the office. Like he has achieved optimum results.

"Take a break, and in an hour we will rejoin for today's final assessment—the Sharing Circle."

I feel a rush of elation.

Eleanor winks.

I think I wink back.

The bathroom pact is officially in motion.

FOURTEEN
All Is True

Lucy and Raheem picked each other's items, Lucy's being the Chanel handbag, and Raheem's the skateboard. They are currently sitting talking on Lucy's bunk, Raheem gently stroking her arm. Malachai is trying his best to chat to Anoushka because he picked her item (the quote book). But Anoushka is trying to talk to Matthew because she picked his (Beats headphones), and he keeps looking at Eleanor.

Celine Dion is playing. A soppy ballad, "All by Myself." Maybe it is meant for Betty, who is on her own, picking her fingers.

I am sitting opposite Eleanor at the table.

We need to show more, she mouths over her pineapple juice as Fluffy watches us.

"More?"

She motions toward Raheem and Lucy, whose faces are a few inches from each other. He is stroking her cheek now and Muscle Man is tapping on his tablet with so much fervor he might combust.

"Like what?"

She'd better not squeeze my butt again.

She shrugs, then makes a face. I think it might be her sexy face.

Kiss, she mouths.

Oh, God.

At that very moment, Raheem leans forward and pecks Lucy on the cheek. I hear Fluffy stifle a delighted squeal.

Eleanor looks impatient.

The screen suddenly lights up, saving me. The voice speaks.

Pod Integrity,
Time for the Sharing Circle.

"Follow me, everyone," Muscle Man says, giving the bunk a gentle kick to wake Raheem and Lucy from their spell.

We get ourselves up, and together we walk out and around to the back of the pod. Everyone is chatting enthusiastically. Like they are actually enjoying this.

There, waiting for us on the fake grass, is a circle of eight beanbags. There is one chair, a Chesterfield, which looms like a throne.

Lindström is sitting in it. A screen above her head in the top of its headrest reads: "The Share Chair."

"What is that?" Malachai whispers.

Lindström's hand is raised in the air. "Welcome to the Sharing Circle, Pod Integrity. Take your shoes and socks off." She loves that, doesn't she? Naked feet. "It is good to be connected to the earth. Nature is important for feeling grounded and whole." Plastic nature, but sure. "Here, in the Sharing Circle, you are in a safe space." *Safe.* "We want everyone to understand that. Anything you say here will remain here."

The Perspex dome above us is going a deep red. It appears that the fake sun is setting again, even though it's only 15:00. We all take off our shoes and stuff our socks into them. I try to hide my hairy hobbit toes as we make our way to the beanbags.

"How is that happening to the sky?" Lucy asks.

"A great question, Lucy. Dr. Stone's work suggests that people are more open at dusk. They are more capable of sharing with authenticity. Hence Serenity is now projecting a sunset."

"That is actually mental, miss," Raheem says.

"It is a wonderful thing, isn't it, Raheem? Serenity is a truly magical place. You are all very fortunate to be here. This experience is specially designed for *you*. So, please, commit to the moment."

"It's quite romantic," I hear Anoushka mutter under her breath.

It is kind of beautiful, actually. Reds and pinks and purples and blues mix above us.

"Now, if you'll all take a seat."

I sink into one of the beanbags and spot the white clipboard on the grass in front of it, holding what appears to be a questionnaire. Eleanor sits on the beanbag next to me. Our secret pact hangs in the air between us. She takes my hand and squeezes it.

Suddenly Finn's blistered palms in fingerless gloves flash into my mind.

Ignore. Ignore. Ignore.

"I have heard great things about your day." Lindström tucks a strand of hair behind her ear. "Some potential is certainly bubbling. Now close your eyes." Her voice is delicate, like she is telling us a bedtime story.

We shuffle a bit; then one by one we shut our eyes.

"Use your senses. Inhale deeply. What do you smell?" Matthew's Lynx Africa. "Hear?" The beanbag crunching under my bum. "Feel?" Like I want to crawl into the ground. "Now open your eyes. The sun is leaving us, so let it take all our insecurities with it. Our fears. Our self-doubt. With me, control your breath. Exhale for five out of the mouth, inhale for three through the nose."

I take a peek. Everyone is doing it.

A ring of Overalls has appeared around the edge of the beanbags. Watching.

I close my eyes, blocking them out.

"Listen carefully. I want you each to think of a story from your past. A story that you feel represents *you*. But it must be based around something *difficult*, something that exposes your vulnerabilities. You must present yourself in an honest way. I have pulled random numbers for the order. Number eighty-one, Betty, you have been pulled first. Please take your place in the Share Chair." Lindstrom stands and moves to the edge of the circle.

I open my eyes to see Betty slumped in the beanbag with her hood up, her sleeves pulled over her hands like this will protect her from what's coming.

"Come on, Betty."

She stands slowly, looking like she might pass out.

"It's OK, Betty. This isn't easy. Can we encourage her, everyone? Let's give her a round of applause."

We all clap.

Betty drops her head toward the floor as she makes her way to the Share Chair. She sits, hunched forward, looking like she wants to disappear.

"Well done, Betty. Now, have a little think about the story you will tell. Everyone else, please pick up the clipboards and pencils at your feet."

We do.

"Please write Betty's name at the top."

Betty

"Now. Repeat after me, Betty," Lindström says. "In the Sharing Circle, all is true."

"In the Sharing Circle, all is true." Her voice is tiny.

"I will not be stopped by shame."

Betty frowns a little. "I will not be stopped by shame."

"This experience is a chance for me to learn and grow."

Betty looks at Lindström with weary concern. "This experience is a chance for me to learn and grow."

"Wonderful, Betty. Have you thought of your story?"

Betty shakes her head. "No . . . Sorry. I can't—"

"Maybe I could give you a hint? Would that be useful?"

A hint? Betty just stares.

"Not to worry, Betty. Some of us need a little guidance to get off the starting blocks."

"OK," she says quietly.

Lindström takes a step toward her. "Tell us about Jenna."

Betty's face goes white. Her eyes widen.

"Jenna?"

"Yes, Betty. Jenna."

Betty drops her head. When she speaks, her voice is smaller than ever. "Jenna was an old friend. We knew each other for a while. . . . There's not much more to say. . . ."

"Don't lie, Betty."

"Lie?"

"Yes. Do not lie."

Suddenly Serenity is not so serene. All the Overalls around us stare at Betty.

"I'm not lying. . . ."

"You are, Betty. You can only break through with honesty."

Betty pulls her hood forward. Eleanor is looking straight at her. She shakes her head. Some of the others shuffle on their beanbags.

Words suddenly flash up on the screen above Betty's head.

Please be patient, Pod Integrity.
We must welcome this vulnerability.

"Betty is resisting. It's difficult to watch her struggle, but we can be with her in the discomfort."

We all watch Betty. Resisting.

And then she begins to speak. "Last year, I . . ."

"Go on," says Lindström.

"I . . ." Betty picks her fingers and twists them around each other. They are beginning to look red and blotchy, like sausage meat. "I had this . . . friend. Her name was Jenna. I would get the train to school, and . . . I met her at the station one morning. She was really . . . confident. She wore this amazing bright purple fluffy coat and big black platform shoes, and it was like she didn't really care. About anything. You know those people? I liked that. I think because . . . we were opposites.

"We got chatting, and we liked the same music. She would buy me coffee. And every morning we met at the station, and we would talk. I would really look forward to it, every day. She was nice to me. Sometimes she would lend me clothes. My bag was falling apart, and she gave me a new one. We began to meet earlier, so we could talk more. I would get up at six in the morning and go to the station. I would tell my mum I had early classes.

"One morning I got there and Jenna said she had these pills. Pills that made everything feel amazing. You just had to take one, apparently. She said I seemed really sad all the time and that it would help. I didn't really want to, but she told me we would do it together. I knew my mum used things sometimes. . . . And I wasn't having a great time at home. . . . And I guess I just felt . . ."

"Continue."

"I guess I just felt lonely. So I took it. Not long after that, I blacked out. I don't know what happened, but I woke up in the hospital and my leg was broken. Someone said they saw me fall onto the train track. Apparently I was lucky. I never saw Jenna again."

Jesus.

"Were you mad at Jenna?"

"No. I just . . . I felt stupid."

"And . . ."

"My mum was mad at me. She was so angry."

"That's enough now. Thank you," Lindström whispers over Betty's sobs.

The screen above her head flashes again.

Now, Pod Integrity:
Answer these questions.
They will come quickly, so be prepared.

My pencil shakes in my hand.

DOES BETTY COME ACROSS AS WEAK OR STRONG TO YOU?

Christ. What kind of a question is that?

Eleanor's demon gaze burns into the side of my head. The bathroom pact. OK. What would Eleanor write? I struggle to make the letters straight and have to push down hard with the lead to keep my fingers steady.

Weak.

DID BETTY COME ACROSS AS HONEST?

No. Dishonest with her mother.

I can't look directly at Betty.

IS BETTY MAKING EXCUSES FOR HER ACTIONS?

Yes. Blaming other people.

USE THREE WORDS TO DESCRIBE BETTY.

Immature.

Fragile.

Lost.

WHAT CAN YOU LEARN FROM BETTY'S STORY?

Don't trust people easily.

HAS BETTY SHOWN SHE HAS LEARNED FROM THIS?

Feeling stupid about her actions doesn't mean
she won't do it again.

Forgive me, Betty.

IS BETTY ATTRACTIVE?

What? Eleanor's eyes flick to me. I can feel their ruthlessness. Shit.

No.

DO YOU FEEL A PHYSICAL CONNECTION WITH BETTY?

No.

GIVE BETTY AN OVERALL MARK OUT OF 10.

3/10

I feel sick. I'm so sorry, Betty.

"Thank you, Betty. Please retake your seat in the Sharing Circle. Everyone, pull out your page and hold it in the air."

We do. The Overalls behind us take them from our hands.

As Betty moves back to her beanbag, she wipes her eyes with her sleeve.

She looks terrified.

Shamed.

This doesn't feel right. . . .

"Number thirty-six, Sebastian. You're next."

Right. I can do this.

"Please step forward. Everyone else, write his name at the top of your page."

I stand. Head rush.

I try to walk like Eleanor might. Strong strides. Head up.

I sit in the Share Chair like I just don't care. Ready to impress.

"Repeat. In the Sharing Circle, all is true."

"In the Sharing Circle, all is true."

I've got this.

"I will not be stopped by shame."

"I will not be stopped by shame."

"This experience is a chance for me to learn and grow."

"This experience is a chance for me to learn and grow."

Lindström leans forward. "Have you thought of a story to tell us?"

"Yep," I say. Confident.

I think Lindström will love it. I think Eleanor will love it. They'll give me tens across the board.

"Great," Lindström says.

"I would like to talk about the time I helped make the bake sale at church a success despite numerous obstacles—"

"Stop, Seb."

"Sorry?"

"Why don't you tell us about the corner shop."

My mind goes completely blank. My whole body numb, like it is no longer mine.

"The corner shop?"

No. Surely—

"Yes, the corner shop."

Eleanor eyes me strangely. *What is this?*

I try to speak, but my voice croaks. My throat is dry. How do I make this stop?

"OK," I say. "But . . ."

"Start from the beginning. Do you need a hint?"

Everyone is waiting. Staring.

"I—"

"Your parents had gone out for dinner, Sebastian. Let's start there."

How does she know about this? Has she spoken to them?

"Yeah. Yes. OK." I try to level my voice, but it is trembling. "When I was . . . God . . . sorry." I can't breathe. A whiteness begins to appear in the corners of my vision.

"You can do this, Sebastian. You must."

I realize I am digging my nails into the skin on my arms.

"I was . . . um . . . fourteen, I think."

"Sixteen." She smiles.

Jesus.

"Right. Around that age. It's . . . hard to remember. . . ."

"Is it?"

Is it? Why is she looking at me like that?

"I don't know how to—"

I'm sweating. Lindström is frowning. Eleanor doesn't look happy either.

I'm sorry. Really, I am.

Why are my eyes filling up?

Stop it. *Stop it.*

Look strong. Breathe.

"It was a . . . a Friday night. I wanted to buy some . . . um . . . I wanted some alcohol. I just wanted to feel . . . good, or something. I wanted to stop . . . thinking." I feel a cramping sensation in my chest. "My parents were out. I put on one of Dad's shirts to make me look older. It was stupid. . . ."

"Keep going."

"I walked for a while to find a shop where they didn't know me. When I went in . . . there was just one other person in there. A boy from my year at school. Connor. I didn't know him well. He was buying cigarettes from the old man who . . . the old man who owned the shop. I thought Connor was going to tell him I was underage. So I chickened out. I picked up a pack of candy instead and went to line up behind him."

"What happened next, Sebastian?"

Why is she doing this?

"Um . . . this man came in. Slammed the door open. He was . . . huge. He pushed himself in front of Connor and asked the shopkeeper for the money in the till. The shopkeeper tried to open it, but he was taking too long, the big man said. Then he just grabbed him. He pulled the shopkeeper over the top of the counter and threw him on the floor. He started hitting him. Connor grabbed the big man's arm. He was screaming at me to help. To help pull him off. To do something . . ."

"And did you?"

"I . . . No."

"Why?"

"Because. I was . . . I couldn't move."

"Why not?"

"I was . . . scared."

I don't dare look up.

"What happened next, Sebastian?"

"There was a lot of shouting. Connor was screaming at me to help. To call the police." God. "I could see the shopkeeper's face was . . . His blood was on the man's fist. All over the floor."

"And during this . . . what were you doing?"

"I . . . Nothing. I did nothing."

Silence.

"Then?"

"The next thing I remember . . . there were sirens. Connor had managed to call for help. Blue flashing lights everywhere. Police cars. An ambulance. The police took the big man away. The paramedics took me outside. An officer asked me what had happened. I could hear Connor saying I hadn't done anything to help."

Silence.

"Was he OK? The shopkeeper."

"The paramedics said he was lucky. That it could have been much worse. If it wasn't for Connor . . ."

"Were your parents disappointed?"

Please, stop.

"They . . . I think they were confused that I didn't call the police."

"And your peers at school? Were they confused?"

Connor told everyone. "Yes."

"You could have done more."

I nod. "Yes."

"Thank you."

I should probably say something now. Something about how the whole experience made me better as a person. That it made me aware of my defects. How I have learned from my weaknesses. Become stronger. More capable.

But I don't. I sit in the share chair, a heat in the back of my head, and watch as my pod mates all start to scribble on their clipboards.

My brain is mush. Like wet paper.

How did she know?

What are they all writing about me? Have I failed?

Eleanor is glancing down at her clipboard with disdain. Like, *what am I supposed to write now?*

She looks up at me. So angry, so *disappointed.*

"Your time is up. Everyone, hold your pages in the air."

I can't seem to stop myself. "Wait!" I cry. "I just need to say something really quickly."

"Sebastian . . ." Lindström puts her hand up.

"I won't be long. I promise. Look, I've learned something today. Something important. I've spent my life being afraid. Some will say weak." She slowly lowers her hand. "But since being here, at HappyHead, I've met someone whose resilience makes me want to change. I think that is the whole point of creating and finding a connection."

Finn. His face. His smell.

"We learn from that other person. We learn their strengths and we adopt them. So we become a team. Together we are capable of being resilient. Of doing the right thing in moments of fear. I want that. I do. I want to learn how to be able to stand up and be strong. Brave. To face what is in front of me, which I couldn't do that day. That has been my life. And I'm sick of it. Here, in Serenity, there's an opportunity for me to change that."

My feet begin to move. Adrenaline has made everything blur. My blood has something inside it that feels chemical, bitter, and it whites out my brain.

My thoughts are gone. I can't hear anything.

My feet are moving toward her. Toward her angular face. I take her hand.

"Thank you, Eleanor," I say, clear as day so they can all hear. "I just want to thank you."

It's like she has got into my brain and summoned me over to her. I can't explain this, any of it. But I do it. I do it because of the pact and because maybe, deep down, I feel like she is right and they are right, and that maybe, just maybe, this could all make me happy. Because I have no idea what that feels like. And I want my family, everyone, to see I can be.

I lean forward. And I kiss her. I kiss Eleanor Banks on the mouth.

It feels like a big, wet slug has just landed on my lips. But I keep going. Because someone is saying something.

"How adorable."

I can hear people clap. I pull away. The slug is gone and in its place is her face. A bit startled.

"Well, thank you, Sebastian," I hear Lindström say. "That was really eloquently put."

And I wonder. I wonder if maybe this place is what I have always needed.

FIFTEEN
The Solution

My mouth is parched, like I slept with it full of sand. There is a crust of dry saliva on my chin. I blink my eyes open to see Betty's black hair falling over the mattress above me. She turns and looks over the side, her eyes red, her face blotchy. For a second, she looks a bit like the girl from *The Ring* when she gets out of the well.

I don't remember anyone else's stories. All I remember is crying. Lots of crying.

I have been awake for a while. Thinking about him. That evening on the balcony. Something about him has stuck to me like chewing gum on my T-shirt that I can't remove.

Why did he show me the perimeter fence? To scare me. Or to protect me?

Why *me*? I hardly know him.

But he is an ache. An ache that keeps persisting.

I hear a sudden noise. There are Overalls entering the room. Lots of them.

"What the—" Betty starts to say, but she is shushed by one of them.

Lindström is standing at the table. "Please, all join me. We have your results."

Results?

"Quickly, now. We have many more pods to visit."

Everyone shuffles their way to the table. I see Lucy standing close to Raheem.

I am trying not to catch Eleanor's eye. Really, really trying not to.

Suddenly she is next to me. "Hey, handsome," she whispers in my ear. A fleck of her spittle hits the side of my face.

"Hey," I say.

I feel her fingers link into mine. I pull my hand away and scratch my nose.

"What's going on?" Matthew asks, and I hear the morning mucus catch in his throat.

Lindström holds up her hand to silence him. "We have assessed your performances. We have looked through your questionnaires and your Reviewers' notes from the day before. Some of it is very promising. As a result, some of you will be invited to participate in one final assessment before we leave Serenity— Couples Therapy. This will involve those pairings we feel have shown therapeutic potential. Not all pods have found pairs. Some had more than one."

There is a whispering throughout Pod Integrity.

"We have identified one couple from Pod Integrity that will undertake the assessment," Lindström continues.

"Only one?" Matthew says. No one answers him.

I avoid Eleanor's death stare.

"The rest of you will watch. This is an opportunity to learn from all the couples and see what it is that makes them therapeutically compatible. Couples Therapy will test their commitment to one another."

She looks at her tablet. "The couple is Eleanor and Sebastian."

Oh, shit.

"You what?" Raheem says.

Lucy's face contorts with confusion.

"We feel that your differences, although at times extreme, have the potential to complement each other. Eleanor's emotionally robust attitude could help Sebastian learn some resilience. Whereas Eleanor might learn from Sebastian's raw sensitivity. You are intellectually compatible and inspire commitment in each other—a real marker for creating happiness. You obviously respect each other and the process. And the physical connection is undeniable. Congratulations."

Eleanor looks like she's in shock. Some people applaud. Others don't.

"Now we want to offer the couple some encouragement before they undertake the next assessment. A well-earned reward. It's going to be quite intense, and there's an element of danger involved."

Hold on, what? Danger?

"Please, everyone, watch the screen."

The lights in the pod dim. On-screen, a woman and a man who both look like Eleanor suddenly appear. They stand outside a large house.

I feel her body tense next to mine.

"Eleanor," the woman says. She is tall with long blond hair, her face sharp like her daughter's. "Darling." Eleanor makes a little noise. "I wish we could see you! You're doing so well. We are so proud of you." Eleanor is staring up at the screen with complete adoration.

She waves. "Mum!"

Lindström whispers to her, "They can't see us or hear you, Eleanor."

"Oh." Eleanor drops her hand.

On the screen, Eleanor's mum then leans down out of the shot and picks up a large, fluffy cat. She waves its paw at us. "Never become complacent. We believe in you. Always."

"Aww," Anoushka says.

"Her mum's a total babe," Matthew whispers.

"Ew, Matthew. Stop," Anoushka says.

The screen changes.

My family.

The three of them are sitting on the floral couch in our living room. Mum, Dad, and Lily, with the familiar beige wallpaper behind them. It's odd seeing them again. Inside Pod Integrity.

Lily is holding a banner. Oh, God. *Go, Sebastian!*

And there are balloons.

Dad speaks. "Well, well, well. Who'd have thought it, hey, son?"

Mum puts a party blower to her mouth. *Buuuuuuhhhh.*

I feel a bit faint, like my knees might buckle. Everyone is looking at me.

Please stop.

"We have heard how wonderfully you're doing, Sebastian. We're proud of you. This journey you're on seems to be so good for you! And . . . this picture makes us *very* happy." She holds up a picture of me in the garden outside the pod. Laughing. With Eleanor. Playing giant Jenga. "Look at that smile!"

Huh? How . . . ?

"Keep doing what you are doing." Mum's eyes fill up with tears.

"Thought you'd be back home after a few days, if I'm honest," Lily puts in. She gives a little laugh. "Well done, bro. Keep it up."

I feel disoriented.

"You keep going, son," Dad says. "Keep pushing yourself. Do us proud."

The video switches off.

I look at the others. Malachai gazing longingly at the screen. Lucy and Raheem still confused. I run to the bathroom door and slide it open.

"Seb?"

We're proud of you.

They've never . . . never said that. Ever.

I push the door shut and slump down in a heap on the floor. I lie there, my cheek pressed into the cool tiles, my heartbeat drumming in my ears. I try to slow my breath.

Finally, there is a knock at the door.

"Sebastian? Are you all right? It is time for the chosen pairs to begin Couples Therapy."

■ ■ ■

On the fake lawn outside the tent, there are two rows of chairs facing each other, about thirty in total. Around them, a crowd is gathering. A crowd of Greens and Overalls and Assessors. Fernsby and Lindström are here. So is Manning, standing on the little mound with a microphone.

I see Antiseptic among the crowd. He isn't smiling. In fact, he looks . . . worried.

Where is Finn? I scan the faces.

"Settle down, please," Manning's voice blares out. "Settle down. We know you are excited. Welcome to Couples Therapy. Could the chosen pairs step forward?"

There is applause. The crowd is applauding *us*.

I feel a bit like an athlete at the Olympics.

The chosen couples line up together in front of everyone. I look down the row. Fridge Boy is here, with his new partner, Ayahuasca. She waves adoringly at the crowd, like she is posing on a red carpet. When I look into it, I notice there are some Overalls wearing little nurse's hats, which is a bit strange. We are directed to stand between the chairs—girls on one side, boys on the other.

"This final challenge of Serenity will test just how far you will go for your therapeutic partner. This is a test of your loyalty and commitment and capacity for selflessness. Please take a seat."

I sit, Eleanor facing me.

Overalls begin to approach, rolling metal stands on wheels toward us—the type you see people trundling around hospitals. A see-through plastic bag is attached to each one, full of some kind of liquid. And attached to each bag are two long clear tubes.

The stands are placed between each couple.

I catch Eleanor's eye. She nods. *We got this.*

"The only rule is that all the solution must be gone from

the bags within two minutes," Manning continues. "It's that simple. In order to draw the solution into your tube, squeeze the pump." Manning indicates a rubber bulb-shaped pump connected to the side of each tube. "Work together to ensure the bag is empty. In life, you must learn to share burdens and you must trust each other to do this in a compassionate way."

In sickness and in health. Till death do us part.

"What's in the solution?" someone asks.

"All will become clear."

Antiseptic has his head down.

"The nasogastric route will be used to administer the solution."

"What's the—"

"Through the nose?"

"No fucking way!" a small boy sitting to my left shouts. "Into our *bodies*?"

"That is correct."

"Nah. No way. I'm not doing this." He stands.

His partner looks angrily at him. "What are you doing?"

"They're not putting that stuff inside me." He turns and strides away. I hear a few people booing him. His partner gives a loud sigh, shoots Manning an apologetic look, then runs after him.

"Anyone else?" Manning asks. "Anyone else want to leave? Now is your chance."

A couple farther down the row gets up.

"The choice is yours," Manning says. "This is a task about trust. Do you trust each other? Do you trust *us*? We cannot progress without trust. The nasogastric route is a proven way to administer fluids quickly, and our medical team is here to ensure safe practice. That way, the Assessors will know it is going directly into your stomach and that you have no chance of pouring it away."

"Why would we pour it away? What's in it?"

There is silence for a moment; then Manning raises the microphone to her lips. "Each couple will be connected to the bag between them. Together you must empty the whole bag."

I can smell surgical gloves. "Hold still," a voice behind me says. And then I can't move my head because someone is clasping it. In front of me, one of the nurses has picked up the clear tube.

"Hold still, Mr. Seaton," the nurse is saying, and I realize it is Misty. She inserts the tube into my right nostril.

I try and focus on anything else. I look at Eleanor.

She nods at me.

I breathe. Calm, Seb. Calm.

"Get off me!" I hear from somewhere. Out of the corner of my eye, I see another couple leaving.

"Almost there," the male nurse holding my head says, close to my ear.

I gag as the tube disappears up inside my face. I feel strange. Dizzy.

"There we go. Nice and easy, see?" Misty slaps what feels like a piece of duct tape over the tube, plastering it to my cheek. "So it doesn't move. That would make things harder for you. . . . We don't want that, do we?"

I look across at Eleanor. Her eyes are closed as the tube is fixed up her nose.

"Just need to check for placement . . ." Misty holds some sort of handheld metal detector up to my chest. The kind they use in airports. "Don't want it to be in the lung . . . That would be very uncomfortable." She presses a button, and it beeps. She scans it over my chest and down toward my belly button. "It's in the stomach," she says, nodding to the nurse behind me.

He gives me a little tap on the back. "Don't try to pull it out. That would be very foolish."

I can see Manning slowly pacing up and down. She smiles at me. *Good boy.*

She stops, and there is an abrupt stillness around the whole lawn.

"Those of you who have decided to stay, please look your partner in the eyes," Manning says.

Eleanor looks at me.

You OK? I mouth.

She nods, but her face is trembling.

The nurses disappear back into the crowd.

"All ready?" Manning asks. "Hands on pumps . . ."

I find the little rubber bulb connected to my tube. I take it in my hand. It feels like the end of a toy trumpet I used to blow in Lily's face when she was annoying me.

"Ready . . . Your two minutes start . . . now."

Eleanor's eyes are fierce. Resilient. "After three?" she says. Her shuddering body shakes her tube, and the metal stand clangs between us.

"Yes."

"One," Eleanor says.

"Two," I say.

"Three," we say together.

I squeeze the pump. The valve opens, and the solution begins to flow down the tube toward my nose.

I squeeze it again. And again.

The line of the fluid moves right up to my face and down. Down into my body.

I feel a small tickle. A *whoosh* in my stomach.

And it is there. It is inside me.

Almost immediately, I feel my body tingle. A strange sensation like little pins pricking all over my skin.

It feels . . . *warm.*

I squeeze. And squeeze. A heat sweeps through me. The volume of solution in the bag between us slowly begins to lower.

I hear shouting farther down. Screaming.

Focus.

The sinew in my muscles begins to feel like it is burning.

"One and a half minutes remaining," Manning's voice says from somewhere.

My vision starts to swim. Blotches everywhere. The bag. The crowd. Antiseptic's face. Eleanor. The yellow of the Overalls. All blending into one.

My mouth is filled with a bitter taste like my body needs to get it out.

I flick my eyes to the left and see Fridge Boy bending forward. His face red. Eyes white. His mouth opens, and he vomits all over the ground in front of him.

"Jamie!" Ayahuasca Girl shouts. "Jamie, stop!"

He continues squeezing the rubber bulb.

God.

"Keep pumping," Eleanor says. Her voice now thin. Weak.

My whole body is swaying, as if I'm on a boat in a storm. My skin burns and itches like I'm being rubbed with nettles. There is a ringing in my ears, and nausea rips against my chest.

The girl to my right is crying, tears streaming down her face.

My hand continues to pump.

I feel myself drooling. It drips down my chin.

A pain in my head.

I can't . . .

I can't breathe.

It . . . stings. Everywhere.

My lungs are heavy, as if molten lead is coursing through them. My lips feel swollen, like they might burst.

There is some kind of disturbance in the crowd. A commotion. Manning is shouting, but I can no longer hear the words.

Eleanor slumps to one side, her body limp against the arm of the seat. Her hand lets go of the pump.

Shit.

The bag still has a few inches of solution in it.

I look at the Assessors tapping away on their tablets.

It burns like hell.

Everything swims.

I pump.

I retch.

I keep pushing.

Squeeze.

Squeeze.

Squeeze.

We're proud of you.

Show them.

Show them.

Show them.

I focus my eyes on the bag emptying.

The solution pouring into me.

A stabbing pain explodes in my chest.

Like my body is screaming.

The ringing in my ears is deafening.

With every inhale . . .

The bag is nearly . . .

Empty . . .

Blood.

Blood is dripping from somewhere.

My nose.

Pooling out over my hoodie, trickling toward the ground.

And I feel . . . calm.

Finn.

Is that you?

His face. In the sea of green.

None of this is right, is it?

I feel myself falling.

Shapes are moving around me.

I can no longer see anything.

Hear anything.

And then . . . nothing.

SIXTEEN

For HappyHead Use Only

Beep.

   Beep.

   Beep.

   Beep.

"He's stirring," someone is saying.

"Sebastian? Can you hear me?"

. . .

Me and Oliver were fifteen when we kissed.

At my dad's party.

It was summer. Boiling hot.

Oliver was actually the son of my mum's friend from church. That's how I knew him. Even though he was in the same year as me at school, we didn't move in the same circles.

That is to say, I didn't move in any circles.

Oliver would never acknowledge me in public, and he made

it pretty clear that if I let on that we knew each other, it wouldn't end well. I was fine with that.

He would come around to our house sometimes on a weeknight when our mums wanted an excuse to have a dinner (get sloshed on white wine) and discuss the current pastoral affairs (bitch about the other mums). They would try and make us play video games, or board games, or any game they thought teenagers liked.

Sometimes we would. Other times he would put on the TV in my room and I would sit there, wearing my headphones. He was nice enough when you got him on his own. He would tell me he was interested in my music and ask me about it.

Sometimes he would look at me funny. Just *look at me,* for ages.

I'd catch him and say, "You OK?" and he'd say, "Yeah, yeah, course," and turn back to the screen, a bit embarrassed. It would make me feel nervous, but in a nice way. Excited, I suppose.

He was tall, a swimmer, and everyone thought he was cool, in a sort of jock way. Popular. With both kids *and* adults. That type.

"Very good-looking," my mum would say. "Really grown into himself."

Our yard is long and has these overgrown bushes halfway down it. Behind them is a little shed and an outdoor seating area and a firepit that Mum had got Dad for his birthday.

The party was to celebrate Dad's promotion. The house was full of their work and church friends, all getting very overexcited. I found the noise overwhelming—*screechy*—so I went outside to listen to my music by the firepit.

It was just getting dark. Mum had put up fairy lights and an ashtray for the secret smokers.

"Hi," I suddenly heard. It was Oliver, by the bushes.

"Hi," I said.

He stepped forward. "What are you listening to?"

"Oh, nothing," I said, pulling off my headphones.

"Let me guess," he said, then laughed a bit stupidly. "David bloody Bowie." He sat down on the chair across the table from me. "You're odd, aren't you?"

"Er, thanks."

"No. I mean, just . . . you're a loner."

"Right."

"I don't mean it in a rude way. I think it's interesting . . . actually." He leaned across the table. His eyes looked like they weren't quite focusing. Fuzzy. "I'm feeling it," he said, then laughed again and nearly fell off his chair. "Dad let me bring my own beer."

I could smell the alcohol on his breath wafting toward me.

"Oh, cool," I said.

He straightened himself up, looking back at the house. Checking. He then turned to me and mumbled something inaudible.

"Sorry, I didn't get that."

"I've been thinking about you." His voice was louder and all slurry.

My stomach flipped. "Right. Cool. Yeah," I think I said.

"I've been thinking about kissing you."

My hands went instantly numb.

"Right," I said, then coughed. "Really?"

He moved around the side of the table.

"Would that be OK?" he said. "You can say no?" He looked back at the house.

"I mean, sure," I said somehow. I don't know how I got there because I couldn't feel my legs, but suddenly I was standing inches away from him. He smelled like beer.

He laughed. "OK. First time for everything, right?"

"Right."

He leaned toward me. "Here goes nothing," he said, tripping slightly.

When his lips touched mine, I felt suspended in a moment of terror and total joy and confusion and excitement and heat and complete shame, all at once.

It was over very shortly.

Because his head turned toward the laughter. The laughter by the bushes.

I opened my eyes.

Lily.

And then he shoved me.

I fell back into the chair.

"Get off me, Seb," he said. "*Christ.* I've told you before, I'm sorry, but I'm not *gay.*" He stood with his arms up by his head like someone who had been caught robbing a bank. He turned to Lily. "Sorry, Lily. I didn't want to embarrass him, but it's getting a bit much. Your brother is always trying to get with me." He made a face, like *Yeah, I know. Can you blame him?* "Look, I've got nothing against gay people, but just because I'm nice to him doesn't mean he can try that shit." He pushed past her toward the house, then turned back and said, "Don't worry, Seb. I won't tell anyone."

My sister looked at me, her eyes glowing. "Makes sense," she said, and then followed Oliver back to the party.

■ ■ ■

Beep.

    Beep.

    Beep.

    Beep.

My eyes open.

I am in a room I have not seen before.

It swims.

I look down at my body.

For HappyHead Use Only

For HappyHead Use Only

For HappyHead Use Only

Repeating green words cover a yellow gown.

I am in a bed I do not know. On my right is a machine. There is a drip in my arm.

    Beep.

    Beep.

    Beep.

    Beep.

"He's here. He's awake."

A hand on mine. "Hello, Mr. Seaton. Don't speak. You must rest."

More voices.

"Check his chip."

"All working."

Light. Blinding light.

A smile in front of me.

Flowers. Plastic flowers.

"Thank you, Sebastian."

"I . . ."

Blackness.

■ ■ ■

Everything is fragmented.

Snapshots.

"Where am I?"

Pain sears through my body.

I'm dizzy.

Where can I be sick?

"You're back in the main building now. Take it easy. . . ."

I look up.

Misty. Misty the nurse. Sitting on a chair at the foot of
the bed.

"You've done brilliantly, Sebastian. Now rest."

■ ■ ■

Don't trust them.

He said it.

He warned me.

■ ■ ■

A plastic cup of water.

I take it and drink it in one gulp.

I am thirsty. So thirsty.

"Excuse me . . ."

I can't . . . I can't . . .

Blackness.

■ ■ ■

"How are the others?"

"The six couples who completed the challenge are recovering nicely."

"Wonderful."

"This is very promising. Very promising indeed."

SEVENTEEN
Into the Night

I blink.

I blink again.

A red glare on the ceiling above me. I look down and see it is coming from the digits of the clock on the desk.

00:02.

I must be back in one of the bedrooms in the main Happy-Head building.

What . . . *What the hell happened?*

My body is heavy on the mattress. My throat sore, like I have swallowed glass. There is a small, pulsating thud somewhere in the base of my skull. Gradually I turn and put my feet on the floor. My muscles feel thin. Weak. Pathetic. My joints stiff.

I feel a tingling on the inside of my forearm, right on the bulge of my vein. I look down and see a bruise, a small gray smudge seeping outward like the first stroke of a watercolor painting.

As I push myself up, I feel like I might vomit. I slowly stand. I sway.

I suddenly notice the size of the bedroom. It's huge. The bed is double the width of the last one. There is a dining table with a jug of water and what appears to be fancy cookies and fresh fruit. There's even a couch. My greens are folded neatly on an armchair. My pills placed on a table next to my inhaler.

I walk to the window and lean over the desk to pull open the curtain. The Astroturf is pooled in moonlight.

What day is it?

There's a buzzing in my ears. A space in my brain. I try to pull my memories into it. A video. Mum and Dad were in it. Lily. Lily was there. With balloons. There was applause.

I shuffle toward the door and open it a fraction. It hurts to move too quickly.

The Harmony Hall is dark.

I step forward, my feet cold on the white tiles.

It is the same. But not.

Something is different.

It is very quiet.

The screen on the wall opposite is fixed with a smiling face.

Bedroom 6: Sebastian Seaton

Six?

There is a noise from somewhere down the hall. A shuffling. I squint. Nothing.

Then the slapping of shoes on tiles. *Pat. Pat. Pat.*

My heart jumps, and a searing pang of anxiety swipes at me. I wobble. Steadying myself with my hand on the wall, I turn. Back into the room. The air is dense, like I am moving through tar.

I pop one of my pills out of the foil and place it on my tongue.

Breathe.

I get under the duvet and lie still. The footsteps grow louder. *Pat. Pat. Pat.*

Then they stop. Right outside my door.

It's OK.

I pull the duvet over my head.

Suddenly the door opens.

Oh, God.

Stay still. Very still.

I squeeze my eyes shut.

Maybe it's Misty again. Misty coming to give me some aftercare.

Go away, go away, go away.

A rummaging. I hear the desk being pulled away from the wall. I can feel the person is very close to me. Very close to my head. A *clunk.* I open my eyelids a fraction.

The red glare has gone.

A voice. "Hey . . . It's me."

I shoot upright.

Finn.

Ice Eyes.

Electric blue, cutting through the darkness. He is crouched down beside the bed, his finger to his lips. "Sorry if I scared you. I think they might be able to listen to us through the clocks." He gestures down to the plug, now lying detached on the floor. "I needed to see if you were OK."

"I—"

"I'm sorry. For what happened to you."

I can't tell if this is some hallucination. He looks me over, his eyes tracking across my face, my body. I swallow the sensation of heat that rises from my stomach.

My voice is harsh and gravelly. "Finn. If they find you in here, we're both—"

"What? We're both what, Seb? *Dead?*"

The word hangs in the air. I wasn't going to say that. I wasn't.

Slowly I swing my legs over the side of the bed, trying my best to hide the pain.

"Careful," he says. When he puts his hand on my arm to steady me, his touch sends a million-watt charge into my body, lighting me up.

"Hi," I say, a little stupidly.

"Hi." He gives a tiny smile and then exhales, the air whistling through his slightly parted lips. "I was worried about you."

"Me?"

"Yes."

"I'm OK. I am. Honestly . . ." I stand but wobble.

"Easy now . . . ," he says, guiding me back down onto the bed. "Here. Drink this."

He pours me a glass of water, and I gulp the whole thing in one go. I must be wheezing, because he passes me my inhaler. He crouches in front of me, pushing his hair out of his eyes, watching me as I put it to my lips and draw the medication into my body.

I feel my lungs expand, and the world around me comes slowly into focus, sharpening, bringing with it the reality of what is happening.

"I want you to come with me." His Mancunian accent rings through the darkness. "You know there is something very bad happening here, Seb."

"It's . . ." I try to gather my thoughts. "It's . . . a little bit . . . strange, yeah."

"You think being encouraged to poison yourself is just 'a little bit strange'?"

I shrug in an attempt to minimize things. To make him think I'm in control. "How did Serenity go for you? You seem in better shape than me."

"I didn't get placed in a pod."

Huh? "Why?"

"Because of the consultation. Because of what I said, I was held in the tent for two days with some other people who clearly didn't say the right thing either. They only brought us out at the end to watch the Couples Therapy. They said it might inspire us. I saw what happened—"

Suddenly there is a noise from the hallway. We both whip our heads to the door. Footsteps. I hold my breath. He puts his hand out between us to keep me from speaking, from moving.

We listen.

Overalls doing their rounds.

We wait until they have passed.

Finn rises and sits on the bed next to me. "I'll explain," he whispers. "But not here. We don't have much time." I look at the side of his face in the moonlight. The way his nose tips up slightly at the end, his cheeks hollow, brow furrowed, intense, like he was made for this time of night. "I need to find out the truth about this place." I hear how strong his voice is. How certain. "And I need your help."

Right.

A wave of panic sweeps over me, so I stand and move to the window, searching for some sort of remedy. I try to assemble my thoughts, but it's as if they have been pulverized in a blender. "Someone else might be better. You hardly know me."

He stands up behind me, and I feel him inches away in the dark. Next to me now.

He takes my hand and squeezes it. "Look at me." I lift my gaze and meet the ice blue of his eyes. "You're a good person, Seb. You are, you know?"

He waits for an answer.

I can't give him one.

As if he expected this, he slowly shakes his head. "Listen, I've met a load of bad people in my life and you're not one of them. You might think you are, but you're not. You're smart; you're funny. The way you are with people. It's . . . You're kind. On the balcony, you made me feel . . ." He pauses. "People don't speak to me like that when they first meet me. They don't."

He pushes the hair off his face, the pale light now shimmering over his skin. "Look at this room. They're trying to make you feel *special* for doing what they want. They're brainwashing you, Seb." He pauses, but I can't speak. "They want you to feel like you're an awful person that they can fix. Like you're broken. So you'll think that all this will somehow make you better. That *they* are the answer. I know you can see that none of this is right." He stops and then says quietly, "If they made you think you have to deny yourself . . . to change who you are . . . you don't need to do that, Seb."

The moon is perfectly reflected in his eyes, making him appear luminescent. Pure.

I suddenly want to cry.

I want to put my head on his shoulder and disappear. Disappear into him.

Eleanor said this person was an animal who needed to be *put down.* A brute.

The skin of the tips of his fingers is soft against the back of my hand. Gentle.

"This isn't what Stone wanted," he says. "It can't be."

"How do you know? She designed all this. . . ."

"Did she? I spoke to her. After I was kicked out of the welcome assembly on our first day. She didn't seem like . . . them."

I remember my conversation with her in her hut in the woods. *My main objective was to give people the chance to see that they themselves are sufficient to achieve happiness.*

"I spoke to her too. In the woods. After I left you by the fence."

"Did you think the same?"

I remember Fernsby pulling me away from her, back to the others. *You shouldn't be disturbing the doctor. . . .*

"Maybe." My whole body is trembling.

"They've been keeping her away from all of this. Keeping her out there in the woods so we can't ask questions." He points out the window. "I tried to go to her after the debrief to speak about the Guided Meditation."

The fragments of a memory of that night begin to align. Finn shouting that they had something of his, something no one had ever seen before, and then his nightmare, him screaming in the Harmony Hall.

"They did everything they could to stop me. They followed me and dragged me back here. I swear Manning doesn't want

Stone to know what's happening. What she's really doing. If Stone created HappyHead to get people agreeing to hurt themselves under the name of fucking *therapy,* I need to find out why." He turns his gaze to me, but I can't bring myself to look back at him. "They kept telling us it was safe. That your health was being monitored. You know, when you finally passed out, you were foaming at the mouth?" I didn't. "Like an overdose."

He stops. I keep my eyes on the floor.

"I tried to stop it. To shout. Anything. But they removed me." I remember the commotion. His face in the sea of green. It *was* him. "Something seriously wrong is going on, and it's only going to get worse. So you can either come with me or stay here and keep pretending that this is what you want. That this is what you need to be happy."

I finally turn to him. "Are you happy?" I hear myself ask.

"I'm . . . trying." He looks scared. Like me.

"Me too. Where are you going?"

"To Dr. Stone's office. To speak to her while it's dark and there are less Reviewers around."

"But—"

"I know how to get out of the building without them seeing us."

I realize he still has his hand on mine.

Holding it.

Holding me.

I can feel the pressure of his fingers on my skin. This reassuring pressure. And he is looking at me in a way that makes me feel something I can't put into words. It removes the whiteness in my brain and dissolves the buzzing in my ears.

There is no panic now.

No fear.

All I see is him.

And I don't want to be anywhere else. And I know that he is right.

So I choose to trust him. I choose to trust him because for the first time since I've been here, for the first time since I can remember, I feel . . .

Alive.

When he lets go, I am emptier somehow.

"Are you coming? We need to leave now, before they do another pass of the corridors."

Before I can think, I am pulling on my greens and stuffing my feet into my shoes as fast as my body will allow me. I follow him out of the bedroom and down the corridor to the staircase.

On the ground floor, there is a door with a green exit light. We push the panic bar, then step through the fire escape and out into the night.

EIGHTEEN
Dead West

I try to keep up with the sound of his feet moving through the fallen twigs and dead leaves, but Finn is much faster than I am. "This way!" he whispers from up ahead. I am only able to see him when he runs through shafts of moonlight that shine down between the gaps in the trees. The branches whip into his greens as he pelts through them.

What the hell am I doing?

"Come on!"

I need a moment. My lungs are still sore, and the heaviness in my muscles is dragging at me, pulling me to the ground. I can feel the residue of the poison still circling in my veins.

"Wait," I say weakly. "Finn . . ." I try to raise my voice, but it gets caught in my throat. I lean forward, putting my hands on my knees, and take in gulps of damp air.

I look back at the outline of the HappyHead building through the trees, the curved roof of Serenity at the very top.

An owl hoots, and I swear it sounds like it's crying. Crying or laughing at how stupid I've been.

"You OK?" Finn calls.

"Yeah. Fine."

We turn and run deeper into the forest. The trees are thicker now, twisting black branches everywhere. The ground becomes wet. Sludgy, gloopy. My socks are sodden.

I drank poison for them.

For *her*.

I *kissed* her.

Eleanor Banks.

I kissed Eleanor Banks.

"We're here." Finn's voice breaks me out of my thoughts. He nods into the blackness ahead, and I see the shadowy outline of Stone's hut. The windows dark, the chimney no longer breathing its smoke into the air above the trees.

He puts his hand out. "Wait."

We listen.

Still. Silent. Nothing.

A cloud glides across the moon, and we are cast into near complete darkness.

"Let's go."

I move forward with my arms outstretched until I feel the brick wall of the hut. I trace my fingers along its rough surface, following it until it becomes smooth.

Glass. A window.

I stop and push my face up to it, scanning for a gap in the floral curtains. I find one, barely a couple of inches wide. I look inside. It is pitch-black.

"Anything?"

"Too dark."

"Come on."

I'm suddenly reminded of that film Shelly made me watch. The one that gave me the recurring nightmare where I'm being slaughtered with a chain saw in the depths of a forest.

Cabin in the Woods. That's the one.

We find our way to the door. "Ready?" he whispers.

That is an interesting question. Before I can answer, he knocks on the door.

Maybe this is a mistake. I could go back. I could.

"Hello?" he calls. We wait. "Dr. Stone?" he says, louder this time. He knocks again, harder, and the force of it makes the door creak open a fraction. "It's unlocked."

He steps into the dark.

"Finn . . ."

Before I can convince him otherwise, he is inside.

I follow him. Total blackness. The door creaks shut behind me.

"Hello?" I hold my breath for a moment.

I can feel him in front of me. He strikes a match and raises it up into the air.

The light settles, and my eyes adjust. The room is pretty much exactly as I remember it, except *tidy.* The books and files and papers that were scattered across the floor are gone. The desk at the back is all neat now; the armchair has cushions placed precisely on it; the long, heavy curtains falling in front of the window are dead straight. Even the Post-its on the walls seem more organized. The kitchenette at the back is clean, crockery stacked up in little piles. I notice the faint smell of cleaning solution.

Finn silently moves across the room to the mantelpiece above the fireplace. He picks up a candle and lights it, holding it out to me. I take the candle, and he lights another.

I weave around the room, taking it in.

Strange.

Very.

"Where's the bedroom?" Finn asks.

"Looks like this is it." She must sleep in the armchair, I am about to say, when my Vans catch on the rug. I look down, and I see something in the half-light of the candle—spots, the color of rust.

"Finn, come and look at this. . . ."

He kneels next to me, his face becoming concerned. Uneasy. "Is it . . . *blood*?"

He brings his candle closer, revealing more rusty dots, and on the wooden floor a dark outline of a patch of crusted red. It's as if someone has scrubbed at the stain but didn't manage to remove the edges.

"Shit," he says, and I can hear the fear in his voice. "What have they done to her?"

A deathly silence follows. Then, "Don't touch it." He hurries into the kitchen, opening the cupboards.

"What are you looking for?"

"Anything. A sign. I don't know. . . ."

I make my way to the desk tucked into the back wall. The books are stacked in small piles, although there are far fewer than I remember. There are still the tasseled lamps, and I notice a paperweight shaped like a bird, a stationery pot with pens and pencils, and in front of it a little antique compass.

I begin to sift through the piles of books, my fingers trembling. *The Mind and the Body . . . The Distracted World . . . Mastering Fear . . .* until I see a small black book with no title.

I flip it open. There are pages and pages of dense hand-writing, each page dated. A journal possibly. Stone's notes.

I fan through the pages. The last entry is September 6, just before Serenity. . . .

Every page after this seems to have been torn out.

I remember our encounter during Survival.

I flick back.

September 4

I scan down the page until I see what I'm looking for. My stomach jolts.

Participant Sebastian Seaton stumbled into my garden today, right into my vegetable patch. Interesting young man. There is a wonderfully open person in there, although I was under the impression he may be frightened to show everything he is just yet. When he does, this will unlock great potential. He has it all there within. Very capable and perceptive. Exciting participant. Potentially restricted by fear of how he is being perceived—

"Anything?" Finn says, startling me.

I slam the book shut and push it away, my heart pounding. "Her field notes . . . the last few entries have been ripped out of it."

Suddenly there is a crunch somewhere outside the front of the hut.

"Behind the curtains," Finn says. *"Now."*

Before I can think, the room goes black as he blows out the candles. He grabs my arm and yanks me so we are pushed back against the wall on either side of the window. He pulls the curtains closed around us.

The door creaks open. Then footsteps.

A lamp clicks on.

Heavy breathing.

The slop of water.

The dull thud of something on the floor.

I lean forward the smallest fraction so I can peer into the room through the tiny gap between the curtains. It's Fernsby. Even in the low pinkish light, I can see he's red-cheeked and flustered. Glasses steamed up, hair messy, a few strands stuck to his sweaty forehead.

He takes off his long black coat and begins to roll up the sleeves of his shirt. He kneels down beside the rug and puts his hands into a bucket at his feet. He stops for a moment. He lifts his head slightly and sniffs the air.

I can just make out faint wisps of candle smoke hovering above him. Shit.

I hold my breath and hear it begin to swirl in my head like when Mum used to put a seashell to my ear on the beach.

We are just outside the reach of the pool of lamplight.

Fernsby's gaze momentarily hovers over the curtains. Then he scratches his nose and his shoulders relax. I watch as he wrings out a sponge and begins to scrub at the rug. At the small rusty dots. The blood.

I can feel Finn next to me, stiff as a board. The air from his nose seeps out onto the window in front of him, cloudy on the glass, before disappearing like a slow tide.

In and out. In and out.

Finn's eyes meet mine, puzzled. *Fernsby,* I mouth.

I can feel myself shaking so much that I think the curtain might be quivering. Suddenly Fernsby grunts. I look back through the gap to see him rubbing his forehead. He mutters something to himself, then stands, drops the sponge in the bucket, and wipes his hands on his trousers.

He stops, looking straight at the curtain. Straight at me?

Oh, God.

He steps forward.

Please, no.

He takes another step, a frown on his face.

A sharp *dum-dum-dum* cuts through the cold air.

Fernsby snaps his head to the door.

Dum-dum-dum-dum.

He grabs the bucket and moves quickly into the kitchenette. I hear the glug of water as he pours its contents into the sink.

"Eileen?" someone shouts from outside.

"Coming!" Fernsby calls brightly. Then low, to himself, "Damn it."

As he paces toward the door, for a moment his eyes catch a redness in the light and he looks pure evil. Then he exhales and smiles widely, like someone has flicked a switch inside him. He puts his hand on the door handle and opens it.

"Oh, gosh. Hello . . . ," he says, his voice somber and warm.

"Professor Fernsby . . . We heard the news. . . ."

I strain my neck but can't quite see.

"Look at you all." Fernsby laughs gently. "I would say come in out of the cold, but I was just leaving."

I lean out a fraction farther and see a cluster of yellow

huddled in the doorway. Overalls. Maybe five of them. Most of them I don't know, but I can see Antiseptic at the back of the group.

"We wanted to see how she's doing," a tall man says. "We're on night duty and thought we'd visit her at the end of our shift. Leave her some soup. We made a flask. It's the least we could do."

"Oh, you're so kind. We're sorting out all her food and provisions. Making sure she is well looked after. But thank you. It's horrible, isn't it? We knew Eileen had been unwell for a while, but she has taken a turn that . . . Well, you know what she's like. Not wanting to *bother* anyone. The illness escalated so quickly, and she didn't want to disrupt proceedings. She has been taken to a hospital, and they will give her the best care we could hope for."

"Hospital?"

"Is there anything we can do?"

"Oh, no. I was just . . ." Fernsby falters for a moment. "I wanted to make it look nice for when she returns. As you know, she isn't the *tidiest*. . . ." A few murmurs of laughter. "It appears you are all very concerned about her, which is lovely. She will be so touched. I will be sure to let her know."

"She seemed so robust. . . . I just can't believe it," one of them says. I catch Antiseptic leaning into the room. He flicks his eyes, scanning them over the shelves like he is searching for something. They settle on the desk. His eyes widen.

"She has left us written instructions," Fernsby tells them, "and we shall continue her work. As I'm sure you would expect, she has asked for Gloria to take complete control of proceedings while she is away."

"How is she?" Antiseptic asks, not moving his eyes from the desk.

"We're hoping for the best, Mark. But it was more serious than she was letting on. We know how much she means to you. We will, of course, keep you updated."

"And Gloria?" Mark asks.

"Gloria?"

"Yes. How is she dealing with the news?"

"She is . . ." Fernsby stalls, as if he can't quite say the word. "Heartbroken. But determined to continue." A pause. "It is incredibly sad. We will make an announcement to the participants tomorrow. We must be strong. For them . . ."

I feel Finn shift next to me. He catches my eye. *Liar.*

"This is what she wanted," Fernsby continues. "For a better future. She is a true visionary. Now, I was going to tell you tomorrow, but since you are here . . . The instructions she gave in her parting letter. Some of the assessments will be changing. They will appear slightly more . . . how shall we put it? . . . rigorous. Eileen felt the participants were responding so well to the treatment that they could handle more demanding assessments to help them acquire even more skills. In light of that, the original schedule will be scrapped and the Hide will begin at five p.m."—he looks at his watch—"today! Gosh, is that the time?"

"The Hide?" someone says.

"Ah, yes. We . . . *Eileen* wants us to really push the participants' resilience and initiative. The aim is for them to remain hidden overnight in the forest, without being caught. A bit of a game, see. To teach robustness. Independence. Oh, and to hopefully have some fun too. She feels they are ready."

"That sounds exciting," someone says. My legs are shaking from where I have been tensing my muscles, straining to hear. "They should all enjoy that."

"Listen, it is so kind of you to come and show your support. But now you must continue your duties and then get some rest. A big day is looming. We will get more detailed instructions to you soon. This is tough for all of us."

"Thank you, Professor. For all you are doing."

"You're too kind. Really. Now"—I hear him ushering them out of the doorway and the slap of feet on the stone steps outside—"look after each other."

He shuts the door behind them. *"Christ."*

The crunch of branches underfoot outside becomes quieter and quieter. I catch Finn's eye. *What now?*

Oh, God. I should never have come. . . .

Footsteps on the carpet. The sound of Fernsby pulling on his coat. I can see his shadow as he leans over the desk. He is looking at something intensely. Then he wipes his finger slowly across the pink lampshade. When he raises it to his face, it is black with dust. "Disgusting," he mutters. "Who could live in this filth?"

I hear him head toward the kitchenette. He picks up the bucket and turns back into the room. I see him nod like his work is done; then he switches off the lamp and briskly walks to the door, bucket in hand.

The door slams.

We don't say anything.

Not for a while.

I think I can hear Finn's heart racing.

Finally, he moves the curtain and steps out. He feels his way to the lamp and clicks it back on. "What the hell have they done to her?" he says.

But I am only half listening because I can see what Antiseptic was looking at. The small picture frame: him with Stone, his arm around her like a son with his mother.

It is upside down.

I pick it up, and as I do I realize the frame is loose. The glass shifts slightly in my fingers and slips away from the photograph. From behind it a folded-up piece of paper the size of a banknote falls to the desk.

I reach for the paper and quickly unfold it.

It is covered in lines scribbled in pen like they have been drawn in a hurry. As I squint at them in the low light, I realize they mean something.

It is a drawing. A map.

"Finn, come and look at this."

I feel him beside me, just by my shoulder.

Next to a sketch of a long building there is an *HH*. Around the building there are trees, sunflowers, and beyond it a large space with an arrow pointing to the left edge of the page—*Go dead west until you meet the coast* written alongside. At the end of the arrow is an *X*, underneath which is what appears to be a drawing of a lighthouse. Then some wavy lines beyond that. The sea. A long vertical line representing what must be the shore. Some words scrawled next to it: *Beneath the lighthouse.*

But the thing that makes the blood pulse in my wrists is the thick black line that begins all the way out in the sea, loops around the HappyHead building and back out into the sea on the other side of the lighthouse like a huge iron horseshoe. The perimeter fence.

"What is this?" Finn whispers.

I turn the map over to reveal a note scribbled on the back:

Mark,

    They are coming for me. I shall resist, but they plan to move me. They will say it is because I am sick.
    She is enacting the Never Plan. The students are not safe. She must be stopped.
    Find me.

                       Stone

The Never Plan?

Finn looks at me. "Mark? As in . . ."

"He was just here."

"She wants him to find her." Finn's voice is slow and considered.

"Yes. But"—I glance over at the rug Fernsby was scrubbing, the stains now gone—"what if she's dead?"

"Guess there's only one way to find out."

The students are not safe. She must be stopped.

"This Hide challenge," I hear myself say. "If everyone is hiding overnight, could we use that to our advantage?"

I glance up. Finn grabs the compass from the desk, then turns to me. He looks otherworldly, framed in the moonlight. His eyes sparkle.

"Dead west."

NINETEEN

Do Not Pass

I look down at the stack of paper they left for me this morning. I have covered the pages with pencil sketches. Doodles. Bowie lyrics. Flowers. A dragon. Hopefully they won't come to collect them, as I have hardly tried to do what they asked. To use therapy drawings to "process my journey so far."

I have, however, tried *not* to do many things.

I have tried not to draw him.

I have tried not to lose my shit.

I have tried not to talk myself out of this insane plan.

Can I even trust him?

I did last night when he was looking all handsome in the moonlight. But right now . . .

The clock beeps.

16:45.

Good afternoon, Sebastian.
We hope you have spent the day recuperating.

*Your chip recognizes that you have recovered to a
sufficient level and that you are well enough to compete.
Please go to the Astroturf for your next assessment: the Hide.
It's another fun one! You will compete individually for this.
Try not to get caught!*

Looks like it's happening, then.

● ● ●

We arrive in a buzz of excitement. One big huddle of Greens,
our yellow HappyHead badges winking from our hoodies. We
are surrounded by Overalls in camouflage gear, all in hiking
boots and with binoculars around their necks. Some are wearing face paint, green and brown streaks, like people in those
army recruitment ads. I can see Mark with his head down, rif-
fling through his backpack.

Finn is a few rows behind me. Hood up.

We spent the whole way back from Stone's hut devising our
plan. I had argued that we should go to Mark, show him the
letter, but Finn said there was no way. That we can't trust anyone, not until we know where she is—if she is even alive. Mark
might be working with Manning. So we decided to find Stone
ourselves. Get to the lighthouse and then . . .

Well, we didn't get past that bit.

We have each been handed a pack, and I watch as the other
Greens search through them, lifting items out one by one. Everyone appears to have something different.

"Hey, I don't have one of those," Malachai says to the girl next to him as she pulls out a flashlight. "Wanna swap?"

"What you got?" she says.

He holds up a small bag of dried pasta.

"Er, no chance."

He slumps off in a huff.

"I'd swap," I hear Eleanor say, to no one in particular. "A flashlight will just give you away. Food is more important." I almost forgot about her. Almost. She pushes up next to me.

"Hey, you. Did you get good stuff?"

Nothing about how I drank poison and nearly died for you? No?

My chest hurts. "I haven't looked yet." Maybe if I don't speak again she will just leave.

I feel in my pocket and find the single foil sheet of pills and my inhaler. And the map. The map to Stone.

"I'm so proud of us, of what we achieved together in Serenity." She is still here. "Shame this assessment is individual, isn't it?"

I can't quite look at her. "Yeah."

"God, you still look pretty dreadful. Did you get enough rest today? I honestly still can't thank you enough. . . . What you did. It was really . . . brave. Did you get my flowers? I brought you some to the hospital wing."

She moves closer, her shoulder pressed against mine.

I try not to recoil. "Oh, it was nothing."

"You're Bedroom 6 now," she whispers somewhere near my ear like an annoying insect. "See? What did I tell you? They *love* you. I'm in room four. A little disappointed it's not a higher ranking, but—"

"Hey, Eleanor." It's Finn.

"For God's sake," Eleanor mutters. She turns to him with a big, fat fake smile plastered on her face. "Oh, hello, Finneas. Right on time to kill the mood."

He fake-smiles back. "Talking of killing things . . . You planning on slaughtering some more defenseless animals today?"

"You know, if you actually took some time off from being a completely useless dick, you might see what it takes to do well here."

"I have a pretty good idea of what they want from us."

I drop my eyes to the floor.

"So you're just actively doing the opposite for the sake of . . . what? Rebellion? You're so cool, Finn. Well done."

"Thanks."

She folds her arms. "I can't understand. . . . Don't you want to be happy?"

"Not in the same way you do."

She rolls her eyes. "Oh, whatever. You'll only have yourself to blame." She inhales sharply. "You know what? I can't be around this negativity right now. I need to prepare. Bye, Seb. Good luck." She kisses me on the cheek, and Finn turns away, scratching his nose. My skin prickles.

I watch as she moves forward to find Ash, who is a few rows ahead, dubiously pulling out a wooden spoon from her pack.

Finn bumps his shoulder into mine. "You OK?"

"Yeah . . . She . . . We . . ."

"Uh-huh," he says.

I don't know what to do, so I just stand still.

I can smell the slight familiar mustiness from his clothes. I want to ask him if he's sure we can do this, but I don't have to because he murmurs, "We will be OK. Trust me."

Trust me.

I feel like I am a swarm of bees stuck in a small box.

People begin to make shushing noises and point to the top end of the field, where a podium has been erected. Fernsby is there, wearing his black coat and his warm smile, standing in front of the microphone.

He taps it. Silence falls.

"We have some very sad news. Our beloved Dr. Stone was taken ill in the night."

A whispering ripples throughout the crowd.

Finn glances at me. It's happening. The knot in my stomach tightens.

"She has been taken to a hospital, where they will be doing all that they can to get her better. She had been suffering from a long-term illness, and in true Stone fashion, she did not want it to affect her work here, so she kept it to herself. We must honor her vision by continuing to go forward with HappyHead as she wanted it."

"Was she the weird lady in the rain boots at the beginning?"

"The lady who created this thing, yeah."

"She was pretty old, to be fair."

I look at Antiseptic. Mark. Head still down.

"Dr. Stone has asked for Madame Manning to step up and continue as sole director of HappyHead. Let us welcome her into her new role. Everyone, please put your hands together for Madame Gloria Manning."

The Overalls begin to part us, ushering us to the sides like

Moses with the Red Sea. Manning is there at the back of the crowd, wrapped in a large black fur coat with a Russian-style fur hat on her head and dark aviator sunglasses. She starts moving through us, lapping up the applause.

The group behind us talks in low voices.

"She's kinda cool."

"I hope that's faux fur."

"She's a fucking sociopath," Finn whispers next to me.

She makes her way up the steps to the platform, Lindström not far behind, like some kind of lady-in-waiting. They join Fernsby by the mic, and Manning turns to face us.

She is absolutely loving it.

"Hello, all," she says. "I am honored to be stepping into the shoes of our wonderful Dr. Stone while she recovers. I am so saddened that she cannot be with us." *Then why are you smiling?* "Now on to the challenge. The Hide. How exciting." She takes off her aviators and does that thing where she stops and looks over us, her children, all hers, eyes glistening.

"You have each been given your items and packs at random. My Reviewers shall, for today, be your *Searchers*. There is one rule—do not get caught until five tomorrow evening. *If* you are in desperate need, you have a red distress flare in your pack. Fire it into the air and we will come to your aid. Obviously, that will end the assessment for you.

"The Searchers will send a blue one up when they have caught someone, and you will be brought to the holding pen, where you will wait until the end. The grounds are large. It is imperative you do not go beyond the edge of the forest, for your own safety. If you are found outside of it, you will be disqualified."

I try not to catch Finn's eye.

Ponytail looks like she has been preparing for this very moment her whole life, donning a yellow balaclava and clutching a pair of hiking sticks.

"When hiding, use your *imagination*. Use your *initiative*. Remain *undetected*. We will give you half an hour's head start, then you will hear a siren and I will release the Searchers. I too will engage in the search." Her eyes twinkle. "As your new leader, I want to show my enthusiasm. And, besides, it sounds like excellent fun. I think my fellow Assessors Fernsby and Lindström might also like to get in on the action." She winks at them. They laugh. "So be prepared to meet your match with any of us! Oh, and there shall be a prize for those who manage to complete the challenge. We are really getting a sense of those who are rising to the top of the pack now. This could be your chance to join them."

People whisper excitedly.

"I'm sure we're all eager to get going, so let's not waste any more time." One of the Overalls gives a little excited *whoop!* "Good luck. A quick demonstration of the flare, to send you off!" Manning holds a plastic orange gun in front of her. "And remember: commitment, growth, gratitude, and obedience lead to a happy head."

Obedience. That's new.

She points it to the sky and pulls the trigger. An orange ball fires up above us.

Pieeeeeeeeeeeeewwww.

We all watch, heads up, as it disintegrates into the gray sky.

Manning leans into the microphone. "What are you waiting for? Go!"

Chaos erupts. Some people start to run off the Astroturf and out into the trees. Others look around, completely lost.

"It's freezing," someone says.

"Are they for real?"

"I'm going to surrender."

"Don't be an absolute pussy, Teddy. Just get going."

"Ugh, pissing hell. Fine."

Good luck, Teddy.

Participants rush past me, banging into one another as they go.

"Watch where you're going, *bitch*!"

Finn turns to me, his voice low. "Let's meet at the top of the stream at the edge of the forest. Just follow it straight up, yeah?"

"You go first," I say.

He nods, then disappears into the mess.

As I wait for the crowd to thin out, I think how young everyone looks. Mum used to sing me a song about lost little lambs, and that's what I think of as I watch them all bleating and scattering unguided into the forest.

I place my backpack at my feet and sift through it.

- A plastic watch
- A single sleeping bag
- What I assume is the distress flare
- A whistle (very useful for remaining undetected . . .)
- Sunscreen (sure)
- A small flashlight (Eleanor was wrong. This is definitely a good thing.)
- A bag of handmade candy
- Some kind of folded-up tinfoil mat thing

I click on the flashlight. It gives off a strong light for its size. I put a sweet into my mouth, sling my bag over my shoulders, and start to walk.

■ ■ ■

As I follow the stream away from HappyHead, I see people digging, making shelters, disguising themselves by rubbing dirt on their faces. Someone is dragging a crate out from some low shrubbery, splitting it open with a rock to reveal tins of food. One boy runs past me full pelt, covered in branches that he has tied to himself with string, like a real-life Groot.

At some point, I feel a thump against my shoulder. A pine cone bounces off me and drops to the forest floor.

"Up here," a girl's voice hisses. I look up. She is perched on a long branch high in a tree. "There's room for two. We could share rations?"

She waves a box of dry noodles.

"No thanks," I say. "I think I'll stay on the ground."

She looks annoyed. "Don't come crawling back to me when you're starved and frozen."

Friendly. I'm not sure how she is planning to light a stove in a tree.

I keep following the stream.

There is a distant wail of a siren. Manning and the Searchers. Coming for us.

I push through the shadows, my flashlight my guide, climbing up muddy mounds and over boulders, slipping on moss as I try to keep as close to the water as possible. The only sound is its flow, bubbling over the rocks. The circle of light in front of my feet shows an endless reel of twigs and mud and roots and soil.

Keep going, Seb.

And then the forest ends abruptly, the stream now little more than a trickle.

I am confronted with the thick wall of sunflowers.

I lift the flashlight shakily. In front of the sunflowers is a large sign in yellow letters:

DO NOT PASS
ANY PARTICIPANT FOUND BEYOND THIS POINT
WILL BE DISQUALIFIED

I stand for a moment, my breath clouding out in front of me. A sudden bang and blue smoke fills the air above. Someone has been caught already.

Where is Finn?

Maybe this is a bad idea. I mean, I didn't really know Stone. Maybe she's dead. And then what? I could go back. I could—

"Oi," I hear.

I spin around. He is standing a foot or so away. Staring at the sign, his eyes narrow.

"You got the map?" Finn asks. I nod. He pulls Stone's compass from his pocket. "Listen, Seb, I just wanted to say cheers."

"For what?"

"Coming with me."

I open my mouth to reply, then stop. There is a low roar in the distance, heading toward us through the woods. A motor.

Vvvvrmmm.

"Shit. *Shit!*" Finn snaps his head around, eyes searching through the gloom. "Follow me!"

I suddenly hear barking. Dogs.

"Come on!" He starts to run along the edge of the sun-flowers, and I follow, keeping low, dipping under branches.

Vvvrrummm.

It is getting louder.

Vvrm vvvrmmmmm.

Through the trees, I see lights weaving toward us, flashing as they cut through the sunflowers. "Finn!"

Voices. Shouting.

I can't see him.

Oh, God.

Vvrm vvrmmm.

Even closer now.

I pick up my pace, breaking into a run.

This is stupid. This is so—

"In here! Now!" He grabs me by the arm and pulls me into the sunflowers.

"Get down!" He yanks me to the ground.

The wind is knocked out of my lungs, and I gasp. His hand is suddenly on my mouth. "Shh. Don't move," he whispers, push-ing his arm right across my chest so both of us are flat on our backs.

There are a million stars above me.

I can feel him trying to slow his breathing.

I turn my gaze down the length of my body and out through the stems. Quad bikes. Their lights blazing into the stems right next to us. I can just make out two men, Overalls . . . Searchers, pulling off their yellow helmets. One is Mark.

They stand, listening. There is not much between us and them. A few feet of sunflowers. That's it.

"We must have lost them," the other one says. "I'll head off down there. You search that way. Professor Fernsby said we should split up."

"All right," Mark says. "I'll take the north section by the forest edge."

I turn my head slightly, trying to see more clearly.

A twig under the back of my head snaps. *Crack.*

Finn's arm presses down on my chest, hard.

A dog barks.

The other Searcher points his flashlight straight over our heads.

"What was that? In there . . ."

"I didn't hear anything," Mark says. "Foxes, I guess. No one will leave the forest."

"Hmm." There is shuffling. The flashlight beam swings away. "Well, if they do, they're going to have to answer to her. Right, let's get hunting."

There is more shuffling.

The kick of pedals.

Then engines.

Vrm.

Vrm.

VrmmmMMM.

Away from us, in opposite directions. Back into the trees.

We lie for maybe ten minutes more.

Until we are sure.

Until there is nothing but a heavy silence.

"Come on," Finn eventually says, pulling himself up. He looks down at the compass balancing in the gloved palm of his hand, its needle pointing directly behind us. "This way."

TWENTY
People Like Us

All I can smell is dewy soil and cow shit. It's all I've been smell-
ing for a while now. And, as Shelly would politely put it, it's
absolutely fuckitty freezing.

Finn stops in front of me. He holds the compass out and
looks in the direction it is pointing.

It is pointing at complete darkness.

Like it has for the past four hours.

Every now and then, a blue streak will dart up into the sky
behind us, the flare signaling that a Searcher has made another
catch. They now look like little blue fireflies.

Sometimes I swear I can hear a dog barking. Closer than it
should.

We make our way down an incline and stop when the ground
levels out.

"What time is it?" Finn asks.

I look at my watch. "Nearly midnight."

"Does that thing have an alarm?"

"Yeah."

"We should stop here, maybe try and get some rest. A few hours at least."

It's difficult to decipher where *here* is. I shine the flashlight around me, its beam of light disappearing over the grass. I turn and see we are near a small thicket of trees.

Finn heads toward them, then takes off his pack and kneels, unclipping it. He pulls out a pack of cigarettes and lights one. He stands, inhaling it, eyes closed. I join him under the canopy of branches, rub my hands together, and blow on them like it will warm me.

It doesn't.

It is so . . . silent.

But I don't try and fill it. The silence.

I pull out the map. I have looked at it approximately three hundred times. "We can't be that far now . . . ," I say, even though I have no idea if that's true.

"You look dead cold," he says.

"I'm good," I try, but my teeth are banging together.

"Hold on. I have this." He pulls out a huge sheet of black plastic from his pack.

"Oh, great. Just what I want to wrap myself in while in the middle of a remote field. A body bag."

When he laughs, I realize I have never heard him laugh genuinely before. It's nice. Really nice.

"I figure we could make some sort of shelter."

We work as quickly as we can. I have to hold the flashlight in my mouth as we throw the sheet over the lowest-hanging branch we can find, pulling out the edges so it makes an upside-down V shape. We weigh down each end with stones, and it begins to resemble a very questionable tent.

I trip over at one point, completely stacking it backward, and Finn laughs so loudly it echoes around the field. I feel stupid, but also giddy. Giddy because we keep laughing, but also because I'm completely terrified. Not wanting to be heard, we shush each other, but that makes it worse and we laugh even more. I try not to think. I try not to overthink any of this, but it's him, *him*. He makes me feel . . .

"Done!" he says, standing back, marveling at our work. "Not too shabby."

When we crawl underneath it, my hands are numb. I lie my tinfoil-y mat thing over the floor like a groundsheet.

"Ta-da," I say.

I shuffle myself into my sleeping bag as fast as I can. Finn sits next to me, crossing his legs. He pulls his hood over his head, then takes a jumbo box of raisins from the bottom of his pack.

He offers it to me. "Dinner is served."

I cup my hands, and he pours some in.

"Why, thank you, sir." I realize I'm starving.

He takes a bottle of water from his pack and swigs, then passes it to me. He shovels in more raisins. "These are actually good."

"I didn't take you for a dried-fruit kind of guy," I say through a mouthful, shuffling on my bum to avoid the bumps.

"I am a man of many surprises, me."

Yes, you are.

He then picks up the compass and begins turning it over in his hands, absorbed. Running the tips of his fingers over the wooden engravings of the curved lettering "N S E W" and

Roman numerals that surround its edges. He seems stiller than I have known him to be. "This thing is really pretty."

It's strange hearing him use that word. *Pretty.* It warms me somehow that Finn, a boy like him, would say that without worrying it sounds . . . I don't know. Like something a boy isn't supposed to say.

"Yeah, it is," I say. "Really pretty."

He nods, his face intense as he turns it in his fingers.

I suddenly remember his nightmare. His screaming. "Can I ask you a question?"

"Yup," he says, still engrossed.

"What did they show you? In your Guided Meditation?" He looks up as if the spell is broken. I wonder if I have gone too far. "It's not my business. I'm—"

"My parents," he says quietly. "They were pictures of my parents. The only way Manning could have got hold of them is by stealing them."

I think for a moment. "Maybe Manning asked your parents for the pictures as part of the entry form?"

"My parents are dead."

"I'm . . . That's really . . . That's . . ."

He rubs his eyes, looking suddenly exhausted. "It happened when I was a kid. They died in a fire."

"Oh . . . I'm so sorry."

"It's OK, really. But thanks." I remember him not wanting to be responsible for fire in the Survival challenge. And Eleanor pushing him to tell us why. "They were *my* pictures. No one else knew about them, other than my social worker years ago." He thinks for a moment. "Not even my new family knew I had them. So when I saw them, I knew something really messed up was going on."

I watch as he bites the skin around his fingernail.

"Is your new family nice?"

"They've always been good to me."

"Ah, cool," I say. "No siblings?"

"Nah," he says. "Just me." He rests his chin on his arms, which are crossed over his knees, like a bird pulling its wings around itself. "They're a little older than Mum and Dad were. I've been with them since I was six. They adopted me," he says. "They're good people."

We sit, and the only thing disturbing the silence is the rustle of the wind against our shelter. I feel emboldened somehow; maybe it's the shock of what he just said or the fact that he told me. "What did you say to them, in Serenity?" I ask.

"Huh?" He snaps his head up.

"In the initial consultation. What did you say that stopped you going into one of the pods?"

"Oh, right." He pops a raisin in his mouth. "They asked me who my ideal girl would be, *female counterpart* or something mad like that, and I said I'm not into girls. I'm gay." He hands me the box of raisins. I stare at him. That was . . . so *easy* for him to say. "They said I couldn't complete the assessment if that was the case." He pauses, thinking. "Maybe it has something to do with this Never Plan. I have a grim feeling this isn't going to end well for those of us that aren't what they want. . . . People like me."

I gulp and my stomach clenches. "People like *us*."

He stops. Smiles. "Yeah. People like us."

"Yeah."

"So . . . Eleanor . . . Your match."

Oh, *God.*

"I don't know what I was thinking. I was just trying to do the right thing. To be liked."

"But you are liked, Seb." He looks at me, his eyes wide. "Can I ask *you* something?"

I clear my throat. "Sure."

"Do you reckon people need someone else to be happy?"

I twist the string pull tie of the hood of the sleeping bag around my fingers. "I think . . . I have always felt better being on my own. I prefer it. If I'm really honest, most other people terrify me."

"Me too," he says then. He turns his body to face me. Bites his lip for a moment. "But you don't. I like being with you."

Holy crap. "That's . . . Thanks."

A pause. A heat in my chest makes it hard to swallow. I really want to look at him.

But also not.

But also yes.

My head hurts.

"I like being with you too." I can't stop my mouth moving before I awkwardly mumble, "I think you're really handsome."

OK, that was bold. Very bold.

What.

Are.

You.

Doing?

"Really?" He seems surprised.

"Yes. In a sort of fallen-angel-type way. You know? A bit like a vampire . . . Not a bad one. Like a good vampire." What? Stop. "Have you been told that before?"

He laughs. "Funnily enough, I haven't." He leans forward slightly, holding my gaze. "You're handsome too."

Dry mouth erupts. Raisins-in-dry-mouth combo. I'm finding it really hard to speak. I swallow hard. "Am I?"

He smiles. "Oh, come on. Give your head a shake, Seb." He nudges my arm. "Course you are. Have you never been told that before?"

"Definitely not."

"You are."

"You don't have to say it just 'cause I said—"

"I'm not. You're really handsome." His Manc accent is *so* . . . "Listen. We're gonna be all right, yeah? And we can . . . we can be there for each other. Help each other through this. If you'd like."

"I would," I whisper.

And we sit, both looking at the arrow on the compass in his hands. My stomach is spinning, cartwheeling. I am trying not to let him see the cacophony of things I am feeling, so I take a hard candy, crunching it so the bits get stuck in my teeth. I realize he's looking at me, the corner of his mouth turned up. A flicker of something in his ice eyes.

A quick pulse, a *charge*.

My heart does a small jump. "What?"

"Nothing." But he is smiling.

"You want one?" I hold out the box.

"Nah, I'm good." He is shivering.

"You can't sleep just in your hoodie; you'll freeze."

"Mancunians are used to the cold," he says, but I can see the cloud of condensation escaping his lips.

His lips.

Then I say something.

"You could . . . I mean . . . if you wanted . . . we could share . . . the sleeping bag?"

He looks at me. And in this moment my whole being feels like it swells, full of everything I have ever felt before, all at once. Like right here under this plastic sheet is the entire world.

"You sure?" he whispers.

"Yeah . . . definitely." I clear my throat. "I mean, I saw this thing on *SAS: Who Dares Wins* that sharing body heat is . . ."

Shut up, Seb.

And I do because he is now moving toward me.

And I am zipping down the side of the sleeping bag.

He lies down on the tinfoil mat, his head next to mine. "Seb?"

"Yeah?"

"I'm glad you're here."

"Me too. I mean . . . I'm glad *you're* here."

He slowly shuffles his body closer to mine.

Slotting his feet down into the base of the sleeping bag.

Pulling himself into me.

Chest to chest.

Legs tangled.

His arms around me.

My whole body tingling.

On fire.

"You're shaking," he says. "You still cold?"

"No," I say.

"You're OK?"

"Yeah." More than OK.

I look up.

Into the blue of his eyes.

His finger on my cheek.

Something happens.

A shift.

The world shifts.

I feel it.

The air changes.

The air between us.

And then.

He kisses me.

Everything else is gone.

And my body splinters into a million pieces.

As if a bolt of electricity has been shocked into my brain.

Like someone is turning a light on.

Its warmth is shuddering through me.

This is what it should feel like.

I am safe.

With him.

TWENTY-ONE
Blood on His Hands

When I wake, he is gone.

No. *No.*

"Finn?"

I knew it. I knew I shouldn't have done this. This was a mistake.

Big mistake.

Huge mistake.

I pull myself out of the sleeping bag and scramble around for my watch.

04:49.

It is still dark outside.

Where is the flashlight? Shit. He took it. He must have taken it.

Leaving me here.

Alone.

The motherfu—

"Ouch!" I bang my head on a branch as I crawl from under the canopy. I step outside onto the dewy ground, rubbing my head. The stars are like pinpricks dotting the inky sky. I look around.

"Finn?"

Silence.

OK . . .

Plan of action, Seb. Return to the woods. Complete the challenge. Pretend nothing happened.

Sounds good.

Why did I trust him?

Suddenly, light. Moving quickly toward me.

"Seb!" Finn. He seems flustered. Frantic.

"Where did you go?" I can hear the panic in my voice. "I thought you'd left, you *idiot*."

He grabs my hand, panting fast.

"Listen. I heard a motor. They must know someone left. They're just beyond that hill." He nods into the darkness, and I can make out the faint outline of where the valley rises up around us, against the purple-blue sky. "We need to leave *now*."

A dog barks.

Finn hands me the compass. Clicks off the flashlight.

Shit.

We pull down the plastic sheet, stuff everything into our packs, and run.

. . .

We run and run.

Side by side.

Dead west.

Following the compass.

Sun rising.

Legs burning.

Not looking back.

Through field after field.

Green.

Gray.

Purple.

Until we stop.

Because the ground beneath us suddenly ends.

We are at the edge of a cliff. And the sea is ahead of us. And on either side of us is the perimeter fence, weaving its way out into the blue, both ends abruptly stopping about three hundred feet off the coast.

Just like on the map.

Trapping us in.

It looks tiny from up here, like you could step right over it.

I turn. Grassy terrain for miles and miles. I have no idea where we are. For all I know, we are no longer in Scotland. Or the UK. Or a reality I am familiar with.

Down on the southern side, what seems like miles away, I see a little inlet. A cove with what appears to be a beach. I turn the other way, to the north. The coastline stretches away from us all the way up, rugged and tall. Right on the horizon, on the top of the cliff edge just inside the fence, is a white mark smudged against the dark sky.

A lighthouse.

"The map said below the lighthouse."

"So . . ." I sense him realizing too. "The only way to get there is . . ."

Down.

I stand next to him on the edge of the cliff and push my foot against a rock. It comes away, tumbling down the slope toward the sea.

It's a long way.

"Might be doable . . . ," I say.

Hunger has started to make me feel nauseous, and we have run out of water.

"I think it'll be fine, if we just take our time," he says. He glances behind him. We last heard the dogs and the quad bikes about an hour ago. "What do you reckon?"

I check my watch. 06:16.

"Yeah. Take it slow," I say.

He turns to face me, his back to the ocean. "Right," he says. "Nice and slow."

He gets down on his hands and knees and starts to climb backward, face to slope, pack to sky, holding on to the tufts of grass with his hands.

"It's OK!" he shouts to me. "Looks worse from up there!"

His feet slide occasionally, and my stomach flips every time they do.

I pop a hard candy and crunch.

"Careful!" I call, but the wind steals my voice and throws it out to the waves.

He stops every now and then, shifting his feet beneath him. Sometimes he wobbles, and his hands grasp, clutching for anything.

The black of his hair descending. Down and down.

I see him reach the shingle below.

He puts his hand up to me. "Come on!"

Seems simple enough.

I slide the compass into the pocket of my hoodie and begin scrambling backward like Finn. My legs start to shake, which isn't useful. I move slower than he did.

"Careful down at the bottom!" I hear him shout. "Some of these rocks are deadly sharp."

Deadly sharp.

My foot presses onto a stone. It shifts. Jesus.

Nice and slow.

Don't panic, don't panic, don't panic.

One foot.

Then the other.

Simple.

Rain suddenly whips around me, lashing at my face, the force of the wind pushing me into the cliff face. I turn my head slightly and look out toward the sea for a moment, the sky the color of mucky paint water.

A surge of fear makes my head spin, and I sway, blinking water out of my eyes.

Something slips.

The compass is no longer in my pocket.

It is tumbling down the slope below me.

I make a grab for it. I miss.

And then I am falling.

It is a strange sensation.

I am no longer attached to the slope by my hands.

I am sliding incredibly quickly.

My back scraping.

The sea a blur.

My body begins to rotate.

Stones.

Sea.

Stones.

Sea.

And the air is knocked out of my chest.

Crack.

My head.

When I hit the rough shingle, I immediately stand up, thinking that's the right thing to do. But then I fall over because there's a searing pain in my leg.

I feel something hot and wet seeping down into my sock.

"The compass . . . ," I say.

I see Finn's face.

He is standing over me, but I can't really understand what he's saying because my brain is all . . .

fffffffff.

White-noisy.

Ffffffffffff.

Everything indistinct.

He is turning me over, and he has blood on his hands. Actual blood on his hands.

He is swearing to himself, but also saying things like, "You'll be OK. It's OK," which definitely makes me think it is not OK.

And I look.

My pants are split open.

And there is a gash.

And it looks deep.

Flappy. A bit like meat at the butcher's.

"The compass," I say again. "For the way back."

I can't see it. I don't know where it went.

And then Finn turns. "Oh, shit." I hear scrambling, and he disappears from view. I'm not sure for how long. But when he comes back, I can see he is wet. He's holding the compass. Which is also wet.

Fffffffff.

The pain from my leg seems to empty my brain.

Things move very jerkily.

Stopping

and

starting

like a reel of old photographs, faded at the edges.

The rocks.

His face.

The sea.

The cliff.

I push myself up, then slump back down. "Typical," I say as casually as I can. "This stuff always happens to me. I'll be totally fine."

Finn is next to me on his knees. He is opening his pack, rummaging through it. I hear a tearing sound.

"This might hurt. . . ."

He is fumbling with my leg. I feel him pull something around it.

"Just need to try and stop the bleeding a bit—"

I can see a faint shooting star in the morning sky. Colors. Pink and orange.

I want to say something, but I can feel vomit rising in my throat. I try to swallow it back down into my stomach. But I can't. . . .

"Sorry . . . ," I splutter.

"It's OK. You hit your head. She'll help. She's a doctor."

"Dr. Eileen. *Come on, Eileen.*" I try to sing it, but I can't remember the tune.

He isn't smiling. "Let's try and stay quiet."

He takes hold of my arm and helps me to my feet.

"Hey, Seb." I like it when he says my name. "It's going to be fine."

He leads me forward, over the rocky beach. One foot in front of the other. We stop every now and then so he can rest for a minute. I don't know how long it takes. I can't see the lighthouse.

"I'm just going to head on for a minute," Finn says. He raises his hand to shield his eyes, looking ahead into the grayness of the rainy mist. "See how far." He sounds exhausted.

"Wait . . . ," I say, then stop. "Yeah, yeah, OK."

"I'll be back," he says. "Won't be long."

As he puts his pack down next to me, I suddenly realize how beautiful he is. His jet-black hair billowing over his chiseled features.

So beautiful.

So . . .

He looks like a moody character from a graphic novel. Like someone has drawn him.

Intense.

I like intense.

I'm intense. I know I am.

My head feels like it is floating off my body.

He starts to take off his hoodie.

"No, I'm fine. I'm fine," I say.

"You're shaking." He puts it over my shoulders. "More than normal."

He then sets off over the rocks, his silhouette disappearing behind them.

Sometime later, he returns. His outline hopping over the rocks toward me. He jumps off the final one and runs across the pebbles.

"She's here," he says. "In some sort of shack. Under the lighthouse, about ten minutes—"

"You've seen her?"

"Yes."

"Lovely," I think I say.

"But there's a man. He came down from the lighthouse. Used a ladder. I hid and watched him. . . ."

"Oh, lovely. Can he help?"

"No, Seb. He had a gun."

TWENTY-TWO
The Never Plan

I can hear a strange noise as I drift in and out of consciousness.

Click. Click. Click.

I blink my eyes open. The clicking stops.

"Hello, Sebastian." Stone. In an armchair directly in front of me. "They let me have my plants and my knitting. Generous of them, don't you think?" She lifts a baby-blue ball of yarn from a linen bag at her feet. Her eyes focus back on her fingers, and the needles begin to move rhythmically around each other.

Click. Click. Click.

There's a cut on her forehead, crusted with a scab.

"Listen now, Sebastian." She talks quietly, her voice more strained than I remember. "Stay away from the windows. Don't make a noise. And if someone comes to the door, get into the bathroom and don't come out until I say. They sometimes come in and have a look around."

I nod.

I am on a rug on the floor of a small room not unlike the inside of my dad's garden shed.

"It's not the most welcoming. I do apologize." She coughs. "How are you feeling?"

I feel groggy as shit. "I don't know. Cold." I look down at my leg. It is bandaged up.

"Don't look so worried, Sebastian. You had a mild concussion, but you should be fine. I'm working on the cut on your leg." On the wooden floor beside me is a small pot with some green gloop inside. "I've used some of my plants. They contain antimicrobial properties, wonderful for keeping things clean. I've applied the ointment, and it should help it heal. Any longer and it might have been serious. You're lucky. Finn saved you."

I sit upright, a sudden ache erupting in my head. I hazily take in the room. There is a small old electric heater giving off an orange glow. A window with a few potted plants on the sill. A small desk. A table. A single bed pushed against the wall behind me.

And there is Finn. Sitting on it, legs crossed. Hair wet, towel around his shoulders.

I try to smile. *We made it?*

He nods at me. But his face is drawn, gray, like the life has been bled out of him.

Do I remember him saying something about a man with a gun?

"Eat. You will need your strength." Stone gestures at a plate next to me on the floor with some bread and cheese.

I don't stop to think and eat it all. I feel the life entering my body again.

"Why are you here, Dr. Stone?" I croak.

"They are keeping me locked away," she wheezes. Her fingers tremble, and she sees me watching them. "My health seems to have taken a particularly unfortunate turn lately. I assure you, I'm typically rather spritely." She shuffles in her seat. "They are monitoring me from the lighthouse above."

"The man with the gun?" I ask.

She raises her eyebrows. "Yes." A silence. Her face hardens. "They took my shoes and my walking cane in an effort to immobilize me."

"I . . . We found your note," I say. "The one meant for Mark."

A pause.

"It was." Her needles begin to move in her fingers once more. *Click. Click. Click.* "Now I am going to tell you both some things. You might not like it, but the fact you are here means you are now involved. You carry a lot of responsibility. More than you can imagine."

She stops moving the needles and places the yarn on her lap. "Too tired even to finish my scarf. Perhaps I am getting old." She looks up, her face wrinkling. Then her eyes darken. "Twelve years ago, I was working in a hospital in London. An inpatient ward for adolescents with severe mental-health illnesses. I saw a generation of young people struggling against the world and systems that they found themselves within and controlled by. The internet. School. Exams. The media. The pressure to be something, to look a certain way. To succeed at all costs. A particular notion of success was prescribed, given to them, *fed* to them. I saw this as a problem that was getting increasingly worse. They were suffering.

"There was a girl at the hospital. I'll call her Hannah. Hannah had been there for months and was terribly unhappy. Seventeen years old. Just like you two. She was put on various medications

262

and given interventions, therapy—seen by psychologists and psychotherapists and doctors. But nothing seemed to change for her. She remained deeply unhappy. She came from a particularly difficult background. Her mother died when she was young—heroin—and she never knew her father. She'd spent her whole life fending for herself. Fighting to keep herself alive in a world that ultimately told her it had no place for her. That she was not a success and never would be. And sadly she took her own life. She . . ."

Stone looks over at the heater.

"I had grown very fond of her. I felt she was let down. Failed, by us. I vowed to do something radical. To find a supplement to effective psychoactive medication. To find a way for young people like Hannah to feel that there was an answer. To feel like they could cope. So I designed HappyHead. Somewhere seventeen-year-olds could go, together, to learn about each other and *from* each other. A place devoid of the pressures of the outside world. A place that would enable them to gain the skills to give them endurance in an increasingly destructive world. Self-confidence. Compassion. Generosity. A place to understand the advantages of looking outside of themselves to those around them. To understand the notion of unity. To challenge what success is and what it means to this society—and to them."

I can hear the wind pounding against the small glass window above the bed, making it rattle in its frame.

"My colleagues at the unit liked the idea—*really* liked the idea. I was given various grants to develop my proposal and ultimately an opportunity to present it to the government. It was taken forward to be established under their guidance over the following few years. *The future of our young people,* they kept calling it. *A real shot at changing the crippling unhappiness epidemic.* I was there at all the developmental meetings, watching my dream become a reality. Potential bases for the centers were found, and the contractors began to build up here, in Scotland, in nature, which was always an essential part of the plan. We began to discuss the logistics. How it would work. How we would get the teenagers together, reassure the parents, create a safe and supportive environment. How the day-to-day structure would look. And so HappyHead was created. And it seemed to be everything I hoped for."

She frowns, the creases in her forehead deepening.

"A woman was brought on board to assist me with the therapeutic side of things. Something I was a little less versed in due to my predominantly medical background. She was a renowned child psychotherapist, and she was utterly brilliant. One of the brightest people I have ever met. And she knew herself, first-hand, what it was to struggle. To be scared. Anxious. To lack self-esteem. So she *empathized.* And because of this I knew she was the right person to help me. To stand by my side. She fully supported doing something about the future of our young people before it was too late. She knew that we were failing the generations after us. She had a core of *decency.* Her name was Gloria Manning."

I hear the bed creak as Finn sits forward.

"We worked with the most dazzling minds from across the country. And the government agreed that this could change the future of our nation. Even of humanity. The world was slowly dying, not only physically—our planet—but *emotionally*—our people."

I look up to see her golden eyes burning in the light of the heater. She is completely still.

"And then, just before the building began, Gloria came to me and said we had been asked to create something called a Never Plan—for *safeguarding purposes.*" She says this like she is quoting Manning, then slowly shakes her head. "The government had asked for it, she said. A document containing warnings of how a system could be abused or manipulated if it ended up in the wrong hands. Hospital wards often have similar documents, highlighting *never events.* Things that should ultimately never happen, things that might be unethical or unsafe for patients."

She looks down at her hands.

"We created one together. Giving many examples of how it could be abused by those in power. Worst-case scenarios. Gloria assured me the document was a way of protecting our program. Of stopping anyone from wrongly using it. This was a way of showing the governing bodies that, if any signs of these scenarios were recognized, the program would be stopped immediately."

Her lip trembles. She sits, still staring into the glare of the electric heater.

"What did it say?" Finn asks.

Suddenly there is the noise of a key in the door.

Stone's face drains of color. "Bathroom, now."

■ ■ ■

We pull the shower curtain around the bath and kneel down. Finn puts his finger to his lips. His face anxious. Quiet. The sun is out now, pushing its way through a low window just above our heads, darkened with some kind of green mold. I lean back against the bath's porcelain rim, Finn right next to me. The plughole is a shade of browny green.

We listen. Outside the door, back in the main room of the hut, there are muffled voices.

"Hello?" Stone says.

"Your breakfast."

"Right."

"Can I bring it in?"

A pause.

"If you must. Please put the gun away. I find it unnecessary."

"I have orders."

"Is that so?"

I hear the man step into the room. "Make sure you drink your fluids, Dr. Stone. You look . . . awful."

"Is that everything? I'm busy."

"Busy knitting?"

"Yes."

"We need to discuss something, Dr. Stone."

"Do we? Is that why you have a briefcase?"

"Yes."

"Could we talk outside? The sun is coming out. I need some fresh air, and it might help me look less *awful*."

"You know your time outside is limited."

"What, you think I'm going to try and make a run for it without my walking cane?"

Silence.

Footsteps.

The front door creaks open, and I hear them both go outside. It slams shut.

We don't move for what feels like a very long time. At some point, I have to shift my position, my leg throbbing.

"What is happening?" I whisper, failing to keep the fear out of my voice.

Not sure, Finn mouths.

I notice that the window above our heads is open a fraction. "Is that how we got in?" He nods. "Jesus. I don't remember much. Sorry if I got a little mental back there."

"You're all right. I enjoyed your singing."

"Oh, God."

He smiles. "Strong vibrato."

"Wow, right." I feel my face flush. "Thank you for, you know . . . For getting me here in one piece."

"I'm glad you're going to be OK. I was worried."

I look at the rust on the taps. Listen to the drip of the water.

Then, out of nowhere, I say, "I'm sorry. That I didn't tell them the truth before Serenity. About me. In the consultation . . . I don't know what happened. . . . I just went along with them. I should have been honest. Last night felt so great. Like . . . amazing . . . I've never really . . . Well, I haven't felt like that before. . . . I just wish I—"

"Hey, *hey,* Seb. Stop. . . ." He puts his hand on my arm. I bite down on my lip. "You don't need to apologize. None of this is easy, is it?"

No.

"And we're here together, aren't we?"

"Yeah."

He rubs his bloodshot eyes. "You tired?"

"Yeah. Extremely. You?"

"Yeah. Can't tell what's real or not at this point."

Shit, my pill. I didn't take it last night. They'd better still be . . .

I fish around in my pant pockets. The foil. Phew. As I pull them out, I can sense him watching me.

"What're they for? You don't have to tell me."

"Oh. Erm . . ." I point to my head and make a twirling motion with my finger.

He doesn't say anything.

"They help me to not freak out, I guess." I guess? "To not get . . . low."

I feel myself go bright red and swallow the pill. The silence is really loud.

"Does it help?"

"I think so. I'm not sure. I've taken them for a while." More silence.

"Whatever she tells us, whatever happens, we have to promise to look after each other. Like I said last night. Yeah?"

Look after each other.

"Yeah," I say.

I hear the key in the front door. Footsteps. Then the bathroom door opens.

"He's gone."

■ ■ ■

A blue plastic tray with a bottle of water and some food has been placed on the table. It looks gray and cold, like some sort of oatmeal. Stone hovers next to it, prodding it with a spoon. Finn takes his place back on the bed, and I sit down on the rug in front of the heater.

"What did he want?" I ask.

"He had me sign an official document for the government to confirm all is going well at HappyHead." She speaks softly but steadily, her tone flat, devoid of emotion. "That everything is going to plan." She is shaking. I can't tell if it's from being outside or from anger. Terror. Rage. "Tricky to say no with a gun pointed at you."

She takes a mouthful of the oatmeal, grimaces, then opens the bottle of water and takes a couple of sips. She screws the top back on and moves over to her chair, where she sits, wiping her mouth.

"So I will now tell you what we are up against." She exhales, readying herself. "When Gloria and I were creating the Never Plan, we spoke of many hypothetical abuses that could happen here. A key therapeutic element of the program was to remove external influence, but we knew that would give a lot of power to those in charge. The Never Plan was a theory of how manipulation of that power might look.

"We worked through the various scenarios. Favoritism. Bullying. Group neglect. Taking a punitive, authoritarian stance. We explored the potential of Stockholm syndrome. Gain the participants' trust while treating them badly and they fall in line."

"Like a cult," Finn says.

"Well, yes." Stone pauses. "I mentioned that perhaps those in charge could become carried away and find a way of manipulating the participants to speed up the results. They could begin splitting up the participants. Identifying those they deemed as successful and grouping them together, in an attempt to separate them out from those who appeared to be resistant to the treatment. There would be a top set of participants—an *elite,* if you will—and a bottom set."

"A favored group?" I ask.

"Exactly." She narrows her eyes. "Manning really wanted to dig deep into this idea. Explore it. She began to ask what would happen if those in charge encouraged *pairing* the elite group. In a way that might benefit future generations . . . And this is how the conversation led to the idea that—at its very worst—the structure of the program could be wrongly used to facilitate a eugenics-style scheme as a means of eradicating the mentally weak."

"Jeez," Finn says under his breath.

"Wait—what?" I ask.

"In brief, eugenics is based on Darwin's theory of natural selection. It encourages breeding out undesirable traits within the human species."

"What traits?" I ask.

"The subjectivity of those who choose what *undesirable* means is one of its many problems. The main principles center on promoting qualities that are deemed superior by those in charge. So, in this case, those who are considered mentally dexterous, prosperous, and happy must breed, repopulate, in order to drown out the inferior. Those who appear to be mentally unwell, those who are struggling or unhappy, are left behind. Or worse."

Breed?

The word lingers like a bad aftertaste.

"Who decides?" I ask.

"Those in charge. Me. Her."

"So, what . . . ?" Finn sits up. "You think she has taken this theory and is now actually trialing it?"

"It would appear so. How much of it, I am still unsure."

Silence.

"She's had us doing mad stuff . . . ," Finn says quietly.

"Yes. I have now discovered that so much you have endured was never meant to be." There is a flash of vulnerability, her eyes momentarily brimming with guilt and shame. "She had been keeping me away. Hidden from the reality. She was the one who proposed the idea of my office being out in the woods. This gave her the ability to exploit the downturn in my health to execute things I would never have allowed."

"Like what?" I ask tentatively, although I'm not sure I want to know.

"The design for the building changed without my knowledge. Moving you around the rooms after every challenge—that was never the plan."

I suddenly realize something she might not know. "The perimeter fence is electrified."

Her whole body tenses. I watch as shock and anger and fear course through her all at once. *"What?"*

"You didn't know that?" There is an edge to Finn's voice.

"No." She looks straight at him. "Of course not. I would *never* . . ." She puts her hand to her mouth, closing her eyes. "How could she?" I hear the fear spilling into her voice, a lump in her throat. "HappyHead was never meant to control people. The opposite."

"But she's doing it!" I say, now panicking. "She's coupling us up, making us drink some weird solution that made us sick. To show our *loyalty.* Did you not know that either?"

"Not until it was too late." Stone clears her throat and quickly wipes her eyes. "Mark kept trying to contact me, but he told me Gloria and the Assessors were making sure he was monitored."

Finn scoffs. "So they're all in on it? We saw Fernsby in your office making it look like nothing had happened."

She frowns, then shakes her head sadly. "Him, yes. And Lindström. Mark thinks Manning also has a select circle of Reviewers to keep the others from asking questions. . . . He managed to come to me while they were distracted during the thing she called Couples Therapy. I summoned her to my office and confronted her when it was over."

"Fernsby must have ripped those pages out," I say.

"Sorry?"

"Your diary. The entries after that time were missing."

"They really do want me gone. Erased. Well, what you might have seen in those missing pages was that I was very upset with how she was putting people in serious danger. I told her I would alert my contacts in the government and the civil service. But she said my mind had become fragile and I wasn't thinking clearly, and that she could very easily convince them of that. There was no way I would be believed." Stone looks wearily at us. "And so she had me put on the back of a quad bike and brought here, in the name of making me well again."

My mind is beginning to reel. "So is she planning on splitting us up?"

"It seems so."

"And then what?"

"Well, I can only speculate as to her intentions, but I remember Gloria was determined to explore how the splitting could be taken even *further*. . . . The elite could become a kind of special group that would be taken for additional development. And the bottom percentile—they would be used, have some kind of purpose too."

"Used how?" Finn asks.

She fiddles with her braid, thinking. "What are your room numbers?"

"I'm in room six," I say.

"Eighty-three," Finn murmurs.

"The bedrooms are clearly her way of ranking you all."

I turn to Finn. "Eleanor kept saying closer to one is better."

"Eleanor?" The wrinkles around Stone's mouth deepen. "What room is she?"

"Four. Why?"

"It is interesting to hear how Gloria's niece is fairing."

What?

"Sorry . . . ?"

Finn's eyes widen. "Of *course* . . ."

"So they're hiding it from people, I see."

I feel like I've been slapped in the face. "Eleanor is Manning's *niece*?"

Then it hits me. The "GM" on the sunflower brooch. Gloria Manning.

"No shit," Finn says. "I always said she knew more than she was letting on."

Miss HappyHead.

"It appears that you, Sebastian, are being primed to be among this elite group."

"OK . . ." My heart pounds against my rib cage. "And what about . . . the bottom? What's their part in this plan?" I look at Finn biting the skin around his nail.

She turns to him. "Finneas. Please remember we were told to create worst-case scenarios. . . ."

"Go on. What happens to the scum in this hypothetical nightmare?"

"Gloria wanted to explore the idea that the bottom percentile could be used to serve the elite. Or with the most hopeless cases, those who pose a threat to the development of the superior percentile, they'd look to remove them entirely."

"Remove them?" Finn glowers. "What does that mean?"

Stone doesn't answer. I can see Finn's eyes burning in the light of the electric heater.

"She wouldn't . . . ," I start to say, but I can't find the end of the sentence because I feel so *angry*. Angry at myself for ever having gone along with it all, for believing Manning when she said I was special. Finn was right all along.

"I am becoming more and more unsure of what she is capable of. . . . How far she will push this."

"She's a total psychopath," Finn snarls.

Stone begins coughing again, hoarse and dry. "Could you fetch me some water?"

"Of course." I walk over to the tray on the table.

"I'm feeling a little lightheaded. . . ."

I stare at the bottle of water. "Wait," I say.

In the top of the plastic screw lid is a tiny puncture mark, barely visible.

My health seems to have taken a particularly unfortunate turn lately.

"Dr. Stone . . . Look at this." I pick the bottle up and take it over to her. "You said you've not been feeling as sharp. You're sick . . . weak. . . . Look."

She holds the bottle up to the light. Then she sees it.

"A needle prick."

"It could be the same solution they gave to us in Couples Therapy. What if she's been—"

"Microdosing me . . . so she can begin the Never Plan knowing I would be incapable of stopping her."

Finn is on his feet now. "She's a total fucking nutjob!" Stone stares silently at the water bottle. "How did you not know? When you were writing that thing? When she was drooling all over it?"

"She was my friend. I never expected . . . Why would I? I trusted her."

"Well, look how that turned out." He is pacing like he can't contain himself. "This is crazy. How do we get out? How do we get out of HappyHead?" He runs his hand through his hair, frantic. "Look, we need to raise the alarm. Tell someone, anyone—"

"It's tricky. . . ."

"*Tricky?* They're trapping teenagers and planning on *mating* them based on some warped idea of mental strength. And then, what—killing off the crap? Do you hear this?"

"Yes. I do."

"How do we stop her?" He looks at us both, eyes wide with panic. "Isn't there someone we can tell? Call?"

"With what?" Stone says, her voice shaking now. "How? Not

even the staff has their own phones; they use walkie-talkies. There's no internet. . . . Just the server she restricts."

"What about getting around the fence to the sea?"

"You'd drown before you freeze to death out there."

"A raft?" I can see Finn knows how desperate he sounds. He leans his head against the wall, then bangs it, so the thud echoes through the room.

I am standing now. "The gate in the perimeter fence. Where's the key?" We both turn to her.

She shakes her head. "It's kept in a locked safe in Manning's office. And you'd need a fob to get into the office itself."

"Does Mark have a fob?" I ask, my adrenaline taking hold.

"No. Only certain people do, of Manning's choosing."

"But he could get one?"

"It's too risky. . . ."

"But he could?"

"Maybe."

"What's the code? The code to the safe?"

"You'd get caught, Sebastian."

"Do you know the code?" I persist. "Please. It's our only chance."

She looks at Finn for a moment, her eyes scanning over him, his helplessness. Then she nods. "You're right. It is. The code for the safe is zero, three, zero, eight. Have you got that? It's Hannah's birth day and month." I glance at Finn, his eyes suddenly bright. "Mark will need to steal a fob for the office. He's the *only* person who can be trusted."

She turns, suddenly energized, and opens a drawer in the desk behind her. She pulls out a piece of paper and a pen and begins to scribble. "You will need to give Mark this. It explains everything. The fob, the safe, the Never Plan . . . He will understand. He will help you." She folds the scribbled note in half and passes it to me. "Keep it safe. Now, Sebastian, if you will crawl under the bed for me . . ."

I stall. She waves her hand at me, shooing me under. "Quickly, now. If we are going to do this, we don't have time to dawdle."

I push myself under the bed. At the back, in among the dust and cobwebs, are two small black electronic devices, about the size of a box of Tic Tacs.

I pull them out.

They each have a screen and buttons.

"What are they?" I ask.

"Radio pagers. You can only communicate between the two of them. Long-distance short messages. Now, listen to me. If . . . *when* you get out, deliver one of these to a man named Tom Jarrow. He's a senior civil servant based in Whitehall, London, and a trusted friend. Have you got that?" We nod. "He can help us. He will know what to do. . . . No one else. Just him. We need to get as much proof to him as possible. Tom can contact me with that." She points at the pager.

She takes my hand. Hers is cold, the skin thin and papery, the blue of her veins little rivers running just beneath it.

"Finn, come here," she says, and he does. "The man will return soon to check I have finished my breakfast." She takes his hand too. "I couldn't forgive myself if she goes through with the Never Plan. I couldn't."

I look into her face, like an old book with wrinkled pages.

Her amber eyes alive and shining, her lip trembling. She speaks quietly but assuredly.

"It's time for you to go now. On your return, you have to act like you know nothing or Gloria will find out and do anything she can to ensure your silence. We must stop her."

TWENTY-THREE
Plastic Flowers

Since leaving Stone, we haven't spoken much. Just alerted each other every time we thought we heard a dog or a motor. We keep following the compass east. Thank God it's still working, after I dropped it in the water. I am beginning to lose my grip on the concept of time. It feels like we have been walking for days. Finn offered me a piggyback. I said I was fine. That I hardly noticed the pain in my leg.

We shuffle on with him supporting me, my arm around his shoulders. He suddenly stops. "Look, Seb."

I follow to where he is pointing. Toppled over in the twisted weeds, something pink. Rusty. With a basket.

A bike. A girl's bike.

I once wanted one just like it.

He yanks it out. There are faded plastic flowers on the basket.

"It must have been from before . . ." Before HappyHead, I want to say.

He inspects it. "It's big enough. The chain seems fine, a little rusty, but fine." He looks up at me, hopeful. "This is gonna work. I'll pedal; you can rest your leg."

I get on the seat behind him.

"Hold on," he says. I place my hands on his shoulders.

We begin to move, wobbling at first until he gets the hang of it. We ride through the fields. We ride and ride, and the wind blows in my hair, cooling the sweat on my forehead.

If this was anywhere else, it would be heaven.

Free.

But we are not free.

"Put your hands around my chest: it's safer," he says.

I do. He picks up the pace, pedaling back along the tracks in the fields between the hills surrounding the valley and into a thicket of trees, just before the sunflowers.

"Let's ditch the bike here," he says.

Together we find branches and leaves to cover it so the bike is hidden from sight.

I sit for a moment, resting my leg. He gets out a cigarette and lights it. He exhales, enjoying the brief pause.

"What's your family like?" he says. "You asked about mine, so . . ."

Family.

My family.

It's strange to think of them.

I wonder what they are doing right now, in this moment, at work, at school, at home, tuna pasta for dinner again. Unaware. A weight of anxiety thumps my stomach.

"They're all right," I say, feeling like I don't know them very well at all. "Very . . . normal, I suppose. My dad works for the council, some boring job he hates but does anyway. And my mum works at a dentist's office as a receptionist. I have a sister. . . . She's fifteen."

"Oh, nice." He looks at me, and I must be making a face. "Oh, OK, *not* nice."

"It's complicated. She . . . she makes them happy."

"And you don't?"

"I feel like I don't."

He pulls off his hoodie and sits with his face in the sun. He closes his eyes.

I look at the ink scrawled across his arms.

The lightning bolt.

A diamond. A clock. Cogs. A skull.

"Who designed them?"

"I did."

"I like the dragon," I say.

"Do you? Cheers. It's my favorite too."

"Why?"

He's silent for a moment. "People fear them. But they're just protecting themselves. They have these horrible scales and they are always drawn weird, kind of ugly, but I think there's something beautiful about them. The fact that they're sort of gross and used as a symbol of evil . . . They're misunderstood. I like that."

"I want one."

"You?" He stifles a laugh. "I'll believe that when I see it."

"What? I'm too *polite*?"

"You said it, not me. . . ."

"I give you permission to design it."

"I'll hold you to that." He looks up at me. "Listen, I'll make a pact with you. When we get out of HappyHead, I'll draw you a tattoo and show you Manchester."

"Deal."

Silence. I watch him turn his face up to the sky again.

"What time is it?" Finn says after a while.

The reality of what we must do hits me. I check my watch. "Three p.m."

"We heard Mark say he would search in the north section by the forest edge." He looks at the compass. "Let's head north and stay low. We give him the note, get him to help us into Manning's office, and take the key to the gate while she is still out searching."

"All in two hours?" I say. I realize I don't sound optimistic.

Finn looks at a loss. "We don't have many options."

He's right. It is our only option.

We make our way stealthily through the sunflowers. It's quiet now. Eerily quiet. I haven't seen a flare for some time.

When we get into the forest, it's like we have reentered some kind of hellscape. The air is heavy. Dark. There is a gentle fog that twists around our feet, as if Manning has cast some kind of spell over the grounds.

"Up this way," Finn says, eyes on the compass. "If we stay at the edge of the—"

A shout rings out through the trees.

Shit.

"I see one! Two! There's two!"

A dog barks.

A motor. Very close.

"Run!" Finn shouts.

But, before I can even move my feet, I feel hands on me, locking together around my chest, my arms, pinning me as I try to scramble free, and I am dragged to the ground.

I can't move anything.

A heavy weight pushes down on me.

My leg. My fucking leg. "Get off me!"

Next to me, on the ground, I see Finn's face slammed into the bark and leaves. He is shouting something. "No!"

No.

No.

I am flipped onto my back, and I see the branches above. And faces, faces of Overalls looking down at me, saying things like *Nice catch!* and *Two at once, baby!*

Then two blue flares are shot up into the air between the trees. Hands pull at me. I am lifted and put into the back of a wooden cart attached to an off-road quad bike. Opposite me, there are two other Greens, although you wouldn't know. They are covered in dirt. Caked in it, like they have been literally hiding underground.

One holds his hand up to me. "So close."

Yeah. You have no idea.

Finn is dragged onto the cart and plonked down on the bench right next to me.

"Get them all back to the holding pen. Searchers. Back to it!" the man who wrestled me to the ground shouts, and the rest of the Overalls scatter back into the forest.

I look at Finn. *What now?*

He shakes his head. He doesn't know.

I don't know.

The driver kicks the pedal.

We begin to move.

We travel no more than ten feet; then, all of a sudden, we stop.

"What's going on?" one of the Mud Statues asks.

I can hear someone shouting, "I'll take them from here!"

"You sure?" the driver replies.

"Yes. You go and get some final catches."

"Thanks!" The driver jumps off the quad bike. "Change of driver!" he calls, then removes his helmet and passes it to someone.

The man he passes it to has dark hair. Neatly cropped. He straddles the seat of the quad bike, then turns to us.

Mark.

"Right, you ready?" He gives Finn and me the smallest of nods. "Let's go."

TWENTY-FOUR
The Safe

The holding pen is actually the assembly hall, but it now looks like a scene from a docuseries about survivors of a natural disaster. Everyone is filthy—clothes torn, cowering in pain, fear, and misery. Some cradling limbs or wearing bandages. Some wrapped in foil blankets. Others crying. One boy is sitting in just his underpants.

"Grab a seat and wait for the end of the assessment," Mark tells the four of us.

"Can I at least take a shower?" one of our mud-caked companions asks him.

"You'll have to wait, I'm afraid."

They shuffle sadly to the far wall and lean against it like a pair of stiff planks. Mark moves over to a table covered in papers, sifting through them, no doubt looking for our names to check off. He is joined by other Overalls. Muscle Man is there, surveying us all with a smirk, admiring how many of us they have caught. Mark keeps flicking his eyes toward us.

Finn and I find a space and sit on the floor. I keep my leg straight, trying not to wince.

Finn looks panicked. "We need to talk to him, and soon. Before the Hide ends. Manning will be back in her office in"—he looks at the clock on the wall—"exactly an hour."

This suddenly feels very real. In Stone's shack, it all felt like some kind of story—a reality that was outside of our own.

But now we are in it.

I stare at the back of Mark's head. We need to do something. Now.

I stand up and try to hide my limp as I walk toward him.

"What are you doing?" Finn whispers.

I don't answer. I just keep limping toward Mark as if I am possessed. I stop in front of him. "Can I talk to you?"

"Excuse me?" He looks at me cautiously.

"Over here." I walk until the other Overalls are out of earshot.

I turn. He is right in front of me. "She's alive," I say, so quietly I'm not sure he's heard.

He stares at me.

"The Never Plan is happening."

His face changes.

I can feel people watching.

I turn away, and as I do, I trip.

I try to make it look as real as I can.

"Shit!" I shout as I hit the floor. The pain from my leg makes it easier to sound convincing.

He stands over me. "Are you OK?"

"Yeah. Yeah."

He holds out his hand. I take it; then I see his eyes narrow slightly.

Bingo.

"Thanks," I say as he pulls me up. I head back toward Finn, having left Stone's note pressed firmly in his palm.

"He's got it," I whisper.

"That was . . ."

"What?"

Finn's eyes are wide with surprise. "Nice," he says.

I bite my lip to stop him seeing how much pain I am in. "Now we wait."

"She'd better be right about him," Finn whispers, watching Mark cautiously. "Or this is all over."

I hadn't thought of that. But it's a little late now.

We watch from our spot on the floor as Mark wanders over to the corner of the assembly hall. He turns to the wall. Pauses. Slowly reaches into his pocket and takes out the slip of paper. He stands for a moment, his hands in front of him, then turns and casually walks back over to the other Overalls at the table.

I check my watch. 16:07.

Time is running out.

Then Mark looks directly at me. He mouths something. *Fob.*

"What's he doing?" Finn says through the side of his mouth.

"He said fob."

Mark points to the pocket on the front of his overalls, then motions to Muscle Man on the other side of the table.

"It's in that man's pocket," I murmur.

"How the hell are we going to get it from there?"

Think, Seb. *Think.*

"Hit me," I whisper.

"Huh?"

287

"Hit me."

"But—"

"Just fucking—"

Whap.

Right in my jaw.

Ouch. That was really hard.

I stand up. He does too. "What the hell do you think you're doing?" I scream as loud as I can. I push him in the stomach. "You're crazy, man!"

Man.

His eyes sparkle with realization. "Don't look at me like that, then, snob!" he shouts back.

The smallest flicker of a wink.

Oh, *burn.*

He pushes me this time, and I stumble.

A crowd is forming.

I look over to see Overalls running up to us. "You two, break it up!" I hear them shouting. Muscle Man is one of them. Mark just behind him.

Keep going.

"It's his fault!" Finn shouts.

"Come on, you fucking prick!" I bellow.

Never said that before.

Felt good.

For a split second, he looks as if he might laugh. I push him so he stumbles backward.

Then he raises his fist. "Let's 'ave it, then!" he yells. "Here and now!"

A swarm of yellow surrounds us. "Easy there!"

Finn tries to jump at me, but as he does, Muscle Man grabs him in some kind of bear hug from behind, trying to dodge Finn's flailing limbs. It's messy. Frantic. Finn keeps thrashing. Other Overalls pile on.

I watch his hands clawing, scratching, *searching* for the pocket.

Come on, come on.

They pull Finn to the floor.

I try to run forward, but people get in the way. I can't see. Too many people now pushing me back.

Greens start standing, yelling.

"Go on!"

"Get him!"

"Stop it, you morons! What are you, twelve?"

From among the chaos I hear Mark's voice. "Enough! *Enough!*" He appears in the middle of us, arms outstretched, silencing the crowd. "Stop this!"

Everyone stops. Silence.

"Get the boy up off the floor."

The Overalls slowly pull Finn up.

"Let him go," Mark says. Muscle Man roughly pushes Finn forward, his face red, breathing heavily. My eyes scan his front pocket. Did Finn get it? Mark switches on his meditation-app voice. "A healing therapeutic conversation will be the best way to resolve this. At HappyHead, we encourage addressing our problems using words."

Muscle Man nods, stepping backward. The crowd begins to disperse. "I'll take these two to the Cozy Room so they can come to an understanding."

And then Mark is leading us out of the holding pen,

grabbing each of us by the arm, and we are moving through the white corridors, just us, the three of us, then quickly up a stairwell, my leg throbbing with every step, in the opposite direction of the Cozy Room.

When he is sure we are out of sight, he lets go of our arms.

"You get it?" he asks breathlessly.

Finn holds out his hand and opens his clenched fist. A small black plastic disc. "This it?"

"That's it."

My heart jumps. Finn actually laughs. "Fucking *yes*!"

"We'll have to hope he thinks he lost it in the forest. Come on."

Mark moves on, and we follow, up and up, my heart pounding against my rib cage, a frisson of excitement reverberating in my ears.

Then, suddenly, he stops right in front of the brick wall in the stairwell.

"The fob, Finneas."

Finn hands it to him. Mark presses it into a groove in one of the bricks. There is a beep, and then the bricks shift as one, swinging away from us.

A hidden door.

"Christ," I say under my breath. "This place is mad."

We step through into a corridor that isn't white.

The walls are red.

Deep red.

And it has carpet. Fluffy beige carpet.

There are chandeliers hanging from the ceiling all the way along.

"Come on," he says. "We don't have long."

We walk quickly, my leg twinging with every step. I look at Finn and see the exhilaration on his face. *Purpose.* We make our way to the end of the hallway, following Mark.

He suddenly stops outside a door and turns to us. "I saw you both. In Stone's office. Behind the curtain. I knew. . . . I knew. . . . *Well done.* Well done for getting to her." I notice his eyes well up, sad, but also relieved, like someone reunited with their family.

"You knew her from before?"

I see him consider answering this. "I was one of Eileen's patients. A long time ago. She is the reason I am alive today."

He swipes the fob again on the wall by the door, and we enter what appears to be a large office. There are deep-red armchairs and a dark wooden desk. There are bookshelves everywhere. Right up to the ceiling. A ladder placed against one of the walls so you could reach the books at the very top. Large picture frames, gold and heavy, surround painted portraits of official-looking men and women in suits, all warmly lit by a number of mismatched antique lamps. At the back of the room is an archway cut into the wall, leading through to a smaller room, a bay of some sort, cast in shadow.

It is beautiful, like something from a Dickens novel.

"There's the safe." Mark points to the back of the room, through the arched wall. Sure enough, there is a large black box on the floor, tucked away in the shadows. "Her note said you know the code?"

I nod. "Zero, three, zero, eight. Hannah's birthday," I say. He looks at me, and I see a flash of remembrance, of pain. Did he know her too?

I study his face.

Slightly waxy skin.

Worn.

Tired.

Afraid.

And I see a real person for the first time.

"Mark," I say. "Thank you."

"Quickly."

But Finn is already there, kneeling in front of the safe. I hear him type in the numbers.

Beep, beep, beep, beep.

He turns the handle. And he stares inside.

"Come on!" I say eagerly, my brain whirring with fear, excitement, adrenaline.

He turns and looks at me, his eyes piercing the shadows. "It's here."

I hurry to kneel next to him.

I look inside, following the line of his pointed finger.

And there it is.

A single key card, right at the back on top of some papers, with two words scribbled on it in black marker: *Perimeter gate.*

I want to grab him.

Hug him.

Kiss him.

"It's there?" Mark hisses from the archway.

"Yes!" I cry, and immediately clap my hand over my mouth, realizing how loud I've been. But Finn doesn't seem to notice. He's still staring into the safe.

"Wait . . . ," he says, his voice oddly cold. "Look, Seb." Finn begins moving the papers. Beneath them is a black file. He pulls it out and holds it up to me. The gold embellished lettering on its front catches the warm light from the lamps in the room behind us.

THE NEVER PLAN.
CANDIDATES

I suddenly feel as if my breath has been stolen from my lungs. Winded.

Finn slowly puts the file down on the floor in front of the safe.

I look back at Mark, who is now standing with his back to us, watching the door of the office. "Mark, you might want to see this."

He turns. "What is it?" He moves quickly toward us. "We don't have time to be—" He stops, now close enough to see the writing himself. His eyes widen.

We all look down at the file.

Finn slowly opens it. He turns the pages. One after the other. Names. Faces.

So many.

I recognize them. From the dining hall. From the Harmony Hall. From around the building and the grounds.

Greens.

And then Finn stops.

SEBASTIAN SEATON

My face, smiling up at me.

My passport photo.

Beneath it, a list of stats and numbers all scribbled in pen, medical things that don't make sense to me. It reads like another language, but it says things about vitamins and blood types and genetic makeup.

I scan down to the bottom.

```
Valuable in his desire to impress those with
authority over him. Could be very useful in
Elite. There is potential, with EB, to be
taken on to Elmhallow as a pair.
```

Elmhallow?

"The Elite . . . ," I hear Mark whisper. "It *is* happening. . . ."
Finn keeps flicking through the pages. The faces of our peers stare back at us. Raheem. Anoushka. Lucy. Malachai. Ayahuasca. Fridge Boy.

He stops.

He glares.

His own face.

Hood up.

FINNEAS BLAKE

At the bottom, below the genetic stats and medical jargon, I see what he is looking at.

```
Ongoing resistance. Unstable, particularly
considering his history. Very unwell.
Dangerous. No potential to be paired
appropriately. Bottom percentile. Possibility
to serve at Elmhallow. Ended if necessary.
```

"Ended?" I say. "What does that mean?" I glance at him.

"What do you think it means, Seb?" I watch his eyes dart over the file. *"Very unwell . . ."* He laughs, a little manic. "We need to get out of here. These fucking hypocrites." He looks at me with such desperation. "This has to be stopped."

He stands.

He suddenly kicks the wall near my head.

Mark moves toward him, but Finn backs away.

"Please calm down," I say. "We can figure this out. We're going to get out." I hold up the key card to him, to remind him of the plan, but he isn't listening.

"Calm down? Easy for you, isn't it? Elite. No fucking issue." He starts pacing, scratching at his arms, his hair. "This is insane. . . ."

Unstable.

Dangerous.

"It'll be OK . . . ," I try.

He looks at me like I'm a liar. "I never wanted to be here— I never . . ."

Then I hear something.

"Quiet." Mark holds his hand in the air. I hear it again. Voices in the corridor. "Manning. Get out of sight. Now!"

Without thinking, I grab the file and the key card, place them back in the safe, and push it shut. I jump behind the little wall on the side of the arch—just wide enough to cover me from the main room. Mark grabs Finn and pushes him up into the opposite one.

Voices. Louder now.

The door swings open.

The lights flick on.

"I knew you would get at least one of them, but *four*," Fernsby says. "I'm impressed, Astrid."

"The *nerve*." Lindström. "Typical man, doubting the woman."

"It would be to his detriment to do that in *this* room." And Manning. The three of them. "Whiskey? A quick one to warm you up? Albert?"

"Why not."

"Astrid?"

Lindström sounds excited. "Certainly. Eleanor is still out there. . . . Brilliant. And Jamie."

Fernsby does too. "And Lucy and Raheem. Both really showing strength now. It was wise not to match them straightaway in Serenity, Gloria. They are fighting to prove their acumen aside from their blatant physical attraction, which is exactly what we wanted from them."

"The twins, Jing and Li, are still out there too," Lindström chips in, to which Fernsby gives an approving grunt.

A pause. Then Manning asks, "What about Sebastian?"

"I think he made it to the final hour," Fernsby replies.

"Not so bad." Lindström again.

"Yes," Manning says. "Could have been better, though. But lots of them continue to impress."

I can smell woody booze mingling with the mustiness of the books. It's like they're a hunting party coming back into the warm after their day out catching things.

Well. That's precisely what they are.

I keep my body pressed into the wall and watch Finn begin to go still in the grip of Mark's arms on the other side.

If they come through the archway . . .

"Wouldn't it be nice to *treat* them in some way? Those who

are doing well. Before they move on?" Lindström's voice is smooth like honey. I can hear the clinking of glasses.

"A treat would be the perfect way to celebrate their achievements." Manning again. "They seem so ready, this top percentile. They are *special*." She sounds animated. Vigorous. Tipsy.

"What are you thinking?" Fernsby asks.

"You'll see."

"Ever the intriguer. No doubt it will be a wonderful way to celebrate their potential."

Potential.

Lindström. "This is the beginning of a new era, Gloria."

"With you both at my side," Manning says. "Right. I can't be drunk at the assembly. Come on, now. There is work to do!"

I hear her ushering them up from their seats and out the door, flicking the light off as she goes.

I step out into the middle of the archway and take in the remnants of their little party scattered over the desk. Finn stands between the arches. He is fizzing. "Good we don't have to deal with that any longer." He turns and types in the code once more.

Beep, beep, beep, beep.

He holds up the card. We both look at Mark, hopeful.

Mark pauses, thinking, then says, "Not yet . . ."

Finn starts. "But—"

"No," Mark cuts him off. "If you don't want to get caught, we must find the perfect time."

"When?" Finn can hardly contain his eagerness.

"Tonight. When everyone is asleep. But that's staying in the safe for now," Mark says, pointing to the key card in Finn's hand.

"What? No way . . ."

"There's no discussion, Finneas. If she finds that card gone, she'll search all of us until it's found. I'll come back and get it later tonight when I know she won't be here, then meet you at the gate with it, let you out, and return it to the safe. That way, she won't ever know it's gone. Zero, three, zero, eight?"

I nod.

Finn looks conflicted.

"He's right, Finn," I say. "If she finds it on us, then God knows what she'll do."

A pause.

He nods. "OK."

"We will meet at the gate. At midnight."

TWENTY-FIVE
Toilet Paper

The Overalls' eyes follow us as Mark leads us back into the assembly hall. Fluffy tuts at me as I pass her and lets out a sigh.

"That wasn't like the Seb we know, was it? Fighting? I hope you boys managed to sort things out."

"Oh, we did," I say. "Don't you worry about that."

"Good." She smiles. "Quickly, now. Take a seat."

The chairs have all been lined up again facing the podium, and the wounded, broken Greens begin to fill them. The front row is reserved for "Unfound."

I look at my watch. 16:59.

We made it.

Just in time.

• • •

"Well . . ." Manning doesn't look her usual pristine self. Her hair is a mess. She looks tired, worn out. Steamed-up glasses. Beads of sweat glistening on her forehead. Mud and dead leaves cling to her. Her immaculate exterior dirtied by twenty-four hours of catching teenagers. "I had hopes for you with this assessment, but I didn't think many—well—*any* of you would succeed in lasting the entire challenge. I thought it too long, too difficult to hold out against my skilled team of Searchers. However"—she holds her hand out to the front row—"seven people remained unfound. *Seven.* Just wonderful." She begins to clap.

Around the walls of the hall, the Overalls join her, and I notice some now have what appear to be batons clipped to their belts.

Where did *they* come from?

"Commitment, growth, gratitude, and obedience lead to a happy head!" Their chant clatters around my brain like a ball in a pinball machine.

I look at the row of Unfound. A big guy with his braided hair pulled into a neat man bun, who looks very pleased with himself. Fridge Boy—Jamie—is there, waving like a gladiator. Raheem and Lucy. Beyond them, two girls with a wildness in their eyes. Twin sisters, it seems, one with her hair dyed blue, the other one with it dyed green. They whisper conspiratorially to each other.

And, of course—Eleanor.

"Please stand up, Unfound," Manning says. "Accept your praise."

They stand. Eleanor gives a small bow to the crowd.

Only a few of us from the Found join the Overalls in applause. I do. I clap like one of those crazy dance moms on TV.

Show that you're willing Seb. Like nothing is wrong. But also, I'm excited.

Midnight.

"And your prize," Manning continues. "You seven will be having pizza and fries for dinner! A little treat—we feel you deserve it."

Pizza. That actually sounds amazing.

Jamie whoops and pumps his fist in the air. Some of the Found groan in jealousy.

"Good job, you guys!" Ponytail shouts. "Go, the Unfound!"

I see Mark smiling from a group of Overalls behind her. He cups his hands around his mouth. "Fantastic work, guys!"

The applause settles.

I catch sight of Finn a few rows behind, head down.

"Yes, yes. Give them the praise they deserve," Manning says. "For this is the program in action. This is our youth succeeding. Resilient. Strong. It is everything I hoped for. . . ." I can tell she is still a little tipsy because of the vigor with which she says each word.

A tall girl with a bruise on her face and a torn hoodie suddenly stands up at the end of the row just behind me. "Don't want to stop the love-in!" she shouts. "But can the rest of us losers shower now, miss? I stink like something crawled inside me and died."

A few people murmur their agreement.

Someone laughs.

I glance at Finn.

"Soon, my dear." Manning's eyes focus on her. "Very soon. And don't be too hard on yourself. No one is a loser. You must not refer to yourself in this way. Everyone did their best."

"Sure," Angry Girl says. "Whatever you say, miss, to make yourself feel better."

A silence descends.

"Excuse me?" Manning asks.

"This whole thing is pretty cuckoo and, let's face it, kind of *creepy*. None of this is exactly thera-fucking-peutic. Did you just fail to mention why your henchmen have weapons now?"

The batons.

I notice a swarm of Overalls have slowly begun to edge toward her.

Manning tilts her head thoughtfully. "Jennifer Beale, isn't it?"

The girl folds her arms, a little taken aback. "Yeah? And?"

Muscle Man is there, a foot or so from her now.

"Perhaps you need a little time-out, Jennifer. A cool-off before your shower."

"What I need is to get out of here."

The hairs on the back of my neck prickle.

"If you could explain where this resistance—"

"Resistance?" the girl shouts and laughs at the same time. "Yeah, I'll *explain*. How is it even ethical for us to be left outside overnight in the freezing cold? Do our parents know about this? Because I'm pretty sure mine would put me on the first train back if they knew the risk you—"

"Risk? We are doing everything in our power to make this experience risk-free."

"Risk-free?" She laughs again, shaking her head.

"All of this is for your safety. To build your—"

"Are you actually kidding? I nearly broke my arm out there trying to find some drinking water in a goddamn tree. I'm sorry, but am I the only one who feels this way?" Angry Girl looks out over us all expectantly.

Manning waits. No one speaks.

No one dares.

"It appears so, Jennifer. I'm sorry you feel this way. I truly am."

She gives a tiny nod. And suddenly, very quickly, Muscle Man grabs her arm and leads her away.

"Gosh," Manning says, "we must hope that Jennifer can find some inner peace at this time. It appears she is really suffering." She speaks tenderly into the microphone. "The cold and exhaustion can make people forget themselves. We must all be empathetic. Treat her with kindness. Thankfully, we can help her here. That is our job. We are here to help you. I just wish you all knew . . . how much we care."

She must have her PhD in bullshitting, because she is exceptional at it.

Tonight. Midnight.

My head fizzes.

"Now I must bring something to your attention. It is regrettably not in the same celebratory vein with which we began. Please, the Unfound, if you will be seated." The seven in the front row sit. Manning takes off her glasses and folds them up. "Sadly, someone here has decided to break the rules."

Silence.

"Not just the rules of the Hide, but the rules of HappyHead itself."

I glance at Mark leaning against the wall and see a look of utter panic flash across his face.

"Someone went into my office."

My stomach feels like it has fallen out and exploded all over the shiny white floor beneath me.

Already?

How?

How did she find out?

I think someone gasps and people are definitely whispering, but the fuzzy heat of shock makes it hard to focus on what is happening around me.

She holds up a yellow HappyHead badge. "This was found on the floor. A participant's badge."

I look down at my hoodie. My badge is still there.

Shit. Finn.

I can't feel anything.

Numb.

I want to look at him, but I don't dare.

We're done. Completely done.

What will they do to us?

"It seems a fob went missing during the Hide and was used to enter my office. The person who did it must be in this room, as we are at full capacity. So I am asking you directly, would you like to stand up and tell us why you decided to trespass?"

Trespass.

No one is moving.

I see Mark out of the corner of my eye, just feet away from her. He is staring dead ahead.

I flick my eyes around the room. To my relief, not many people are still wearing their badges. People must have lost them in previous trials, or out in the forest. The few who still have theirs on look around them eagerly, some pointing to their yellow smiley face, proclaiming their innocence.

"No? We promote practicing the principle of honesty here.

There is no punishment. Just the opportunity to grow. You were asked to stay within the authorized zones, and it was merely to keep you all safe. We have a responsibility here, to your family. To you. And that safety has now been jeopardized. There are important private documents in my office with personal details about every single one of you in this room. If this person has somehow looked at them, that is a serious breach of confidentiality and I need to know immediately."

Silence. Earth-shattering silence.

"Does no one want to own up?"

Why is she looking at me? *Is* she looking at me?

I stare at my pale, shaking hands.

"That is a real shame." Manning lets out a long sigh. "I hope that if anyone has any information or knowledge of who it might be, you will come forward. Do not be scared."

I look toward Eleanor, her posture rigid with tension. Anger, perhaps. That someone could do this.

"From now on we will be upping our containment protocol. I am left with little choice. I didn't want to have to do this, but feel I must, for your protection. Firstly, we will be recalibrating everyone's chips as soon as you return to your rooms this evening. The recalibrated chip will trigger a sensor if you go through a door into any unauthorized zone. It will then send an alert, and we will immediately know exactly where you are. This includes the staff quarters, or if you step outside the building."

What? No. *No.*

"You will also notice that we shall be installing some cameras around the grounds and along the perimeter fence. Room searches will commence later. It is in all of your interests for me to find out if anything has been taken. All fobs and security codes will be changed. Please do not worry about your personal details being exposed. I will have my office guarded continuously."

I turn to catch Finn's eye. But his gaze is fixed on the ground. "Now, everyone, to your rooms. It is a big day tomorrow."

Shit, shit, shit.

No. We can't leave.

There's no way out. . . .

As the Greens begin to pile out of the hall, I linger for Finn. I wait until I can feel him right next to me. I notice his badge is no longer on his hoodie.

"What do we do?" I hiss.

"Meet me at the bottom of the stairwell by the fire escape. Midnight. We need a new plan." He sounds terrified.

"No talking!" an Overall shouts.

Finn pushes past me into the throng of teenagers all desperate to get back to their rooms and take a shower to clean themselves of the last twenty-four hours.

●●●

Back in Bedroom 6, I sit and try to slow my breathing. The adrenaline must be leaving me, and I suddenly feel aware of my body. I feel raw. My bones cold. My skin sore.

My *leg*.

We're done. Of course we are. How could we not be?

I stare at the plate of chicken and rice and vegetables on the dining table next to the clock.

I take my pill, my hands trembling.

Come on, Seb. No time to think. They are going to search your room.

I wrench myself up and empty the contents of my pockets onto my bed. I grab the radio pager, pull off my dirty sock, and push the pager inside it. Then I hurry into the bathroom and dislodge the top of the ceramic tank above the toilet.

Clonk.

I place the sock in the cistern just above the waterline, lodged between the lever and the tube. It fits. I place the lid back down. I then go back and sit on the bed and try to calm the incessant fluttering in my chest.

There is a knock at my door.

I stand. "Yes?"

My stomach flips.

They know.

They know it was us.

They saw us.

This is it.

When Mark enters, my knees go wobbly with relief and I grab the side of the table.

"Hello, Sebastian, I am here to search your room and to recalibrate your chip." His voice is stern, emotionless. He holds his finger to his lips, points to the clock on my desk, then touches his ear.

Finn was right. They are listening.

He steps inside, shutting the door behind him.

"Please take a seat." He pulls out the chair from under my desk, and I sit. He raises his hand, and I see that he is holding some kind of metal scanner. I recoil slightly, remembering Couples Therapy.

Trust me, he mouths. He clicks a button, and it begins to make a whirring sound. He holds it up to my clavicle. To my chip.

The machine makes a strange beeping sound, then stops.

I suddenly feel a searing heat emanate from the chip inside me. Then the thing in his hand speaks with an American accent. "Recalibration complete."

"Thank you, Sebastian." Mark begins to pace around the room, moving things, rustling about as if he is searching, the desk, the bed, the couch. He then heads into the bathroom. He is in there for a while, clonking around. I feel the heat dissipate into the extremities of my chest, coursing through my body.

Then. "Your room is clear," he says. "Good luck with your assessment tomorrow. It will test many of your skills that are instrumental in generating a foundation for happiness. In life, we must endure so much, and this test will help prepare you for when that inevitably comes." He sounds like he is reciting a script. His face looks somber. "Good night, Sebastian. And eat up. You need to replenish your energy levels."

He leaves, and it is quiet.

I look down at my cooling food, and my stomach turns. But then I see something poking out from beside my fork. A small scrap of toilet paper with black ink seeping through it.

I open it.

STAY FOCUSED. DO NOT BE DISCOURAGED. THERE IS A CHALLENGE IN TWO DAYS. A CHANCE TO ESCAPE. BUT FIRST YOU MUST COMPETE IN ABCD TOMORROW.

YOU MUST SUCCEED AND FINNEAS MUST FAIL. PUT YOUR SUPERIORS BEFORE <u>EVERYTHING</u>.
FLUSH THIS NOW.

· · ·

Even though I'm beyond exhausted, the mixed emotions of telling Finn the new plan keep me awake until it's time to meet him.

Telling him he must fail.

I have gone over almost every idea of what failing might look like a hundred times. But he will be pleased to know that there is still a chance . . . surely. . . .

When I finally get to the fire escape at the bottom of the stairwell, he is not here.

I look at the panic bar under the green exit light.

NOT FOR PARTICIPANT USE

I instinctively place my hand on the bar. If I step outside, they will be alerted. My chip will tell them exactly where I am.

What will they do to me? What is the worst they can do?

I don't want to think of the answer.

I slowly lift my hand and look around the ceiling and the walls for any sign of a camera. Nothing.

"Psst."

I jump.

He is all shadow.

"Jesus," I say. "You scared me."

"I have an idea," he says, and steps forward. "Look." His body is practically humming with eagerness. He holds up a small piece of broken glass.

"Whoa," I say. "Careful."

"Let's cut them out and run." What? "Cut out the chips and run. Now. So they can't track us." He begins to pull his top over his head. The curve of his stomach. The line of hair above his boxer shorts.

"Wait," I hiss. "You need to calm down, Finn. This is stupid."

"No, what's stupid is staying here a second longer."

"But even if we do cut them out, how are we getting over the fence? The key card is back in the safe, and we have no idea where we're going. . . ."

"But . . ."

"Finn, listen to me." I put my hand on his arm, which is now across his bare chest, the glass hovering next to his clavicle. I can see his pulse just above it by his neck, drumming like a hummingbird. "Mark has a plan. He said in two days there will be an opportunity to escape. . . ."

"*Two days* . . . Seb, it's all right for you. I just can't do this anymore. . . ."

"Who knows if we even *are* going home after HappyHead finishes?"

He stops. I realize I have his attention now. His face darkens. "Elmhallow."

"Yeah. Whatever that is. And I sure as hell don't want to find out."

I watch as the reality of this dawns on him. He exhales slowly. "So . . . what's this *opportunity*?"

"Mark left me a note when he searched my room. I must

succeed, and you must fail in the next challenge. Then we can get out."

I feel the skin of his bicep under my fingers, the ripple of his muscle tensing. "You trust him?"

"Yes, I trust him. He wants us to have the best chance of escaping. Sticking some dirty glass in us and hoping for the best isn't going to work."

"But . . ." He is desperate.

"Mark wants us to get out. So we can do this for all of us." I nod upward, indicating the others asleep in their rooms. "For other people like us."

For a moment, he leans his head on my shoulder, and I can smell his hair, soap, and smoke. "It needs to work. Whatever it is. It needs to."

"It will. I really think it will."

"You'd better be right." He looks up into my eyes.

To serve at Elmhallow. Or ended.

I'm shaking. "I am. I know it."

He drops the glass and it clatters onto the concrete beneath us. He steps away and pulls his top back on.

"So I need to fail."

"Yes. The challenge is called ABCD. He said I have to put my superiors before everything to succeed. So I guess . . ."

"I should do the opposite."

"Right. That's all his note said."

"OK." A pause. Then he says, "It was my badge. I'm really sorry."

"Don't be. We promised to look after each other." I smile at him. He slowly nods. "We'd best not get seen down here," I say. But really I want us to stay.

"Yeah," he says, and he stops for a moment, and I watch his eyes momentarily flick up and down me.

"What?"

He falters. "Nothing. I'll go first."

Then he is gone.

TWENTY-SIX
ABCD

05:30.
   This morning, the Jackson 5 blares out.
   A, B, C . . .

Good morning, Sebastian.
Please have breakfast, then make your way to Bedroom 23.

Piss it. I have gone down.
   I mean, I knew this would happen, but I didn't expect to fall out of the top twenty. I immediately wonder what room Finn has been moved to—I assume he has gone into a better room, since we only got caught in the final hour yesterday. They'll probably think that is an improvement for someone who had seemed not to give a damn about the assessments until now.
   So, to accomplish what Mark's note said, we have work to do.
   With the sock from the toilet cistern in my pocket, I make

my way down the corridor. I do everything I can not to draw attention to myself. To blend in. I've always been good at that.

I can hear some Greens whispering to each other as we march down the Harmony Hall in single file. But there are more Overalls loitering today, far more, and the Greens are immediately silenced.

We are quickly ushered into our new rooms. I hardly have time to put the sock in the cistern before the clock does that thing it does.

Today's assessment is ABCD.
Please make your way to Assessment Room 7 on the ground floor,
where you will join Acid Green again.

Here we go.

I don't know what it is, but this morning I feel . . . I mean, I don't want to say *strong* because that's a word I would never use for myself, but I feel something.

Alert, maybe.

Like my senses are heightened.

Galvanized by Mark's note.

Stay focused. Do not be discouraged.

We still have a chance.

On my way down the stairwell, I stop for a moment by the window. Outside, some Overalls are standing beneath a tall pole that wasn't there before. It has a large orb at the top like a big black eye. A camera. Then I see more poles, lining the pathway and out into the forest.

I shudder and duck away.

On the ground floor, our cohort is congregating outside the row of assessment-room doors. I make my way to the door of Assessment Room 7. Mark is there, leaning against one of the walls, smiling like nothing has happened. Like nothing has changed. He looks squeaky-clean as always—the wax in his perfectly coiffed hair shining.

Just act casual, Seb.

No one knows anything.

There is nothing to know.

Just act chill.

You can do that.

I see Finn a little farther down. Where is Ash?

"Hey . . ." Eleanor appears next to me.

Eleanor.

She looks upset, her face red and blotchy. Not her usual flawless cover-girl skin. There are bags under her eyes.

OK, Seb. Show her.

"Hey, Eleanor. Well done on the Hide," I say, my voice coming out all weird. I think I might be trying to be seductive. I notice Mark watching us.

"Thanks," she says. "You too. You did well." She smiles. "I do think you can do better today, though." She winks.

"Yeah, I intend to."

"Good." She squeezes my hand and I nearly pull away, but I don't. I squeeze hers back. She side-eyes me, and her eyelashes flutter.

"You look really lovely," I say, and she blushes. For a fleeting moment, her eyes open really wide and it is like I see beneath her, into her, for the first time, her defenses no longer there. The stone wall that surrounds her has been breached, fractionally . . . and she is exposed.

And, in that moment, I don't hate her.

"Oh, don't be silly," she says, and I wonder if she has ever been told that before.

"Which room are you in now?"

"Twenty-three."

"Twenty-three?" She gives a strange little laugh.

"You?"

"Two."

Oh, shit. "That's amazing."

"Is it? *Is it?* It's not number one." She folds her arms and looks at the floor. She scuffs her shoe on the white tiles.

"Are you OK, Eleanor?"

"You know . . . I put *everything* into this. . . . It's just so . . ." She stops.

"What? What is it?"

"It's just frustrating, isn't it? I know I'm good enough. This whole thing . . ."

"Good enough for what?"

"Never mind. Look, sorry."

"Don't be. You're making people proud. Your parents will be. They seemed like they really love you, in the video in Serenity."

"Really?" she says, oddly hopeful, her eyes gleaming at the prospect. I see that crack in the stone wall again. Scared. Just trying to impress.

Like me.

"They know how good you are."

"No, they don't." Her voice quivers. "But I am better than *that,* and I'm under so much . . ." She catches herself, shaking her head. She inhales, then smiles at me. "Oh, God. Sorry. This is silly." She wipes her eyes, and tears begin to fall. "God, how embarrassing."

"Eleanor . . ."

"Don't be nice to me. Don't. I can't deal. . . ." She suddenly refocuses, looks at me, and smiles. "You're so sexy," she says, slightly robotically. And then it's gone. "Can you believe someone did that during the Hide? Absolute nutter. What were they thinking?"

She is back.

"Yeah, idiot," I say.

"Putting us all at risk like that. I wonder *why* they were in there. . . . Thank God for the new security."

"Yeah. Thank God."

A voice chimes over a speaker, and the screens on the walls light up.

It is time to enter your assessment rooms.
Good luck.

■ ■ ■

At the back of Assessment Room 7 is a long table. Fernsby is there, sandwiched between two Overalls, Fluffy on one side and someone I don't recognize on the other.

No Mark.

Which makes me nervous. Well . . . *more* nervous.

You must succeed and Finneas must fail.

Put your superiors before everything.

But what is really strange is that in front of the desk there are three different poles running from floor to ceiling. The middle pole is metal and is surrounded by three chairs with their backs pushed up against it. In front of each chair is a screen facing upward.

The pole on the right is made of wood and has a woman tied to it. Ponytail. Her arms are hugging it and her wrists are bound with rope. She turns her head, and I see she is wearing a blindfold, across which the word "Jane" is written. Ponytail has a name. Jane. So . . . *domestic.* For a moment, I imagine her in an apron with oven mitts at home, removing a roast turkey from the oven.

I look at the pole on the left. Metal. Someone else is tied to it. Blindfolded.

Ash.

What?

"Do not be alarmed," Fernsby says as Fluffy pours him a glass of water from a jug, cucumber slices floating inside it. "Everyone here is a willing participant. Do not talk to anyone. Take your seats at the middle pole." He indicates the three empty chairs. "Chop-chop."

As we walk toward the chairs, I slow down and look at Ash. She seems almost serene, her cheek pressed into the cool metal of the pole that her arms are hugging. Her hands have a wire circling them, some kind of lock holding it together.

I feel Finn next to me.

Eleanor chooses the seat facing the door.

"Something doesn't feel right," Finn whispers behind me.

"Please, boys, let's not waste any more time." Fernsby sounds impatient.

I take the seat facing Ash.

"Ashley" is written on her blindfold.

Finn takes the final seat, facing Jane.

"Hi, Ash," I whisper. She doesn't reply.

Fluffy appears in front of me and holds out what appears to be a straitjacket. One of those white ones you see in films about the old loony bins.

"Just need to get you in this. Don't worry—it's nice and comfortable. Arms out." She begins to hum something. Out of the corner of my eye, I can see the other Overall and Fernsby doing the same to Eleanor and Finn.

Obediently I lean into it, and she pulls it on like a backward shirt. The sleeves are long, twice the length of my arms. One arm has four padlocks attached down the length of it; four holes line the length of the other. "These will clip together up here, on to these," Fluffy says. She sits me down with my arms crossed around me and locks them on to a series of hooks that run up the middle of the pole behind my head. With each clip, I can feel the jacket pulling me in, tighter and tighter.

"Nearly there, Sebastian," she says. "Wonderful. Now, if you just kick off your shoes, fantastic, and I'll take your socks. . . ." I flinch as she pulls at them, peeling them off my pale feet. I hadn't anticipated such intimacy with Fluffy. It's probably not the time to tell her about my lifelong battle with athlete's foot. "All set," she says with a smile, and goes back to the table.

"Welcome to ABCD," Fernsby says. "This challenge will test

your knowledge, observational skills, and honesty. Using your feet, answer the questions on the touch screen in front of you. Each question has one correct answer: A, B, C, or D. Each correct answer will unlock one of the padlocks in your sleeves. If you get it wrong, you will have to answer a series of bonus questions to continue. But don't worry: these are a little easier. You have ten minutes. You will probably want to get out of your chairs as soon as possible to help your two companions." He indicates Ash and Jane. "To complete the challenge, everyone needs to be free before the horn. So a nice short one for you today. Ready, set, go."

The lights above us switch off. A digital clock on the wall begins to count down from 10:00. Music booms throughout the room, plonky and electronic, like something from *Space Invaders* or *Pac-Man*. The screen beneath my feet suddenly lights up.

WELCOME TO ABCD
Rule one: Do not discuss questions with others, or your entire
team's clock will lose valuable time!
Rule two: Look after those you feel need it!
Rule three: Beat the heat!

09:32.
09:31.

Right, let's get started.

QUESTION 1
WHAT IS THE LARGEST LAKE IN THE WORLD?

Four squares pop up with an answer in each:

A: LAKE SUPERIOR   **C:** LAKE TANGANYIKA

B: CASPIAN SEA   **D:** LAKE BAIKAL

I push B with my toe, ever grateful to Shelly for boring me about that in the library one lunchtime.

CORRECT! CONGRATULATIONS!

Balloons burst onto the screen. I feel a ping behind me as one of my padlocks opens and my straitjacket loosens slightly.

OK, this is easier than I thought.

QUESTION 2
WHAT IS 12 X 17 X 8?

A: 1,634   **C:** 1,632

B: 1,362   **D:** 1,326

Shit. Math. Hate math.

That's *hard.*

The music isn't helping.

Right, ten times seventeen is one-seventy. . . . Two more, times that by ten . . .

I look up at Ash, her cheek still pressed into the metal of the pole.

I see the clock on the wall behind her. 07:32.

Oh, shit.

Sod it.

I push my toe onto square C.

CORRECT!!

Wow. OK. Good guess. Confetti this time. Another ping as the next lock comes free.

QUESTION 3
WHAT IS THE MOLECULAR FORMULA OF 5-HYDROXYTRYPTAMINE?

Huh?

A: $C_9H_{13}NO$ **C:** $C_{21}H_{30}O_5$

B: $C_8H_{11}NO_2$ **D:** $C_{10}H_{12}N_2O$

6:57.

6:56.

Shit. Absolutely no idea.

I push A with my toe.

Why is Ash tied up?

WRONG!

A sad face of a clown. He shakes his finger at me. Damn it.

THE CORRECT ANSWER IS D.
FUN FACT: 5-HYDROXYTRYPTAMINE IS SEROTONIN, A NEUROTRANSMITTER THAT KEEPS YOU HAPPY! REMINDER: DO MORE LEARNING ABOUT THE THINGS THAT MAKE US HAPPY!

I'm starting to feel very warm.

Ash is pulling her face away from the pole now. She is scrunching her nose up in a way that suggests she's uncomfortable.

Something doesn't feel right. . . .

BONUS QUESTION!
WHO IS THE MOST LIKELY TO BE A LIAR?

OK. Wasn't expecting that.

A: ASHLEY   **C:** FINNEAS
B: ELEANOR   **D:** MYSELF

I feel a warmth behind the back of my neck.

06:02.

I hover my foot over Eleanor. Miss HappyHead . . .

My stomach churns.

I move my toe and push C.

Finn.

He needs to be as far down the rankings as possible for the plan to work.

BONUS QUESTION!

WHO IS THE MOST MANIPULATIVE?

A: ASHLEY   **C:** FINNEAS

B: ELEANOR   **D:** MYSELF

I need to succeed.

How would *they* think?

How would the niece of Manning think?

I push C again.

BONUS QUESTION!

WHICH OF YOUR TEAMMATES HAS THE MOST
POTENTIAL TO HARM THE REST OF YOU?

A: ASHLEY   **C:** FINNEAS

B: ELEANOR   **D:** MYSELF

Shit.

Shit.

"Guys! Guys." I hear Finn's voice somewhere behind me.
"The poles are—"

"No talking!" Fernsby shouts.

I push C.

THANK YOU! BACK ON TRACK, SEB.

A pricking on the back of my neck.

Ash is moving in a strange way. She seems to be squirming,
trying to twist her body.

QUESTION 4

JANE'S POLE IS SAFE. BUT IF ASHLEY STAYS ATTACHED
TO HER METAL POLE, SHE IS GOING TO . . .

A: WIN A PRIZE   **C:** SING A SONG
B: DO A DANCE   **D:** GET BURNT

My back feels incredibly hot.

Ash is twisting her head away from the pole. She is pulling her body in the other direction. "Help!" she shouts. Her voice is wobbly, terrified.

"Guys!" I hear Finn cry. "The poles are heating up!"

Sweat is dripping from my forehead.

"I said no talking!" Fernsby snaps. "Thirty seconds off everyone's clocks!"

The clock suddenly drops to 04:35.

I watch as Ash tries to pull her wrists apart, the wire digging into her skin.

What the actual . . .

I push D.

Holy shit.

I feel the ping of the third padlock releasing.

CORRECT! METAL CONDUCTS HEAT, WHEREAS WOOD DOES NOT.

Fireworks explode across the screen.

One left . . .

04:12.

04:11.

"Help me! Please!" Ash's voice is small. I can barely hear her over the music. The skin on her cheek is turning red. Tears are starting to fall from under her blindfold.

Jesus.

Is this how far Manning is willing to go to find her favorites?

The lunatic bitch.

Stay focused, Seb. . . .

QUESTION 5
HOW MANY KNOTS ARE USED TO TIE JANE TO HER POLE?

A: 2   **C:** 4

B: 3   **D:** 5

I didn't look.

Why? Why didn't I look?!

Observational skills. I try to twist my head to get a look at Jane, but she is out of my line of vision.

"My arms! Help me! Please!" The small voice is louder now. Desperate.

Come on, Seb. Get this right. Come on.

Probably more . . . To make it harder.

I push C.

WRONG!

No.

Shit.

Sad clown wags his finger again.

I hear someone's straitjacket fall to the floor.

Eleanor rushes past me over to Ash and pulls her blindfold off.

"Oh, God. OK . . . Don't worry, I'm going to help you get out of this," she is saying. I watch as she begins to pull at the wires around Ash's wrists.

"Please help me!"

"I will. I promise I will—"

BONUS QUESTION!
WHO IS THE MOST UNHAPPY?

A: ASHLEY   **C:** FINNEAS
B: ELEANOR   **D:** MYSELF

Come on, come on, come on.
I push C.

BONUS QUESTION!
WHO IS THE MOST LIKELY TO UNDERMINE THE PROGRAM HERE?

A: ASHLEY   **C:** FINNEAS
B: ELEANOR   **D:** MYSELF

God.
C.

BONUS QUESTION!

WHO IS THE MOST LIKELY TO ACT IN THEIR OWN INTERESTS
TO THE DETRIMENT OF OTHERS?

A: ASHLEY   **C:** FINNEAS
B: ELEANOR   **D:** MYSELF

C.

THANK YOU! YOU ARE BACK ON TRACK, SEB.

03:21.

QUESTION 6

WHAT KIND OF LOCK IS USED TO KEEP ASHLEY'S HANDS
TOGETHER?

A: LOCK AND KEY   **C:** BIKE LOCK
B: NUMBER   **D:** NO LOCK
COMBINATION
LOCK

I suddenly realize this isn't about math. Or geography. Or
each other. It's about them. It's about loyalty.

I look up and see Eleanor fiddling with the lock, trying to
twist the numbers, her fingers shaking.

I push B.

CORRECT!!

Put your superiors before everything.

I feel the final padlock ping open, and my straitjacket falls to the floor at my feet.

"Seb, help me!" Eleanor shouts. "We need to break it off!"

Finn is still in his straitjacket.

I dart to the Assessors' table, where I can see them tapping away on their tablets. I grab the jug of water and drop it to the floor. It smashes, water spilling everywhere.

I grab a shard of glass.

And I run.

I run to Jane.

"Seb!" Eleanor screams. "What is wrong with you?!"

No, Eleanor. *You're* wrong.

The music is getting louder. Its electronic beat blares into my head. Its vibrations.

I can't hear Ash screaming anymore.

02:31.

02:30.

I use the shard of glass to start cutting Jane's rope.

"What are you doing, Seb! Seriously? Help us! Her skin!" Eleanor's voice is a blur.

Jane is inhaling steadily, hugging the wooden pole. I saw at the rope with the shard.

The rope snaps open. I pull off her blindfold.

My hand is bleeding.

"Quick!" I shout.

Jane's eyes are bright. Surprised.

01:03.

01:02.

Jane runs around the central pole toward Ash and pushes Eleanor out of the way. I watch as she turns the combination lock. Jane knows the code. She has to.

They want us to know that without them we have nothing. We can achieve nothing. Despite our instincts, *they* are the answer. We need ultimate trust in our leaders.

Ash falls backward as the lock opens.

The horn sounds.

Eleanor looks at me. Upset. Angry that she didn't know. That she didn't realize.

The bloodied shard of glass slips out of my hand and drops to the floor at my feet. A team of Overalls pours into the room, taking Ash out through the door in that familiar yellow haze.

The music stops. All I can hear is our panting.

"Interesting," Fernsby says. "Very interesting."

Muscle Man enters through the assessment-room door. He makes his way over to Fernsby. They talk in hushed voices. Muscle Man nods.

He goes to Finn, who is still strapped into his chair. "I'm going to unlock you," he says. "Then you need to come with me."

TWENTY-SEVEN
A Ghost

They know.
    Don't they?
    They know it was him.
    It was us.
    They must.
    Ended.
    It was his badge.
    The HappyHead smiley face.
    Smiling.
    Because of me.
    My answers.
    Run.
    Run.
    Is he hurt?
    Bird fluttering.
    Squawking.
    In my chest.
    Trying to get out.

Out.
Out and away.
Ended.
Ended.
Ended.
Shit.
I can't.
I can't.
I can't.
Breathe.
My chest.
I can't.
Catch.
My.
Breath.
My inhaler.
I need my inhaler.
Where?
Where?
God.
Oh, God.
There.
There.
Click.
Pshhhh.
Hold.
3 . . .
2 . . .
1.
God.

Breathe. Breathe.

Spots. Dancing spots.

Breathe.

In.

In.

In.

Head between knees.

Easy now. Easy.

OK.

OK.

That's it.

Late-night asthma attack while sleeping. Hello, old pal. Not seen you in a while.

I am drenched.

I tiptoe across the room to the bathroom and flick on the light. I splash cold water over my face, then sit on the toilet seat and breathe in the cool air. I turn and open the cistern.

Donk.

The pager is still there. In the sock.

Deliver one of these to a man named to Tom Jarrow. He will know what to do.

As I head back to bed, I hear voices in the corridor.

"Go straight back to your room, Mr. Blake." Someone coughing. "Get some sleep."

The slam of doors. I put my ear to the door. Nothing. For a long time. Then I hear a single set of footsteps padding gently on the cold floor outside. I hear them coming closer.

Then they stop.

Outside my room.

And I feel a small tap on the other side of the wood.

The footsteps start again.

I slowly open the door a crack and look down the length of the corridor, where I see a ghostly figure leaning against the wall far down in the distance.

Head down, hair falling over his face.

A dark, fragile ghost.

Him.

I tiptoe forward.

He turns, his face pale as the moon.

He looks . . . different.

Drained.

Hollow.

I point to the doors that lead to the stairwell. He nods and turns. It's as if he is floating. Guiding me.

I tiptoe behind him all the way down to the bottom until we reach the fire escape.

NOT FOR PARTICIPANT USE

He stops just beneath the green light. I hardly recognize him. It's as if someone, some*thing*, is possessing him, hovering by him, drawing out the life from his body. There is the low murmur of voices somewhere far above. The hum of an extractor fan. He pushes himself into the corner next to me.

He flinches.

"Finn? Are you OK?"

He nods tentatively, like his body has been put on half speed.

"Jesus," I say. "Are you sure?"

When he speaks, he sounds older somehow. "I'm fine . . . ," he says, but I can tell he is in pain.

"I didn't know where you had gone. I had no idea what they would do to you." My voice quivers, but I don't care.

"They took me to be questioned. They suspected I was the one who went into her office. Apparently Acid Green's answers didn't help."

"I'm so sorry—"

"You did what you had to."

He looks like a drawing with no depth now, just an outline. I want to put back inside him whatever it is they took. "Did you tell—"

"Of course not."

Silence.

"Mark . . . ," he says.

"Mark?"

"He was there. . . . Part of the interrogation."

"What did they ask you?"

He inhales deeply and closes his eyes. "If it was me. If anyone helped me. How I got in. How I got hold of a fob. They asked if I took anything. If I read anything. If I think it's OK to put everyone's safety at risk."

"What did you say?"

"Nothing. Denied it all."

"Good . . . That's good."

"I said that during the Hide I hid the whole time on the far edge of the forest. That I didn't move until I was found. Mark confirmed that I was caught there, so it would have been un-likely for me to be able to get into the building."

"Right."

"They mentioned you."

A pause.

"What did they say?"

"They said how wonderfully you are doing. How I'm a bad influence on you. On the whole team. Pulling you away from the promise you are showing. Stopping your chances of being truly happy."

The noise of a pipe creaking somewhere above us.

"They don't suspect . . . *us*? Do they?"

He shifts slightly, wincing once more. "No. I said I hated your guts and hope we never see each other again." He laughs, then drops his head. "It worked. That big man I stole the fob from confirmed that we don't see eye to eye. That we had a fight and we resolved it in the Cozy Room. Thank fuck for that. I thought he might have known and was gonna turn me in. Seems he didn't have a clue."

I nod. "That's good. . . . And it's really good that they don't think we're . . . you know. If they found out—"

"I know." He looks dejected. Broken.

I hate this place. I suddenly feel so trapped.

"You did amazing," I force myself to say. "We're on track. Everything is as it should be."

"Is it?" He doesn't even look at me. We stand in silence for what feels like a very long time. All I hear is the wind outside, lashing against the fire-escape door.

Finn turns, his eyes blazing like he has been set on fire from the inside. "Let's just leave, Seb. Come on. Me and you. What's the worst they can do if they catch us?"

I want to. I want to run with him. But we won't even get as far as the fence. The cameras. Our chips.

"Mark's plan is our best chance of escape. Only one more day to wait . . . ," I say instead.

He shrinks back into the shadows. "And what if this plan of his fails?"

"It won't."

"You don't know that."

I want to tell him he's wrong. That I do know. But I say, "You're right, I don't."

A door slams somewhere above. We push ourselves farther into the corner. Into the darkness. Close. "We will get out, Finn," I whisper now. "We're nearly there."

I put my hand on his arm. Squeeze. Hold. And I suddenly realize how much I care about him.

I want to close my eyes.

For us to dissolve together.

Into the air.

And float away.

"You look like shit too, by the way," he says.

I smile.

Voices, a few flights above. The change of shift.

"Hey." I put my hand on his cheek. He turns his face to mine.

I look into his eyes. His ice eyes.

A lump in my throat. I pull him toward me. "Can't wait for my tattoo. Any ideas for what it will be yet?"

I watch him soften: the thing haunting him letting go of its grip ever so slightly. "I did have a thought."

"Go on."

"Maybe a flower."

"A *flower*? Bottom of my back? I could see that."

"Ha. No. I was thinking maybe here." He touches the inside of my forearm.

"OK . . . What kind of flower? Don't you dare say a sunflower."

He laughs gently. "There's a flower called a gladiolus. It means 'sword' in Latin. Courage. I guess it's how I see you."

I pause. "I like that." And I feel a little breathless.

Then he says, "It's my birthday today."

"What?"

"Yeah. Nice way to spend it."

Oh, God.

"Happy birthday, Finneas. Many happy returns."

He turns his body into mine with a hint of a smile. "You're weird. In a good way. I like you," he says quietly, and he puts his hands on my shoulders and twists my body to face him.

He takes my face in his hands.

I like you.

He leans forward. Pushing his forehead into mine. And my whole body is alive.

"Is that OK?" he asks.

I make some kind of noise that I think sounds a little like "Yeah. That's . . . that's more than OK."

And this time, I kiss him.

And it feels truly insane.

And then.

Then.

There's a noise behind us. A shuffling.

I turn. "What was that?"

He is looking too. "I think . . ."

Footsteps?

We pause for a moment.

"Rats?" I say, uncertain.

"We should get back to our rooms," he says darkly, the thing possessing him returning, latching its claws back on. "We can't take any more chances. Not after nearly being caught in her office. We're putting Mark in danger too."

"So we stick to the plan?"

"Yes. But, if anything goes wrong, we meet back here the same time tomorrow night, and we cut our chips out and run. Deal?"

"Deal."

Don't go.

I don't want this to end.

He leans into me again, and for one final moment, everything stops.

TWENTY-EIGHT
The Treat

A different song is playing this morning. ABBA today. "The Winner Takes It All."

Bedroom 3.

Yes yes yes yes yes yes.

Fucking ace-balls.

I wolf my breakfast, eager to beat the Harmony Hall rush. I then grab the sock with the pager inside, tuck it neatly into the waistband of my joggers, and draw the string tight. I make my way past Greens looking longingly at me as they walk in the opposite direction.

Someone calls my name. "Hey!"

It's Ash, outside Bedroom 15.

I stop. "*Ash,* oh my God. Are you OK? After yesterday?"

"Yeah, I'm fine." Her eyes are strangely dull, but she has a huge smile plastered on her face. "I've jumped from Bedroom thirty to fifteen for my bravery. They said they're so proud of me."

"Ash—"

"Keep moving, please!"

I am pulled away from her, into the throng of Greens.

I see Raheem and Lucy stopping outside 7 and 8.

"Hey, Seb—nice work!"

"Yeah, you too, guys."

I keep moving.

Last night was . . .

Kissing him again . . .

And we could get out of this place.

Today.

The two of us.

Together.

Gladiolus. Why is that so . . . *hot*?

Focus, Seb.

When I get to the door of Bedroom 3, it is already ajar. I linger outside for a moment.

Voices. There are people inside.

Jane and Misty.

Oh, God.

I step inside, immediately very aware of the sock tucked into my elastic waistband.

"Hi," I say, waving. The room is massive. Huge bay windows and an actual chaise lounge.

"Good morning, Sebastian!" Misty is perky as anything this morning, rivaling my own excitement.

"Just doing the morning checks," Jane says. She looks hardened somehow. Less ditsy. "You did a really good job in the challenge yesterday. We were just talking about how much you are growing. You've surprised us all. I'm not sure I would have put any bets on you on day one, but look at you now."

"Oh . . . Thanks."

"Empty your bag, please. Sorry, you know the new rules."

"Sure, no problem." I take my backpack off my back and unzip it, turning out the contents onto the bed: my pills, my inhaler, my T-shirts and underwear falling out of it. As I do, I feel the pager slip down the inside of the leg of my joggers. It stops at my ankle.

Oh . . . shit.

I hesitate.

Shit.

"What's wrong?"

"Oh, nothing. I just . . ."

I stand up straight. Jane leans down and begins to root through my things, separating them. I edge myself to the chaise lounge and perch on the end of it. Misty watches me from the window.

I glance down to where the pager has slipped. I can see a rectangular lump at the bottom of my joggers by the ankle band.

"All clear," Jane says to Misty. "Thank you, Sebastian."

"No worries."

No worries at all.

None.

"Sebastian," Misty says. She looks at me. Then doesn't speak for a moment, which makes me feel like I should look away. But I hold her gaze.

"Yeah?"

"I've noticed you're limping."

"I hurt my leg a little during the Hide. It's OK."

"Can I take a look?"

"Honestly, it's fine. Just a scratch."

She looks me up and down.

Please just leave.

She tilts her head slightly. "You're tougher than you look, aren't you?"

That's a weird thing to say. "I s'pose . . ." is all I can come up with.

"Well . . . ," Jane says, breaking the weirdness. "You are robust. You're proving that."

"Thanks, I'm glad."

Misty is still staring. "If there's anything you need to tell us, Sebastian, you should. We don't want to worry about you."

I can feel the pager digging into my ankle. "You absolutely don't need to."

"No?"

"No."

"Well, that's what we want to hear. You don't want to let us down, do you?"

"Absolutely not."

"That's what I thought." Jesus, Misty's showing her interrogative side this morning.

"Right," Jane chimes in. "On to the next room. Sorry to disturb you. However, you will be pleased to hear that we have something a little different planned for you today. A reward."

"That sounds exciting."

They both nod and head for the door.

"I hope you find whoever did it," I say.

They turn.

"Sorry?" Misty gives me a funny look.

"Whoever trespassed. They deserve whatever punishment they get."

They both relax in unison. "Thank you, Sebastian."

"And I just want to say I feel like I've grown so much as a person at HappyHead. I only wish there was more time. I really feel like I'm finally finding myself."

"That's all we want for you," Jane says.

"I know."

They turn and leave.

I exhale, then look at the clock.

Something very special is planned for you today.

You will be given a treat.

A date. With Eleanor.

Isn't that exciting?

Because you have both done so well, Sebastian.

Because you deserve it.

And Madame Manning is so proud of you.

Meet Eleanor at the track by the Astroturf at 12:00.

And so Mark's plan begins.

I hide the pager in the cistern, wrapped in the sock.

There is a knock at the door.

Muscle Man. He is holding a clothes bag on a hanger. "Time to get ready. You'll need to put this on."

"What is it?"

"It's for your date."

Play the game. Like nothing is wrong.

"What's your name?" I am feeling more confident that I thought.

"My name?" He looks surprised.

"Yes. I realize I don't know it."

He pauses for a moment, crossing his arms. "Sean. My name is Sean."

"Thanks, Sean." I unzip the bag.

His expression warms momentarily. "No worries, Sebastian."

I pull out a suit. A black suit with a crisp white shirt and a tie.

"Put it on. I'll give you a minute."

"Great, thanks."

He goes back out into the corridor. I pull on the clothes. They smell fresh. Lavender. Shiny black shoes.

Oh, God.

God.

I leave the tie because I've never known how to do one. And maybe she will think I look cool in a suitably rebellious kind of way if I keep the top button of my shirt undone.

I look in the bathroom mirror. I hardly recognize myself.

Stay focused. Tom Jarrow. Whitehall.

I grab the sock from the cistern and push it into the inside pocket of the jacket with my pills and my inhaler. This is the last time I'll see this room.

I hope.

The last time I will be inside this building.

Sean knocks. "All set?" His voice through the door.

I open it. "Think so . . ."

"You'll need this." He is holding a rose. I take it. "Where's your tie?"

"I don't . . ."

He looks at me. "You can't go on your date without a tie, Sebastian."

He picks it up from the bed and puts it around my neck. I feel like it's my first day of school.

"There. Now you look the part. Enjoy today. It's going to be very special."

● ● ●

Waiting on the running track next to a row of five small trucks are nine other boys in suits, and ten girls in dresses. Floaty floral dresses like it's a summer's day. It is not so bitingly cold this morning; in fact, there's a warmth in the air. Some of the Greens I don't really know, but others I recognize. Raheem and Lucy, Matthew Parry-Brokingstock, the twins, and Man-Bun Boy from the Unfound. Fridge Boy. Ayahuasca Girl. Eleanor. Eleanor is there. Her hair falls loosely around her shoulders and is gently wafting over her face in the breeze.

I am led toward her by an Overall.

She looks so different. So . . . informal.

She is smiling at me.

As I join her, she takes my hand and I smile back at her. I then kiss her gently on the cheek.

"You look beautiful," I say, handing her the rose.

"That's so sweet." She is wearing makeup. Lipstick.

The Overalls pair the others up.

Some of the participants look surprised at their pairings. Others pleased. Lucy and Raheem. Fridge Boy with Ayahuasca

Girl. Matthew with one of the twins. Man-Bun Boy with the other. We stand in a line, eyeing each other up.

And then Manning appears, stepping out of one of the small trucks parked on the tarmac. She has her sunglasses on and a navy-blue Breton jacket with gold buttons. She is wearing a large floppy hat, striped blue and white. Nautical.

She is followed out by ten more Overalls. Mark is among them, smiling as if nothing is amiss.

She waves at us with a white-gloved hand. "Well, look at you all," she says, her red lipstick like a bright rose petal against her pale skin. "Don't you clean up nicely? You all look so happy." She shakes her head proudly. "Now, to reveal your treat. A day at the beach."

Some people make oohs and aahs; one of the girls gives a little clap. "Aw, romantic!"

"But don't worry . . . there's no challenge today. You can just sit back and enjoy yourselves because someone else will be doing the work for you." Manning points to the Astroturf.

A line of ten more people has appeared. Heads down, eyes on the ground. Silent. Like a group of criminals in a police lineup.

All of them look exhausted, unkempt, their clothes dirty, unwashed, their room numbers plastered on their hoodies.

And there he is. Finn.

Betty. Betty is there.

Jennifer Beale. Malachai.

Some others that I don't know.

I feel odd. Woozy. Suddenly flushed with anger.

Is this the bottom percentile?

I swallow it.

"You can each pick someone to help you. We need to be kind to them." Manning nods solemnly in their direction. "For they have found it incredibly difficult here and I would like to give them a chance to keep trying. To show their commitment, even when things haven't gone so well. To give them some responsibility and purpose so they can know their worth. It breaks my heart to see them unable to recognize it, to struggle." Her voice cracks, perfectly timed. "But that is why we're here. To help each other." She beckons them over. "Join us, please!"

I catch Eleanor looking at the approaching line, and I notice a flash of something I haven't seen before. Empathy.

For a brief second, she looks confused. Upset. But then she senses my eyes on her and snaps her face to me, hardening again. "If that was me," she whispers, "I would be so ashamed."

"Yes," I say. "Me too."

I can feel my back sweating.

The ten of them line up in front of us by the trucks.

Manning begins to walk between the two lines, her hat flopping in front of her face. Every now and then, she stops to look at us, to take us in, nodding, like we're a part of something incredibly special. "Each of the couples will have an assigned Reviewer to keep an eye on proceedings."

The Reviewers begin to line up behind the couples. I watch as Mark heads toward me and Eleanor.

He stands behind us.

He doesn't look at me.

"One at a time, the couples will choose one of the less fortunate." *Less fortunate.* "Only five of them will get this opportunity, so"—she looks at us—"choose wisely. Lucy and Raheem, please step forward."

They do.

The Overalls start clapping. Someone whoops.

Lucy blushes, flattered.

Raheem puts his fist in the air, clutching her hand. Proud. Someone cheers.

Manning raises her hand. "There will be time for celebration in due course. Now, choose who you would like to accompany you today. Someone who you feel will be able to learn from you. Who will use you as an example of how to achieve your acquired happiness."

I look at the *less fortunate*.

Hands clasped in front of them. Hardly looking up.

Raheem and Lucy whisper conspiratorially, making their decision. They nod at each other, then Lucy says, "We choose number ninety-three, Betty."

Betty looks up, terrified.

"Please join them, Betty."

She shuffles toward them. She looks like Finn did the other night. Haunted. Hollow. An outline.

Lucy puts her hand on Betty's shoulder.

"Sebastian and Eleanor, please step forward."

Someone, I think it might be Matthew, shouts, "Yes, Sebeanor!" and suddenly I want to put my head in a microwave at full blast. Eleanor's eyes dart around the lineup before us.

I try to smile. *Sorry,* I want to say. *I'm sorry.*

"Please pick someone to accompany you at the beach."

"OK," Eleanor whispers into my ear. "What do you think?" She sounds strong. I feel Mark's eyes on my back. And I suddenly understand. We need to pick Finn.

I open my mouth. "What about . . . ?"

"I think a female."

Shit.

"But . . . what about someone we know? We might have more chance of influencing them, if we know what they're like."

"Hmm. What, so Malachai . . . or *Finneas*." She spits his name.

"I mean, if it was Finn . . ."

She turns to me, with a strange look in her eyes. She pauses, studying my face.

I shrug. *Take the bait. Your sadistic side wants it. Come on.*

She then smiles. "We could make it quite . . . difficult for him." Her smile turns to a smirk. "Time to get our own back for him nearly ruining everything." Without consulting me any further, she steps forward and points to Finn. "We pick number ninety-four, Finneas Blake."

I turn and look at Mark.

Bingo.

Not long now, Finn. And then we'll be out of here.

We'll be free.

. . .

We are in the back of the truck. Mark keeps his eyes fixed on the road. Finn is in the front seat next to him, head down.

Next to me Eleanor keeps pointing out the window and saying how pretty everything is. How stunning. I don't mention that I have seen most of this before, except in the pitch-black while running from the sound of hunting dogs. I also don't point out the spot where we made our shelter.

Where we first . . .

We drive through the valleys, the fields that Finn and I cycled across. The fence is ever-present, running alongside us in the distance.

What now? What is the plan?

After maybe fifteen minutes, we round a corner and are greeted by an expanse of ocean. And a beach.

I have seen this before too. It is the cove I saw from the cliff top before I fell.

On the shore, just where the water laps onto the sand, there are ten boats. Rowing boats with parasols attached to the back of them—big yellow umbrellas, with the HappyHead smile. Each boat has a tartan picnic blanket over one of the small wooden benches crossing its width. The waves are much calmer than when I last saw them. And the fence, running down on our left, much taller than I remember, jutting out into the blue.

But not as far as I thought. Perhaps two hundred yards, max.

I get a little jolt of excitement. Of hope.

"Here we are," Mark says. He gets out and opens the side door for us.

"Thank you," Eleanor says, and we exit to see the rest of the couples arriving in their trucks. Each pair, with their less fortunate other, begins to surround the edge of the sandy cove. Manning is already here with a team of Overalls.

She holds up a yellow megaphone and speaks. "Isn't this just beautiful? Please have someone from each couple come and take a basket. They have been personalized to contain your favorite foods."

Eleanor is looking at me.

"Eleanor?" Mark says.

She frowns, and I think she is about to protest, but then the frown disappears. "Of course," she says, and swans off to her aunt.

The three of us stand waiting for her to be out of earshot.

"The boat?" I say.

Mark nods.

I look at Finn. His eyes narrow. *The boat.*

"You two will overpower Eleanor," Mark whispers quickly. "And I'll fall off the boat with her like it was an accident. I'll then swim with her back to the shore. You two will take the boat and row it around the side of the fence."

And before they can catch us, we will have disappeared.

Into the Scottish wilderness.

Because the good thing about the Scottish wilderness is that it's huge.

And we will make our way back to London. Find Tom Jarrow.

And we will somehow stop this.

Stop her.

And we will be free.

Yes. This could actually *work.*

Eleanor practically skips back. "We've got chocolate cake." She winks and kisses me on the cheek.

"Oh, yum."

Manning waves us over before sitting down on a gingham picnic rug. An old gramophone has been placed next to her and is playing warbling classical music. The megaphone squeals on.

"Gather around, gather around." We do, in a buzz of anticipation. "Welcome, couples. Welcome to your first date," Manning says, sunlight glistening from the rippling water behind her. She radiates an eerie calmness. "I would just like to say a few words before I let you enjoy yourselves. It is my absolute pleasure to be here with you couples. I know this might sound odd, but I am so grateful to you all. I am grateful to have met you. You have proved something that Dr. Stone"—her voice wobbles, perfectly timed again—"and I were so hopeful we could do. Many people doubted us, but we have shown that her vision works. That there are teenagers in this country with the capacity to be strong and happy. To be well. You are the future." She stops and takes off her hat. The surrounding Overalls clap.

"Enough from me. Your treat is to have an hour out at sea, relaxing. Being waited on by the person you selected. They will serve you, row for you. And hopefully learn from you." I catch Finn scowl. "Enjoy it. You deserve it. You have your Reviewer should you require assistance, but even the sun is smiling on us today. Could the Reviewers please take the rowers to the boats?"

I watch as Mark takes Finn by the arm and leads him down to the boat in front of Eleanor and me. The other Reviewers do the same. I see Jennifer resisting, trying to break away, but a prod from a truncheon stops her. Others are numbly led forward, their expressions blank.

One fair-haired boy stays rooted to the spot. A large Overall stands over him. "Move, Killian."

Killian glares at him. Eyes dark. Distant. "No."

"Excuse me?"

"I said n—"

But before Killian can finish, the Overall abruptly grabs his shoulders, so his whole body jerks, and leans down into his face.

"You're lucky to be given this chance. All right? Do you understand me? We are trying to help you."

For a fleeting second, Killian looks like he might spit in the man's face. I watch him hesitate, his eyes seething. Then, slowly, he nods and drops his head.

"Good. Well done." The Overall smiles like he is proud of himself, then leads Killian forward toward a boat.

Betty. She looks like a shell of herself.

It's OK.

It is.

We can stop all this.

I watch as Mark pushes Finn onto the wooden bench at the back of the boat and signals for him to take hold of the oars. Finn complies.

Oh, God.

What if I'm not strong enough? Or they catch us before we get around the side of the fence? Surely they will be patrolling. . . .

Breathe, Seb.

It will work.

I catch Manning watching me.

You can do this, Seb.

The megaphone blares. "Couples, your turn."

Two by two, the couples walk toward the sea and begin to clamber into the little wooden boats. I watch Raheem take Lucy's hand, and she giggles as he guides her carefully onto one of the benches. Betty sits behind them, oars in hand. She is now quietly crying. Lucy doesn't look at her.

"What are you waiting for?" Eleanor says, tugging on the sleeve of my jacket. I suddenly realize how warm I am. There is a bead of sweat running through my hair behind my ear, and I realize my back is now completely sodden. I walk with Eleanor across the sand.

She is humming gently.

The sunlight is glimmering off the surface of the water.

When we get to the boat, I put my hand out for Eleanor like Raheem did, and she takes it saying, "Oh, what a *gentleman*." I follow her, but as I put my foot into the bottom of the boat, the whole thing wobbles. A surge of panic pumps through my body.

"Whoa!" Eleanor says. "Steady now . . ."

I perch on the bench in front of Finn, who has his hands clamped on the oars. I don't dare look at him. I tap my jacket pocket, by my chest. The pager is still there. Everything is in place.

Nearly there.

I can hear a strange revving noise coming from somewhere.

Eleanor opens the little wicker basket and begins to root through its contents. The other couples are all doing the same. Glasses, strawberries, a bottle of fizzy fruit juice . . .

"Oh, how *cute*," she says, tucking a wayward strand of hair behind her ear. "Sebby, look."

The revving noise is getting louder.

"What's this? Oh my *gosh* . . . ," Eleanor says, and she lifts out a small booklet, the size of an envelope. "Sebby, look. It's a photo album!"

"No way," I say, but my voice doesn't feel like my own. She begins to flick through the booklet, her hand over her mouth.

"Get ready to leave the shore, rowers!" Manning is giving

orders into the megaphone. "When I say. Final checks, please, Reviewers."

"This is too much," Eleanor says. "Oh my gosh, look at this one." She holds up a picture of us holding hands in the gardens of Serenity.

"Yeah," I say. "Nice."

The revving is now coming from the beach.

"And *this*." She shows me a picture of us kissing, after the Sharing Circle. "I mean, I know we don't look our best, but this is our first kiss, Sebby!"

I can see something behind her head, moving down the dirt track to the cove. A quad bike.

Something isn't right.

It speeds down onto the sand and grinds to a halt. Three people step off.

Jane.

Misty.

And Sean.

"Look how handsome you are here," Eleanor is saying.

This doesn't feel . . .

"What is going on?" Ayahuasca Girl calls from the boat to our left. Eleanor stops and turns, her eyes suddenly widening. I watch Manning stand up from the picnic rug.

"Ah! Right on time," Manning says into the megaphone. "Please, could I have everyone's attention?" Jane, Misty, and Sean join her. She nods at them solemnly. "Please, if you will." Then she points.

In our direction.

To our boat.

And they begin walking toward us.

Manning's voice booms out. "I would like you all to know that we have found the person who put you in danger. The trespasser."

My stomach twists in a way that it never has before. The anxiety hits me like a tidal wave, knocking the air from my lungs.

"No . . . ," I hear Finn say from behind me, and I turn to see his face drain of color.

The megaphone blares. "It was important for me that this particular group of participants witness this. Witness that there are consequences for those who put the safety of the rest of you in jeopardy."

Sean, Misty, and Jane are just yards away.

Then Sean leans into the boat.

He grabs Finn by the back of his hoodie and pulls.

"That we are, and will always be, wholly committed to keeping you safe," Manning's voice rings out. "That you can trust us."

"No!" Finn screams, thrashing, clawing at Sean as he drags him over the side of the boat and down onto the sand. They struggle, and Sean throws Finn down so that he lands on his back.

"Don't fight," Sean orders, now standing over him. And I notice Sean's hand reach to something tucked in his waistband. A leather sheath. The glint of metal.

A knife.

"Wait!" I shout, but Finn has already seen it. I watch his eyes lock onto it, and as they do, they empty. They go completely gray.

Sean leans down and speaks quietly into Finn's ear. "I

wouldn't want it to accidentally slip and hurt you, would I?" Stop. Please. "Come with me. Now."

Finn looks at me, and I want to jump to him, to pull him toward me, but he shakes his head: *No. Don't.* He nods at Sean, who pulls him up and turns him away from me, leading him back up the beach.

I look for Mark, but Misty and Jane are already with him, holding his arms, pulling him out of the boat. Together they begin to drag him toward the quad bike. He struggles for a moment, but then Misty whispers something in his ear. And he stops.

"And disloyalty must be rooted out."

I watch helplessly as they put Finn and Mark on the back of the bike. Then, in a shower of sand, they turn the bike around and head back up the dirt track.

And they are gone.

I blink.

My mind is blank.

I can't . . .

How?

Things begin to blur.

Manning's voice. "The good news is we are safe now. All of us. There is no need to worry anymore."

Clapping.

Eleanor is clapping.

I look around, and others are too.

Matthew. Fridge Boy. Lucy. Ayahuasca Girl.

Manning is walking toward us. Nodding, as if to say, *Thank you, yes, I promised we would keep you safe.*

The boat wobbles.

Manning steps into it.

"How about a little picnic on the sea, then?" She looks at me and Eleanor. "Good. I will be your rower for today. This is going to be *so special.* Off we go!"

...

"You know," Eleanor says, taking a sip of her sparkling fruit juice, "since the first day I met you, I always knew we had a connection. Didn't you?"

Manning has stopped rowing now that we are away from the shore. The end of the perimeter fence is only a few yards away.

So close.

Manning watches us, nibbling on a strawberry.

She looks just like her niece.

Same cold eyes. Same hard exterior.

Same little family secret.

"Yeah." I try to keep my voice steady. To remove all emotion. "I often felt like there was something going on. Something between us."

"Me too! I'm so glad you felt the same way. And when you kissed me . . . it confirmed everything." She takes my hand.

"I know exactly what you mean," I say, and as I hear myself, I feel sick.

This is hell.

I am in hell.

I want to take the oar and hit myself with it over and over and over until I am nothing.

I'm so sorry, I want to tell him.

I told you to trust me. But you were right. We should have run.

"Would you like a hot chocolate?" Eleanor asks me. She pours steaming brown liquid into a mug. "And you have to try these brownies. They're vegan." I feel myself nod. She smiles and pushes my hair out of my eyes with her fingers. "You're quite romantic, really, aren't you?"

Nothing could be worse than this.

Nothing.

"Yeah, I can be."

"I see it in you." She leans forward. "You're a little softy at heart."

Gladiolus.

I put my hand on her shoulder.

She leans closer.

I feel her chocolate breath against my face.

She presses her lips against mine.

I wait for it to end.

And I think of him. I think of him in the forest and his bruises and his blistered hands. I think of his tattoos and his arms and his back. His eyes. And how I thought we would be gone by now. On our way out . . . together.

When it is over, she leans back and wipes my lip. "Oops, lipstick!" She giggles. "Let's talk about something interesting. Do you want children?"

Is this real?

"That *is* interesting," Manning chimes in. She then smiles and gestures as if she is zipping her mouth shut.

I can't bear it.

"I haven't really thought about it," I say. "Children. Yes.

Maybe. I don't know. Long way off." I laugh. But nothing is remotely funny.

Eleanor makes an ambiguous noise. "Hmm."

"Why are you asking?" I try to sound casual. I feel Manning's attention on my words.

"I just think it's nice to know if we're on the same page. About family values. They're so important to me. I know I want a very traditional family. One day . . . of course." She adds a breezy smile and a flick of her hair.

"Yeah," I say. "That's incredibly important to me too."

"I'm glad."

The sweat drips from my hair into my eyes.

She is waiting again. I can feel it.

I lean forward.

She sticks her tongue in this time. Like a fat oyster.

When this one ends, she makes a little *aah* noise.

"It's so pretty here," Eleanor says.

Pretty.

"Yeah."

Manning shuffles on her bench, making the boat rock.

"I would like to tell you both something. A little secret."

Eleanor looks up. "Yes?"

Oh, God. No. Please just let this be over. All of it.

"There is something special we want for you both. We see strong leadership qualities in each of you, and we think together, you could be a force to be reckoned with. We have decided that your time at HappyHead will not be over. You will be . . . progressing." Eleanor's eyes light up. "You will embark upon a course of further *training,* shall we say." I feel my face drain of all blood. "We have informed your parents, and they are, of course, thrilled by the news."

"I can't believe it!" Eleanor squeals. She puts her hand on mine.

"Yeah, wow. Me neither." I muster my final ounce of will-power and plaster a big smile on my face. "I'm so happy."

"Right, it's getting late. Please keep this news to yourselves for now. We don't want any of the other participants getting jealous."

"Oh, of course not." Eleanor squeezes my hand as Manning turns the boat to row us back to the shore. "Sebby, I'm so proud of us."

I keep thinking of his face through his black hair, all messy, as I watch the end of the fence moving farther away, until it finally disappears.

I think I am crying.

I turn and look out into the wind, over the ocean, so the wetness on my cheeks can't be seen.

TWENTY-NINE
Like Lead

I try to steady my hand as I lift my fork to put the grilled chicken into my mouth, but I can't stop it trembling.

I have been staring at it for . . .

What time is it?

22:36.

A very long time.

I have no appetite. I put down the fork.

I push myself up and feel myself move to the bathroom.

It's as if I'm not here. No longer occupying my own body.

Watching myself from above as I take off my clothes.

The crust of blood seeps through the bandage on my shin.

Stepping into the shower. Trying to balance. Not to get it wet.

I can't.

I sit. My legs out in front of me.

The heat doesn't shock me. My skin goes pink. Red. Purple blotches.

My muscles burn.

Wait.

Wait.

He said . . .

What did he say?

If anything goes wrong, we meet back here same time tomorrow night.

The fire escape.

I have to try.

He could be . . .

Same time, same place.

He will. He has to be. He will be there.

And we can leave. Go. Run.

If he isn't, I will run myself.

He was right all along.

I exhale.

I wait. I wait for the same time as last night.

■ ■ ■

00:00.

I creep along the hallway. Down the stairs. My shoes slapping against the concrete floor.

Pat. Pat. Pat.

Please be here, please be here.

The creak of pipes from above.

I feel for the pager in my pocket.

Pat. Pat. Pat.

He dropped the shard of glass on the floor. We can use it. We will cut out our chips like he said, exit through the fire escape and leave. . . .

We can try.

We have no choice.

A noise from above.

My heart surges.

Pat. Pat. Pat.

Keep going.

Down. Down.

The green of the exit light.

Come on. Come on.

I can hear something.

Some*one.*

At the bottom.

Yes.

I run.

Pat. Pat. Pat. Pat.

I round the corner.

Pat. Pat.

"Finn!" I say, and I am loud because I can't control myself. I am so excited to see him, to be with him, to jump on him, to hug him, kiss him—

But

wait.

No.

No.

Under the exit sign.

Next to the panic bar.

Staring.

Eyes bright with anger.

Eleanor.

"Looking for someone?" Her voice is hoarse.

I am breathless. "What . . . ?"

"I knew you'd be back." Back? She lingers in the half-light, arms folded. "I saw you here with him last night." Her face looks suddenly sickened. *Last night.* The noise. The shuffling behind us.

She looks like she is burning.

"What are you doing here?" is all I can say.

"I knew. I just knew. The way you were looking at him on the beach today . . ." Where is he? He should be here. . . . "How could you? How could you be so selfish?"

Oh, God.

And then I suddenly realize. "It was you. . . ." My voice is distant. I feel heat rising. Anger. Rage.

She steps toward me, the green light making her appear inhuman. "They needed to know he was the one who trespassed. I did it for all of us. To keep us safe."

"How did you know?"

"I heard the end of your . . . conversation." I catch a glint of the glass shard on the floor. The one Finn wanted to use. "So yes, I told them he was the one who went to the office. And that it was Mark who helped him."

I lean down, running my fingers across the floor. Her eyes follow me. I feel for it, *there*. When I stand, I hold the shard of glass in the air between us. "You're wrong."

"Oh, tough guy now, are we? Don't embarrass yourself, Seb."

The dirty glass trembles in my hand.

What will they do to him? To us?

"Why . . . why didn't you tell them I was there?"

She steps forward, closer to the shard. "You think I'd be stupid enough to ruin this for myself?"

"What do you mean?"

"I need you, Seb. And I'm not going to let your little crush fuck this opportunity up for me, OK? So you can either take that piece of glass, cut yourself open, leave, and get caught by the cameras before you even reach the forest—and God knows what she will do to you then—or you listen to me." She steps forward again, the shard nearly touching her hoodie now. "Or I guess you could kill me, but I think we both know that's not going to happen."

"Shut up, Eleanor."

"He's not who you think he is, Seb."

"What the hell do you know?"

"A lot more than you think."

My body clenches. The shard is digging into my hand.

She tilts her head. "Do you know *anything* about his past?"

"I—"

"About the deal he made to be here?" What? "Oh, I see. He didn't tell you. He lied. That's so un*like* him. Finneas is here as part of an agreement. He came to HappyHead instead of serving a sentence."

"That's not . . ."

"True? Yes, Seb, it is. It's time you stopped kidding yourself."

"How do you . . . ?"

"I've read his file. You would not believe what he did, Seb."

"But . . ."

"Have you even thought—just once—that I might be protecting you? Trying to look after you?"

I . . .

My body is like lead.

I drop my arm.

Why didn't he tell me?

"Do they know . . . about me and him?"

"Of course not. That would be the end of it for both of us. So we need to keep it that way. Understand?"

I drop the shard of glass, and it shatters on the floor.

"I'll see you tomorrow, Sebby. Can't wait to continue on this journey with you."

■ ■ ■

I've tried to block it out. What happened after Lily saw me kissing Oliver when I was fifteen. What she did.

She didn't tell my parents like I thought she would.

Instead, she told everyone at school. And, by everyone, I mean everyone.

When Oliver found out, he thought it was me. He thought I had told people myself because I *loved it so much.*

He said that because I had been so obsessed with him for years, he had let me kiss him as a favor. A kindness.

He waited for me by the bus stop after school. He told me he wanted to talk about it, if I had a few minutes, to try and clear the air.

I said sure, but I didn't want to miss the bus.

He said it wouldn't take long.

"Where are we going?" I asked.

"Follow me."

He walked me around the back of the school, past the science classrooms and the outdoor shed where the bikes and athletics equipment were kept, and he took me to the reeds by the pond. No one ever went to the pond. It stank like shit, and there were flies everywhere.

"What are we doing here?" I asked.

"I want to give you something," he said. "Hold out your hands."

And so I did.

That was when he pulled out the rope and began to tie them together.

I tried to wriggle free, I did. But all of a sudden there were other boys holding me as well as Oliver, and then someone was pinning me to the ground and tying my legs together too. And they were laughing.

They threw me into the water.

It was cold.

Shockingly cold, considering it was summer.

But the thing that really made me panic was how deep it was.

I began to sink to the bottom.

Sink.

Like a deadweight.

Like lead.

And I couldn't move.

Because of the rope.

And then they ran.

I don't remember much more, except waking up in the hospital. Apparently the art teacher, Mr. Baxter, had seen me struggling when he had come to get his bike to cycle home.

Thrashing, he said. Gasping.

I remember the police asking me if I wanted to press charges.

I obviously said no.

And that was it.

No one ever discovered who it was.

Some people said I did it to myself to get sympathy. Which

was a little annoying, but I half expected that. When I asked Lily why she did it—told everyone, I mean—she said that she was helping me. That she wanted me to be *out* because no one should have to live in the closet. Especially in the twenty-first century. Everyone is so accepting these days. She told me that she thought it would help make me happy. She had never known me to be happy, and something needed to change.

Things did change after that.

I vowed never to kiss a boy again because it seemed only to make very bad things happen.

THIRTY
The Ten

There is an abrupt knock on the door.

05:30.

There is no song today.

No "Shiny Happy People."

No ABBA.

Just a cold, hard knock.

"Number three?" It is Misty's voice. "Sebastian?"

"Hi, come in," I say, and stand up by my bed.

When Misty enters, she isn't smiling. "Top off," she says.

I do as she asks.

"Let's see." She looks at the stitch in front of my chip. "OK, time to say goodbye. Sadly, no anesthetic today."

I hear her speak, but the words don't seem to sink in.

She pulls out a scalpel from her bag, then slices the thread so my flesh opens.

I clench my teeth together and stare at her straight in the eyes.

"Does it hurt?" she asks.

"Yes," I say flatly. "Very much."

"Oh, that's a shame," she says, then squeezes with her fingers so the chip pops out into her hand. "Well, you're much tougher than you were the last time we did that. I see this place is working for you." She slaps a bandage on top of the cut. "Now, you need to get dressed and come with me."

"Right . . ."

"Immediately."

"Where are we going?"

"The assembly hall," she says. "There's going to be a special announcement."

■ ■ ■

When we get there, something feels different.

Everything is quiet. Too quiet.

Misty stops outside the assembly-hall door and turns to face me. "This is where I leave you."

"OK . . ."

"Good luck, Sebastian."

"Wait. . . . Do I . . . need anything?"

"No. Not today." She turns and leaves.

I feel for the pager in my pocket. Thank God I took it from the cistern.

When I push the door, the first thing I notice is that the lights are not on. It is dark. Just the light spilling in from the hallway behind me. And all the chairs are empty.

"Hello?" My voice echoes back at me.

I step inside. The door bangs shut behind me.

It feels so *big*. So oddly purposeless.

There is the faint buzz of the air-conditioning.

Something's wrong.

Then I see them.

At the back of the room.

A small crowd of Greens. Where is everyone else?

They all turn at once.

"Seb!" It is Raheem. He waves. "Any idea what's going on?"

I recognize them. Some of the couples from the beach. Lucy, Fridge Boy, Man-Bun Boy, Matthew Parry-Brokingstock, Jing and Li, Ayahuasca Girl.

And Eleanor.

She hurries toward me. "Hi, I'm so glad you're here."

She takes my hand.

"What is this?" I ask as she leads me toward the group.

"No idea," Lucy says with a shrug.

We stand in silence, looking around the room as if an answer might suddenly appear from the darkness.

"Is this an assessment?" I ask.

Suddenly there is a noise.

A *clunk* from the ceiling.

We all turn. The screen above the stage is slowly being lowered into place.

It flickers on.

Words appear.

LIVE FEED.

Why do I feel something terrible? Something terrible in my stomach.

Then there is a face looking directly into the camera.

Stone.

But . . . she looks . . . so different. She looks healthy. Her hair washed and neatly placed in a bun at the back of her head, her face full of color. She is wearing earrings and a necklace and expensive-looking glasses. She is no longer shaking, her body calm, poised, strong.

She is standing in front of a grand fireplace, her hands neatly crossed in front of her.

She smiles. A smile I do not recognize.

She speaks. "Hello, all. Commitment, growth, gratitude, and obedience lead to a happy head. Please repeat."

Obedience.

A sudden surge of fear hits me.

"Commitment, growth, gratitude, and obedience lead to a happy head," we repeat.

She speaks again. "I am so delighted to see you all again. You look so well. I am sorry that I have been sick, but I am feeling much better now. I am indebted to my wonderful friend Madame Manning for taking over and making sure everything has run so smoothly in my absence." She looks off camera and nods. Manning steps into the shot.

No. No.

This can't be—

"We couldn't be happier that you are feeling well again, Doctor." Manning turns to the camera, and they both stare into the lens. "Before we tell you why you are all here, we have a short clip we would like you to watch."

Have they got to her? Is she with them?

I glance down the row of Greens. Everyone staring, transfixed by the screen.

It suddenly changes.

Music. "Shiny Happy People."

Shots of the HappyHead building. Manning shaking the hands of tired-looking Greens as they board buses. Our fellow participants. Back in the outside world. Running toward their parents. Hugging them. Crying. Happy tears. There is Anoushka, with her arms around her parents. Her HappyHead badge glinting in the sun.

Parents talk to the camera. How proud they are . . . How pleased. How different their children seem. For the better.

Then Ash.

Ash. She holds up a HappyHead certificate. Says something about getting offered a place at the university she wanted. Her mum hugs her. Her dad beams.

More shots of reunited families. Laughter. Then a group shot. Outside the building. All the leaving participants cheer.

I search the faces. Where is Finn?

I can't see Betty either.

Or Malachai.

Or Jennifer.

Or the blond boy from the beach. Killian.

Where are they? The bottom percentile.

What have they done with them?

The montage stops. The screen snaps back to Stone and Manning, but they are no longer alone. Fernsby and Lindström are next to them. All standing in a row in front of the fireplace.

Stone is smiling. "Your peers have arrived safely home, ready to face the world. Happy." My body goes cold. Completely numb. "But as you may have realized," she says, "the ten of you will not be going home today."

"What?" I hear Jamie whisper.

"No way," one of the twins says.

Manning speaks now. "I am thrilled to inform you that you have been selected to move forward. You will be going somewhere incredibly special."

The screen changes again.

Aerial shots of an island in the middle of the sea.

"This is Elmhallow," a voice-over chimes out. "Elmhallow will be your new home for the foreseeable future. You are about to embark upon what will be the most important journey of your life. You have been selected to be leaders. Champions of this program."

The drone shots continue.

Flying over the ocean. Glistening blue. Over long, beautiful pebble beaches. Woods surrounding a shoreline. Fields. Plush and green. A group of stone cabins in a circle around a large tree.

Then more faces of parents flash across the screen.

But this time . . . *our* parents. Waving. Clapping.

"Go, Raheem!"

"We are so proud, Matty!"

"Good luck, Lucy!"

Mum and Dad. "Well done, Seb!" Tears in their eyes.

I feel like my legs might give way.

Eleanor squeezes my hand.

I look down the line of nine people standing next to me. Hands over their mouths. Shocked. Amazed.

"The rest of your lives are about to begin. So it is now time to follow us. Please turn around."

The screen suddenly goes black.

I think about him kissing me. My face in his hands.

We all turn.

There are others in the room with us now.

A group of half a dozen people wearing black. All black.

Waiting at the back.

They look . . .

Official.

Suits.

Ties.

We said we would look after each other.

"This way," one of them says sharply.

Where is he? Where have they taken him?

There is a murmur from the Greens. But, before anyone can speak, they surround us. "This way, please. Now."

And we follow them.

Outside.

Out through the back door.

I can see a bus.

People are getting off it.

New people. Shiny people. Trailing out of the bus.

Coming toward us. Looking up at the building.

Excited. In awe. The next one hundred.

"Seb!" I hear. *"Seb!"*

I turn.

And there among them is Shelly. My Shelly.

Heading toward the air lock door.

She waves. "Oh my God! Oh my God, Seb! This is so exciting!"

"No, wait. Wait, Shelly. . . ."

"What?"

And then I feel a hand on my shoulder.

Rough.

Gripping.

Pulling me away, up to the track by the Astroturf.

And before I can call out again, Shelly disappears through the air lock.

"This way. Come on."

We are told to stop next to another bus farther up the track.

Someone opens the doors.

I am ushered roughly into a seat.

Eleanor is placed in the one directly in front of me.

She turns and smiles at me. "Are you OK, Sebby? You look kind of sick."

I can't . . .

I don't know.

I feel a small vibration in my pocket.

The pager.

"I'm fine. Really."

"Oh, good. Because you're white as a sheet."

As she turns back around, I slowly pull the pager from my pocket, careful to keep it out of sight in the gap between my leg and the seat. Carefully, I check the screen.

1 NEW PAGE.

I press the OK button.

The message opens.

SEBASTIAN.
SEE YOU AT ELMHALLOW.
STAY STRONG.
STONE

I hear the tires crunch on the gravel, and we begin to move.

JOSH SILVER
in his own words

Tell us about your life so far.

I was born in Southampton and moved to the Lake District before I started school. I then moved to Salford, Manchester. I loved being creative, so I wanted to be an actor, and I was accepted into the Royal Academy of Dramatic Art at seventeen. After graduating, I appeared in some theater—at the Donmar Warehouse, Shakespeare's Globe, on Broadway in *Wolf Hall,* and opposite Nicole Kidman in *Photograph 51* in the West End. (This was a high point for me, as I had spent my younger years dancing around in a leotard to the *Moulin Rouge* soundtrack.) I featured in a BBC adaptation of *The Moonstone* and other smaller TV roles.

I decided to change career paths at thirty and began training to become a mental health nurse. I've just graduated, actually. While training, I worked in acute and intensive adult inpatient settings, in adolescent wards, and with younger children.

What was the inspiration for *HappyHead*?

The world now seems to be a bit obsessed with wellness. *Happy-Head* was born through me wondering what it would be like if the wellness culture had darker undertones. Could it be used as a façade for something way more sinister? In the context of how much we trust the powers that be, how far would we go to get what we're told is the ultimate reward?

I began writing the book while working in a mental health inpatient unit. I was watching the patients undertake a therapeutic exercise and one of them looked at me unconvinced, like *Is this going to make me better?* And I said yes because that's what we'd been taught to say. This is part of the treatment. This will help make you better.

It got me thinking about the trust we put into all our systems. I was intrigued by the question, Could these systems manipulate us and get people to do pretty much anything with the promise of a reward? The reward of happiness. Are systems already doing this?

Is happiness just an illusion?

Working in mental health units has been enlightening, and it has fed lots of aspects of my book. I've often heard people say "I just want to be happy." And this sounds great, but I began to wonder what the definition of "happy" is to people. Is it universal? Is it obtainable? Is it actually real? Maybe not, if someone else is telling us what it looks like.

The notion of happiness is prescribed to us. It's everywhere. I mean, social media says I should make loads of smoothies and film myself drinking them. Those people look happy. Or do a dance to a song I hate so people like my stuff and follow me. Those dopamine hits will help. I can apparently care about the climate and important things, definitely, just need to make sure I look hot while I'm out protesting. Then post about it. If you're gay, be a cool one, please. Effortlessly cool. Like it's not been difficult.

How did you find the writing process?
After stopping acting, I needed an outlet to be creative, so I started writing. I had never written before. But I loved it. I once read a George Orwell quote, something along the lines of writing a book is like a horrible exhausting struggle or a long bout with some painful illness. I love George Orwell, so I was fully prepared to fall into a hole of despair and warned my boyfriend to buckle up—I was about to be a total fucking nightmare.

However, that just wasn't the reality for me. I loved writing the book. I would look forward to finding moments before work, during work, breaks on night shifts, sitting in my car, in the local greasy spoon, on walks with the dog. . . . I would just write. And it was an incredible escape for me. Something that became addictive. I loved being inside the world with the characters. It was just a lot of fun.

What do you think is unique about your book?
This book challenges our society's prescribed notions of happiness, wellness, and success.

What do those words really mean? Ultimately, what is more important—being ourselves completely, or attempting to fulfill the expectations of others?

Mental health has certainly been a prominent topic over the

past few years. LGBTQ+ books are gaining more recognition. *HappyHead* puts these two things together in the context of a bizarre and terrifying facility where the process of curing unhappiness elicits dark truths. The book has an LGBTQ+ love story, but I didn't want it to be the entire focus of the book. I always wanted a gay hero.

In writing the character of Seb, did you draw on your own teenage experiences?
I had a very distinct need to be liked when I was younger. Seb has that. And, like Seb, I have struggled with my own mental health since I was an adolescent. I have taken various medications to help since I was sixteen. I was always called a sensitive boy. The phrase "wet blanket" springs to mind. I definitely struggled to deal with stuff/reality. I was a very intense person. Overthinker.

I didn't find growing up gay to be easy. Spent a lot of my time pretending and wishing I wasn't. However, unlike what the HappyHead facility is proposing, my adolescence was not one that had much "wellness." Sadly, I chose to abuse substances as my coping mechanism. That didn't work out well for me. Naturally, things fell apart and the wheels came off. Then I did have therapy. That worked much better. I now am sober and have been for a while. I smoke nicotine occasionally because sometimes an herbal tea just isn't going to cut it.

I always felt the need to prove myself to others. I definitely cared a lot about what other people thought of me, and I thought being an actor might make them think I was doing something very interesting and exciting. My mum told me when I changed my career to nursing, "You have to stop trying to fulfill other people's expectations of you." I will always remember that.

What does happiness mean to you now?
I grew up in a world where the idea of happiness was very clearly set out. It still is for lots of people. I remember when I was about twelve, I made a list of all the things I hoped I never would be: out of work, broke, alcohol abuser, drug user, gay—all on there. As I began to tick them off, I thought that I was pretty much destined to fail/never be happy. Sometimes those two things meant the same thing to me.

I eventually managed to find a path that allows me to be myself with healthier coping strategies. Writing is one of them. My brain runs at a million miles an hour. It's sometimes a bit like sitting in a shopping trolley going down a hill. Chaotic, at times. It means I obsess and I struggle to settle, which can be useful when writing. Writing gives me that outlet, that release of energy that I need to be able to move through the world without being completely nuts. I loved writing this book; it feels like different aspects of me are there in all the characters. I hate the word, but writing it was pretty therapeutic.

ACKNOWLEDGMENTS

There are many amazing people who helped me bring this book to life. I am forever grateful.

Firstly, the team at Delacorte Press and Penguin Random House USA, who have believed in this story with so much passion since we met. Kelsey Horton, my incredible US editor— I am very grateful to get to work on this with you. Joe, Lili, and Beverly, for being so kind.

My agent, Becky Bagnall. For championing this story with an enthusiasm that blew me away from the day you first read it. My British editor, Katie Jennings. I feel very lucky to work with someone whose instincts match mine, and who always guides me into the uncomfortable. You are a wizard. I would also like to thank the assistant editor, the amazing Molly Scull. This wouldn't be where it is without you.

The whole team at Oneworld and Rock the Boat, including Kate Bland, Lucy Cooper, Mark Rusher, Paul Nash, Laura McFarlane, and Deontaye Osazuwa. Thank you for being so kind and making this all happen.

To Hayley Warnham for designing the cover. To my brilliant publicist, Liz Scott. Also to Hamza Jahanzeb for the authenticity read, Susila Baybars for copy editing, and Jane Tait for proofreading.

Kinx for your support and notes and for early proofreading.

Jessie for your kindness and thoughtfulness with the first draft. Nomes, Millie, Eliza, James, Christian, Brandon, and Taron for always encouraging me.

My brothers, Tom, Ben, and Dan. You are the best.

To Liz Hall. When I was seventeen you told me I should start writing and you helped me understand its ability to channel my thoughts.

To Dil. Those days on shift together when you just kept telling me to go home and write.

My parents. For continued support and a desire to make the world a more inclusive place.

To the incredible patients I have worked with across the years, and to those who have encouraged me to keep writing this book and for telling me they would read it.

The Lake District for opening my brain up.

The girls at Jenny's café for letting me stay late to write.

Jordan and Chris. Thank you for being the best Fortnite squad members. And for all your support.

To David. You have inspired me to try to fight for a better world through the power of creativity.

To my dog, Dodger.

Finally to Seb, Finn, and Eleanor. I've really enjoyed escaping with you.

Or not escaping.

Let's see.

ABOUT THE AUTHOR

Josh Silver is the debut author of *HappyHead,* which was short-listed for the YA Book Prize and nominated for the Carnegie Medal, and its upcoming sequel, *Dead Happy.* Before becoming an author, he worked with teenagers as a mental health nurse, which inspired the critically acclaimed duology.